Address to Die For

A Maggie McDonald Mystery

D0374163

Mary Feliz

LYRICAL UNDERGROUND
Kensington Publishing Corp.
www.kensingtonbooks.com

LYRICAL UNDERGROUND BOOKS are published by

Kensington Publishing Corp.
119 West 40th Street
New York, NY 10018

All Kensington titles, imprints, and distributed lines are available at special quantity discounts for bulk purchases for sales promotion, premiums, fund-raising, educational, or institutional use.

Special book excerpts or customized printings can also be created to fit specific needs. For details, write or phone the office of the Kensington Sales Manager: Kensington Publishing Corp., 119 West 40th Street, New York, NY 10018. Attn. Sales Department. Phone: 1-800-221-2647.

Lyrical Underground and Lyrical Underground logo are trademarks of Kensington Publishing Corp.

First Electronic Edition: July 2016
eISBN-13: 978-1-60183-663-2
eISBN-10: 1-60183-663-5

First Print Edition: July 2016
ISBN-13: 978-1-60183-664-9
ISBN-10: 1-60183-664-3

Printed in the United States of America

For George.
For my parents, who introduced me to the world
of books.
For Jim and Michael, who never doubted and
laughed in all the right places.

ACKNOWLEDGMENTS

No one writes alone. People who become authors begin by learning to read, punctuate, and juggle grammar. So, thanks to all educators everywhere, including all parents who are, first and foremost, teachers. Authors also need cheerleaders, cohorts, colleagues, friends, advisors, and family. I can acknowledge some, but not all. My family suffered the highs, lows, obsessions, and distractions that are part of the roller coaster a writer chooses to climb aboard when she says, "I think I'd like to write a book." They came along for the ride and provided chocolate, coffee, hugs, solitude, and support. If they questioned my sanity, dedication, or ability, they kept their doubts to themselves. They were my first readers and great editors.

My editors, Jennifer Fisher and Mercedes Fernandez, helped Maggie and her family evolve far beyond what I'd imagined while keeping them true to themselves. My friends—the ones I write with, walk with, exercise with, drink coffee with, and those I only email—have been mentors, role models, fashion advisors, brainstormers, calmer-downers, and revver-uppers.

And there's George, who always, always has my back. I couldn't have done it without you, and wouldn't have wanted to try.

Chapter 1

When moving or traveling, pack last the things you'll
need first.

*From the Notebook of Maggie McDonald
Simplicity Itself Organizing Services*

Thursday, August 28, Morning

"Awesome! I bet it has bats!" My fourteen-year-old son, David,
exploded from the car and mounted the steps of the old house
three at a time. He peered through the grubby porch windows.

"Is it haunted?" Brian, my twelve-year-old, leaned into my side
as we stood in the front yard. I eyed the dust motes cavorting in a
light beam that had escaped the shrubs and overgrown trees surrounding the 100-year-old California Craftsman house. I put a reas-
suring hand on Brian's curly mop of hair. "I doubt it, honey." I hoped
it was true.

I swallowed hard and watched my husband, Max, ease his long
legs out of his Prius. Like my minivan, Max's car was overloaded.
We'd packed both cars with everything too fragile to transport in the
moving van. In among the breakables, our two kids, one golden retriever and two cats, we'd tucked picnic food, cleaning supplies, and
sleeping bags.

Today was Thursday. The plan was simple. The movers would arrive tomorrow. Since Monday was Labor Day we'd have four days to
get settled. The kids would start school on Tuesday, and Max would
begin his first full day at the new job the same day. I was giving myself
a month to focus solely on house and family. After that, I was determined to restart my career as a professional organizer.

Two minutes into the plan, it was unraveling.

"Max, didn't Aunt Kay's lawyer say the house was in turn-key condition? Is this the same house we looked at in February?" I stared at the weedy front yard, dusty porch, and drooping gutters. I wondered what we'd gotten ourselves into and what had happened to the spotless house and garden I'd last seen five months earlier.

Max's feet crunched dead leaves that covered ruts in the gravel drive. Belle, our two-year-old golden retriever, bounded to him.

"Hmm." Max tilted his head and squinted at the house. "His exact words were 'shines like a showpiece.'" He scratched his head. "A handyman was supposed to be coming a couple of times a week to fix things. The house looked perfect when I saw it in April."

Max picked up a dead branch from the walkway and swiped at a weedy flowerbed, beheading some wild carrots. "Needs a little work, doesn't it?" He took my hand and squeezed it gently.

"A little work? I'm not sure it's safe." I looked at the house again in professional terms, calculating how big a team I'd need to whip it into shape. At first glance, I could tell it wouldn't be easy. A film of silt covered everything, but that was normal for a dry August day in Northern California—nothing a hose, broom, and some window cleaner couldn't fix. But I counted three broken windows.

David poked his battered sneaker at a gaping hole in the floor of the porch—a hole that begged to break the leg of an absentminded new homeowner. I wanted to gather the kids, jump in the car, and hightail it back to our plain vanilla split-level in California's Central Valley. I was scared. Afraid of spiders, bats, and the huge to-do list this ancient house presented. I was even more terrified that Max and I had made a terrible decision and were in way over our heads.

Max put his hand on my shoulder—his calming gesture. "Maybe it's better on the inside and the problems are superficial. It was fine a few months ago. How bad could it have gotten? Let's wait, take a breath, and check things out before we panic."

That was Max. Always confident that things would work out. My approach was the opposite of his. I tried to anticipate problems and organize my way out of them.

I took a deep breath and pulled my shoulder-length hair into a ponytail. I should have checked the house out more recently myself. We'd peeked in the windows in February before we had the keys, and Max had done a walk-through in April. Both times, the house looked fine. After that, wrapping up Max's work, my business, and everything else had consumed every spare minute. Pressed for time, we assumed our earlier examinations of the property would suffice. It looked as if we'd been wrong, but there was nothing we could do about it now.

Today, my job was to move my family into this house and get started on our new life in Orchard View, a small town in the hills above Silicon Valley. Efficient organization is my passion and my profession, and I was eager to get started.

I clutched my binder filled with the phone numbers I'd need to set up the phone, Internet, cable, electricity, and gas. It held the kids' birth certificates and school records and my growing list of the things we needed to accomplish in the next few days. It was my security blanket.

"Honey, wait," I called to David, who tugged at the windows and searched for a way in. "Dad's got the key. Let's go in together."

Max patted the pockets of his rumpled jeans like a caricature of the absentminded professor he'd been until a few weeks ago. He held up the key, tied to a grubby cardboard tag with gray twine. The steps creaked as he joined David on the porch. Sidestepping the hole in the floorboards with a dance move worthy of Fred Astaire, he brandished the key and flung open the door, bowing low and waving his arm to invite us in. This house—Max's great-aunt Kay's home—featured large in stories from his childhood. He'd grown up here and loved every inch of the house, the grounds, and the surrounding countryside.

I squeezed past Max and peered up at the oak-beamed ceiling and the fireplace that dominated one end of the expansive front room. I hoped the skittering noises I heard were dry leaves and not mice. From Max's stories and from our earlier sneak peeks, I'd imagined the house with polished wood paneling and comfortable, welcoming rooms that were free of rodents and insects. I shivered. I hate spiders. One encounter with a web makes my face itch for a week—or a couple of minutes, at least.

I crossed my arms, gripping my elbows with my palms. This was the first room we'd seen. What lurked beyond? If the visible parts of the house were this neglected, what did that say about the parts we couldn't see, like the electricity and the plumbing? I needed a house inspector. I needed to find a hardware store. I needed my head examined.

"Max . . . honey? Didn't the title company require an inspection?"

"The lawyer said he'd be out of the office the rest of the week, but I'll call him. We'll straighten this out."

I took a deep breath to center myself and stall my runaway thoughts. We had to make this work. There was no going back. Max had left his job at the university in Stockton to take an upper-level management position in software engineering at Influx in Santa Clara. He'd worked part-time from home since wrapping up his teaching responsibilities in May.

This move was a dream Max and I had shared for ages: Getting away from Stockton. Leaving the university community where I'd lived all my life and Max had lived since his freshman year in college. Where my parents were part of the fabric of the university and everyone knew me and still thought of me as a child. Max wanted proof that his knowledge base wasn't ivory-tower nonsense and was valuable in the global technology marketplace.

Max grew up in Orchard View, a small town straddling the freeway between San Jose and San Francisco. He'd always wanted to go back. For years, his only relative had been his reclusive great aunt Kay. She'd died in her sleep just shy of her 100th birthday in February, and left the house and the rest of her estate to Max. At Silicon Valley property rates, the house, barn, and two acres of land backing up to an open space preserve were worth more than fifteen million dollars. Without Aunt Kay's generous savings we wouldn't have been able to afford the taxes, let alone the house.

As soon as Aunt Kay's house was officially ours, we'd put our Stockton house on the market. Max resigned his job at the university and I stopped taking on new clients. Once launched, the plan took on a life of its own. Our belongings were sardined into a moving van that would groan up the hill tomorrow.

I rubbed what I hoped was an imaginary spiderweb from my nose, turned to Max, and gave him the best smile I could muster.

"Are you going to introduce us to your dream house?" I said. The only time I'd been inside for any length of time had been years ago, before we were married. I'd been preoccupied with wedding plans and meeting Aunt Kay and barely spared the house a glance. After that, knowing how busy we were with kids and work, Aunt Kay had come to visit us. Before we knew it, years had passed and she'd moved to assisted living. A Stanford professor had rented for a while, but the house had stood empty for several years since then.

"I know this isn't what we expected, Maggie," Max said. "But it's got good bones."

"Even good bones get broken," I muttered under my breath. I tried to drum up something more positive to say to Max. Tried and failed. I sneezed. The house was stuffy, dusty, and smelled as though a squirrel, rat, or bird had died somewhere. I crossed the room, unlocked a window, and struggled to push up the sash. Max helped open the rest of the many windows and a pleasant breeze wafted into the room. Chalk one up for old houses. In the absence of air-conditioning they relied on thick walls, graceful porches, and cross-ventilation that worked whether we had electricity or not.

"Mom, Mom, Mom," called Brian, rubbing at the tiles on the fireplace, his hands and face covered in greasy soot. "There are knights!" Nearly a teenager, he was still 85 percent small boy.

"Nights?"

"Knights! With lances! On horses! Fighting!"

Max dashed across the room, knelt next to Brian, and rubbed at the copper tiles himself. Sure enough, armored knights on horseback charged full-tilt across the top of the fireplace.

"I'd forgotten about these guys," Max said. "Aren't they great? In the firelight, it can look like they're moving."

Brian beamed at Max and Max grinned back. I knew that if there were knights on the fireplace, the house undoubtedly had other hidden treasures, and I'd need a lance and armor of my own to get anyone out of here tonight.

Belle barked in the back of the house. Her insistent, needing-to-go-out bark. I remembered the cats in their carriers in the car had similar needs.

"Brian, can you find a room upstairs where we can get the cats settled?"

Brian leapt up from the floor and wiped his hands on his jeans, smearing black handprints the length of his thighs. With feet huge like a growing puppy's, he clomped up the stairs to join his older brother. David, running from room to room over our heads, sounded as though he'd invited a herd of elephants to help him explore.

"This is going to be my room," David called down the stairs. "It's got its own fireplace. How much you wanna bet it's got bats?"

I looked at Max, still gazing at the knights. I could tell that he wanted to show me the world that encompassed his childhood dreams, but we had a ton of work to do.

"Max, can you check on the electricity? And see if we've got hot water or any water at all? I need to let Belle out and I want to clean at least one room to sleep in."

"Yes, m'lady," said Max, still inhabiting the world of Camelot. "I'll see if I can round up the knights-errant and arm them with brooms, mops, and paper towels."

"I brought some of that stuff in the car," I said. "I think it's close to the top layer. Don't bring anything else inside until we've got a clean place to put it down."

Finding my way through the gloom to the back of the house, I opened windows as I went. I felt overwhelmed. Fixing up this house would be the largest project I'd ever undertaken, and the condition of the house had shaken my confidence in my ability to get it all done. My Stockton organizing business had been busy, but my projects were small—bringing order to the offices of absentminded professors. They were nothing like this house with its dignified historical significance and rapidly expanding list of renovations.

The dining room had nice windows, a built-in sideboard and china cabinets, and a long oval table surrounded by a dozen chairs. To my right was a swinging door that I expected led to the kitchen. I pushed the door, which opened halfway and stopped. My forehead wrinkled and my mind scurried in wild directions as I imagined what I might find on the other side of the door.

Get a grip, Maggie! You've watched too many episodes of *Masterpiece Mystery*. I peered around the door, relieved to find an innocent pile of old newspapers. I'd heard they were good for cleaning windows, so we were set if we ran out of paper towels. I was working hard to stay positive. As soon as I'd scooted the newspapers out of the way, the door swung open into a narrow pantry connecting the dining room to the kitchen. Each wall was lined with cupboards and a long counter. I'd dreamed of having a room like this for projects and homework and storage. No one designed houses like this anymore.

The kitchen was well lit with windows over the sink and across the south wall, opening the room up to the vista of a sloping lawn, an old red barn, a creek, and golden rolling hills. The gnarled trunks of coastal oaks dotted the hillside. The view was drop-dead gorgeous. Soothing. A red-tailed hawk soared and glided on thermals. A breeze started at the house and moved downhill across the grass, rippling it like someone shaking out a silken roll of fabric. No wonder Max loved this place.

Belle barked sharply. I unlocked the back door and pulled at the knob. The door didn't budge. I braced my feet and pulled, praying that the knob wouldn't come off in my hand and send me sailing across the room. The door screeched open as a jagged piece of flashing caught on the metal threshold. I added *Get back door to fit* to my growing mental list. But I pushed the list away for a moment and stood on the covered back porch, imagining bringing my coffee out here in the mornings and sitting with a blanket on a rocking chair while watching Belle explore. I had no rocking chair, blanket, coffee, or even a mug, but I enjoyed my delusional moment.

Belle raced through the tall grass, invisible except for her tail. I turned and went back into the house, enjoying the sound the wooden screen door made as it banged against its frame. It was an old-fashioned sound, straight out of *The Waltons*.

I pushed an early twentieth-century two-button switch on the wall and waited. Nothing. I pushed it twice more, whispering: "Please." It was a hope, prayer, or incantation, but I wasn't sure which.

"Max . . . honey? Any luck with the electricity?" I tried not to panic. The electricity was probably fine. This light was the first I'd tried to switch on. It might have a burned-out bulb or be linked to a fuse that had blown.

I'd grown up as the daughter of professors in a house near the university campus. If we wanted electricity and didn't have it, we called maintenance. I knew how to change a lightbulb, but my electrical expertise dwindled to nothing after that.

Plumbing wasn't my strong suit, either. I turned the cold-water knob over the white farmhouse sink. Nothing. My shoulders drooped. I stepped away, rubbed the small of my back, and jumped as the faucet jerked with a bang. Swampy gurgles that sounded as though the house had severe intestinal issues erupted from the tap, and dark-brown water poured into the sink. Just when I was starting to think there was something about the innards of old houses that I didn't want to know, Max stuck his head through the pantry doorway. He carried a ladder and a bucket filled with lightbulbs.

"Oh, good," he said. "Leave the water running for a few moments until it clears. It's a bit rusty, but the plumbing seems solid. I'm taking the ladder up to David. He's going to check for burned-out bulbs and replace them."

"Good work. What's Brian up to?"

"He's getting the cats and their litter box organized."

I followed Max up the stairs and was delighted to find a built-in window seat and cupboard on the landing. Above the seat, the top of the windows held stained glass. Late-morning sun shining through the glass wisteria vines spilled lavender and green splotches of light on the stairs. The house was doing its best to charm each one of us.

As we turned the corner at the top of the stairs, Brian crested the top of a second staircase, lugging a cat carrier in each hand. Back stairs? Just like *Downton Abbey*! I took one of the cat carriers as Brian held it out. Holmes, our grumpiest cat, growled his disgust with the lurching trip from the car.

"We'll get you settled as soon as we can, Holmes," I said, trying to comfort the four-year-old orange tabby. "Brian found you a great hidey-hole."

"I did!" Brian said. "I swept out the closet and put Dad's old sweatshirt on a shelf in there."

I knew that Holmes's partner, Watson, would be the first to explore. A small female, Watson had large splotches of white in her orange coat, including one on her face that made her look as though she'd had a comic encounter with a dish of whipped cream.

It would take time, but if we kept the cats contained to one room for a few days, I was sure they'd settle in. I hoped the same would be true for the rest of us.

Max carried the ladder and bucket down the hall. "David? I've got the ladder so you can get started on the bulbs."

"In here, Dad," David called from the bathroom at the end of the hall, his voice echoing off the tiles. "Look at this toilet! The tank is way up there and you pull this chain to make it flush. Gravity! How cool is that?"

David perched on the curved edge of a voluminous claw-foot tub. He stepped from tub, to sink, to toilet, and jumped down.

"This house is great, Mom," David said, beaming. "There's a desk that turns into a bed—the bed comes out of the wall—in the next room."

David would be starting high school next week. He'd been reluctant to leave his Stockton friends and seemed wary of starting the next chapter of his school career without them. His enthusiasm for the new house was a welcome change from his sadness over leaving the old one.

Holmes howled and the normally quiet Watson joined in. I put a hand on David's shoulder to stem the flow of questions, surprised anew at how fast he was growing. He was almost as tall as I was. I straightened my posture and turned to Brian.

"Did you get their litter box set up?"

Brian nodded.

"Food? Water?"

"Yup."

"And the closet is secure?" I didn't want the cats escaping and freaking out before they'd had a chance to learn they were home.

Brian nodded and rolled his eyes like the young teen he was becoming. "All checked out and ready to go, Mom."

"Perfect, go for it, then."

He disappeared into the bedroom with the two complaining cats and shut the door behind him.

Max's new work phone rang with the doom-filled Darth Vader's theme. Apparently we had cell service.

"Hey, Jim," Max answered the phone. "Yup, just arrived, thanks. Really? You're kidding, right?" Max looked at me, covered the phone, and mouthed, "Be right back." He walked down the hall with his head down.

Uh-oh. Something was wrong.

I turned to David. "Can you open that window? It's still a bit whiffy in here."

The window screeched and stuck, but David muscled it up.

"Can you flick that light switch?" he said. "This should be working."

I pushed the old-fashioned two-button switch. Nothing. I hoped the problem was as simple as a few blown fuses.

From the bathroom, I could hear tension in Max's voice as he paced in the hall and talked to his new boss on the phone. "Okay, Jim, I see. Let me talk to Maggie and I'll call you back . . . yes, tomorrow . . . that's right . . ." Max looked up at me, grimaced with a *What can ya do?* look, and ended the call.

I lifted my eyebrows.

"I'll fill you in later," Max said. "I need to check out the fuses and see if we can get some lights on in here before it gets dark."

I headed down the back staircase, delighted to find that it ended in the kitchen. I assumed the narrow, utilitarian stairs had been planned as a way for children and staff to go about their business without disturbing the serenity of the living room. To me they seemed as much fun and as full of possibility as a secret passage to Narnia. I was a self-proclaimed gluttonous reader, prone to quoting from both children's and adult literature without warning.

My next step was lunch. It was time to grab the cooler from the car and dust off the back porch to set up our sandwiches and drinks. Belle joined me on the walk to the car. She butted her nose into the back of my knee. I scratched behind her ears.

I grabbed the cooler from the backseat with my right hand, tucked a nested set of pet dishes under my arm, and grabbed a bucket of cleaning supplies with my left hand. Loaded up, I headed back to the house.

"Maggie!" Max called from somewhere inside the house. I picked up the bucket and struggled to open the kitchen door, giving it my shoulder and some muscle.

"I've got lunch," I called to Max, thinking he must be in the next room. "There's a cold beer with your name on it."

"Maggie!" Max said, clomping up the basement stairs. He flung open the door at the top of the stairs and a dreadful smell wafted up. I gagged as Max yelled "Call 9-1-1!"

Chapter 2

The unexpected happens when you're moving. Make
sure your cell phone is charged.

From the Notebook of Maggie McDonald
Simplicity Itself Organizing Services

Thursday, August 28, Midday

I raced to the top of the basement stairs. Max had a white-knuckled
grip on the banister, was sweating, out of breath, and grayer than
I'd ever seen him. I grabbed the doorframe and reached for him.

"How can I help? What's that god-awful smell?"

"Don't come down here. Call 9-1-1," said Max.

"It'll be faster to take you to the hospital ourselves." I stuck my
head around the door and called up the stairs. "Brian! David!"

"Huh?" Max's face wrinkled. Was confusion a sign of a stroke,
heart attack, or both? I couldn't remember.

"Is it a heart attack?" I asked. "Let's get you in the car. Boys! Get
down here!"

"Keep the kids out of the basement. And keep Belle in the
kitchen. Call 9-1-1. He's dead."

Dead? "Who's dead? Are you okay? Max, are *you* okay?"

He shook his head. "Me? I'm fine. Oh, no, sorry. Didn't mean to
scare you. I'm fine. It's some guy. Dead. Bottom of the stairs.
Tripped. Fell." Max grabbed the counter and slid to the floor, still
looking as if he were having some sort of cardiac event.

"Dead?" I said. "Are you *sure* you're okay?" I closed the door to
the basement, wishing I had a towel to stuff between the door and the
floor to keep the odor from escaping. I reached toward a cupboard to

grab a glass and get Max some cold water before I remembered our glasses were packed in the moving van.

David and Brian clattered down the back stairs. David took them two at a time and jumped over the last three to land in the kitchen with a *thud* that rattled the windows.

"What's up?" David asked, his gaze flitting from his dad, to me, and back. "What's that smell? Dad, what's wrong?"

Brian stood on the bottommost step and peered over his brother's shoulder. "What stinks? Is lunch ready?" His voice petered out and his eyes widened. "Mom, what's wrong? Is Dad okay?"

"I'm fine," Max said, patting his pockets. "Hand me a phone." Max took the phone I gave him. I moved between the boys and the basement stairs.

"Everything is fine, guys," I said. "Let Dad talk. We'll have lunch outside in a minute."

"Who's Dad calling?" asked David.

Brian shoved past David, grabbed Belle's water dish, filled it at the sink, and put it on the floor for her.

"I'm on hold," said Max. "Everything's fine, but I'm calling 9-1-1. I found a guy in the basement. He may have fallen down the stairs. Umm . . . he's dead."

Brian paled.

David laughed. "Seriously? You're kidding, right? What did you find? Let me see." He moved to get past me.

I blocked his way. "David. Listen. You can't go down there. Grab some paper towels and take the cooler and the sandwiches out on the porch. Dad and I will be out in a minute and tell you what we know."

David craned his head around me to look at his dad, who sat on the floor with his head on his knees.

"Hello? Yes, this is Max McDonald." Max took a breath and stretched out his legs. "I'm calling from twenty-one eleven Briones Hill Road, Orchard View, cross street Monte Viejo Road, to report a dead body in my basement."

It took a while to get everyone calmed down and set up with lunch on the back steps, but performing ordinary tasks helped calm my horror over the fact that there was a dead man in our house. I was torn between wanting to see what Max had seen and not wanting to go anywhere near the basement. I'd come down on the side of taking a peek, but the stench had me gagging before I'd taken three steps. I retreated to the kitchen. I'd leave any necessary action on the body to the professionals Max had summoned with his call to 9-1-1.

The kids fired questions at their dad, who hadn't taken more than a bite of his turkey sandwich. He'd sipped at his beer, then asked for cold water and held the plastic bottle to his forehead instead of drinking it.

"I was going downstairs to find an electrical panel," Max said. "There was this pile of what I thought was dirty laundry blocking the bottom step and the stench was awful. Laundry made no sense, since no one has lived here for years, but I kicked the clothes with my foot to shove them out of the way." Max took a sip of water and pushed his thick, dark curly hair off of his forehead.

David started to interrupt, but Max talked over David's question. "I knew I'd kicked something more solid than clothes, but I didn't put it together. I wanted to find whatever dead animal was making that stench and get rid of it before your mom freaked out."

"Are there, like, flies and worms?" David asked, wrinkling up his nose as if he didn't want to hear the answer. He looked relieved when Max assured us there weren't.

The sound of emergency sirens ended our discussion. Max grabbed Belle's collar while I found her leash and snapped it on. She was usually good with strangers, but we were cautious. In a situation like this one, where a dog's family was tense and in an unfamiliar location, it was hard to know how any dog might react.

In less than a minute our weedy drive and overgrown lawn were covered with dozens of emergency vehicles. What on earth had Max told them to bring out this enormous response? Our quiet yard looked like a scene out of *Homeland* or *24*. I half expected Jack Bauer to leap from an SUV, talking to the president on his cell phone.

Doors slammed and trunk lids thudded as members of the various emergency teams called greetings and instructions to one another. They moved in a practiced, choreographed dance and I admired their organized attack as they converged on the house carrying toolboxes, aluminum suitcases, and other equipment that looked industrial, scientific, and more than a little creepy.

I couldn't shake the feeling that I'd stumbled into someone else's nightmare. I wanted to start the day over from the beginning. I knew it was important to plan for disasters and expect the unexpected when you were moving, but . . . a dead body? Who plans for that?

A man Max's age separated from the crowd and approached us. "Detective Jason Mueller, Orchard View Police," said the man in an authoritative bass voice, showing us his badge. "Mr. McDonald?"

"Thanks for coming." Max shook the detective's hand and introduced the rest of us. I shook his hand too, but I was growing impatient. I needed the crime-scene circus to do its job. I wanted them to remove the body so we could get on with our job—settling into our new home and town.

And then I panicked. On TV, when someone dies everything gets blocked off with police tape. Would we be able to stay? If not, where would we go? Before we'd moved, I'd tried to find a local hotel to use as a home base during the first few days of our move. I'd looked for one that would permit us to take Belle, Holmes, and Watson, but the closest one was on the far side of the San Francisco Bay. None of the pricey Silicon Valley hotels wanted to risk three animals and twelve muddy paws on their 500-thread-count sheets.

"Nice to meet you," said the detective. "We'll be out of your hair as quickly as possible."

"Is this necessary?" I asked, lifting my chin toward the swarm of vehicles, which had been joined by a Subaru with a neon-yellow kayak attached to the roof rack. "Max said the man fell."

"We investigate every unexpected death," the detective said. He nodded to two jumpsuit-clad workers lugging a generator. "It's going to get noisy around here. Do you have somewhere else that you can go?"

"We're moving in," Max said. "Arrived an hour ago."

"The moving van's coming first thing in the morning," I added. "We've got a ton of work to do . . ."

Detective Mueller nodded and asked, "Where's the body? In the basement?" He gestured to the team with the generator and then pointed toward the basement door. A gangly young man wearing a bright blue neoprene jacket, fleece tights, and water shoes joined the team. He'd jumped out of the Subaru and must have come straight from kayaking.

"Look," Detective Mueller said. "I understand this is disruptive. A violent or unexplained death takes a toll on everyone. After our team goes through the house, and after the medical examiner has a chance to look at the body, I can let you know more. Right now, I can tell you it will take us several hours before we clear out. It will be noisy and lit up like an operating room. You might want to take off."

I looked at Max and raised my eyebrows.

Max ran his hand through his curls, looked up at the house, then across the yard to the barn. "Detective, we've got some thinking to do—decisions and arrangements to make."

Max grabbed my hand. "I think we'll head down to the barn, finish our lunch, and figure out our next step. Our cats are closed up in a closet in the big bedroom at the top of the stairs. Can you make sure your people don't let them out?"

The detective nodded. "We'll need to interview you later. Please let us know if you need anything from the house or if you need to go anywhere."

He turned toward his team and took a few brisk strides toward the house before turning back.

"Mr. McDonald, did you know the dead man? Had you seen him before?"

Max shook his head. "Once I realized he was dead, I cleared out. I didn't get a good look." He furrowed his forehead and stroked his chin. "I suppose he could be Javier Hernandez, my aunt's caretaker. That would explain a lot." He wrinkled his nose and his skin turned an alarming shade of greenish gray. "Would you like me to take another look? Or I can call my aunt's lawyer and find out if anyone else had keys, if that would help. He's out of the office for the long weekend, but I can call him next week."

Detective Mueller jotted something in a dog-eared notebook with a stubby pencil. "If you can get me the lawyer's name and number, I'll see if we can get hold of him sooner than that." He held up his cell phone. "Can you both give me your contact information?"

While Max and the detective exchanged numbers, I focused on the kids, hoping that chores and clear instructions would provide a sense of normalcy.

"David, take the lunch cooler down to the barn. Brian, take Belle. Dad and I will be there in a minute."

The kids took off at a run. Max grabbed my hand and squeezed gently. "It's going to work out," he said.

We packed up the rest of our lunch, stopped at the car to grab a package of Oreos I'd been saving for later, and walked down the pathway of trampled grass, dirt, and gravel that led across the yard to the barn and the dry creek beyond. Any physician would have taken one look at us and prescribed Oreos all around.

"I can't believe this," I said. "I thought this was going to be so easy: move into a turn-key house and tell the movers where to place the furniture. We unpack, make the beds, fill the refrigerator, and get the kids in school—a done deal."

Max stopped and looked at me. "Man plans. God laughs," he said. It was a Yiddish proverb, passed down from his Aunt Kay. She'd spurned religion but peppered her speech with idiomatic expressions from a wide range of cultures.

"So, I'm delusional." I shrugged, fighting off tears of frustration. "I expected a few things to go wrong, but today has been the opposite of what we'd planned. All this mess . . ." I waved my arms to indicate the chaotic mass of people and equipment that had transformed our house and yard. "And now a dead body. A *body*, Max. Who plans for a *dead body*?"

Max took me in his arms and hugged me, kissed the top of my head and said, "That dead body may not be our biggest problem."

Chapter 3

Establishing organized systems makes it easy for
most people to handle routine cleaning. But when
you're in over your head, there's no shame in calling
a professional.

From the Notebook of Maggie McDonald
Simplicity Itself Organizing Services

Thursday, August 28, Afternoon

I pushed Max away and stared at him, convinced his words were an
unfunny joke or that I'd misheard him.

"What?" I asked.

"The body might not be our biggest problem." Max stuck his hands
in his pockets and kicked at the ground like a kid who knew he should
tell the truth, but who knew the truth would get him into trouble.

I opened my mouth to speak, but questions flew around my head,
forming sentences and breaking apart. Forming again and exploding.
I closed my mouth and stared at him.

"That phone call? The one from Jim, from Influx?" Max said.

I waited. He looked at the ground.

"They want me in the Bangalore office on Monday."

"India?"

Max nodded. "I told them I needed to talk to you. That we hadn't
moved in yet and I didn't know where my clothes were."

"And?"

"The moving company called. Their driver had emergency surgery
last night, and they can't get a new team together until Monday, and
Monday is Labor Day."

"And?"

"They don't work on Labor Day."

"And?"

"They'll call later to reschedule."

"And you'll be in Bangalore?"

Max bit his lip, stared at me, and said, "I told Jim I'd talk to you and call him back. I wanted to discuss the ramifications without the boys around so we'd have a chance to think about it together, first. But then I found the guy in the basement and the police arrived. Jim's called twice since, but I let it go to voice mail."

I shook my head, trying to recalibrate my expectations for the week. "I don't even know what the time difference is or the travel time. What time do you have to leave here to be in Bangalore on Monday morning?"

Max's mouth dropped open and snapped closed. I guessed it wasn't the question he'd expected. I suspected it wasn't a question he'd thought to ask. I looked at him. I had nothing to say. And no idea where we went from here, except that I needed an Oreo.

Without warning, I started laughing and sort of crying. I couldn't stop. I laughed until my stomach ached. I bent at the waist, put my hands on my knees, and turned my head to look up at Max. He was laughing too. What else could we do? Crying wouldn't help. Our plans were a mess. I'd need to scrap my priorities, schedules, and lists, and start over.

After days of packing up our belongings and wrapping up our lives in Stockton, we were exhausted—too exhausted to nimbly adjust to drastic changes. I fell over and sat on the ground, still laughing, snorting, and wiping my eyes. Belle bounded up from the barn, not wanting to miss a minute of fun. She bounced around me and licked my face, then head-butted Max, wanting in on the joke.

My laughter died out to a few maniacal giggles. Max stood, reached out a hand to help me up, and said, "Let's go talk to the kids. Figure out how we're going to make this work."

I stood, brushing off my jeans and wiping my hands on my shirt, surveying the neglected landscape that the caretaker had promised would be in perfect condition when we moved in.

"Oh, Max. Do you really think the man in the basement could be Javier? He was so nice when I phoned him about the measurements." My eyes filled with tears and my throat tightened. I'd called the caretaker months earlier, worried that my grandmother's antique wardrobe wouldn't fit in the house. Javier provided the measurements of doorways, hallways, and stairs, but also asked for the dimensions of the old armoire. A few days later he sent me a short video of his grinning nephew carrying a refrigerator-sized cardboard box into the house, up the stairs, and down the hall to the master bedroom. They'd crossed out *refrigerator* on the box and marked it *NANA'S CUPBOARD 4' x 3' x 8'*.

I smiled, sniffed, wiped my tears, and refocused my attention on Max.

"I hope not, Maggie, but it has to be Javier, doesn't it? Who else would it be?" Max brushed something from his eyes and scraped the ground with the toe of his shoe. "He was a great guy. Not only when I came to inspect the property in April, but back when I was just a kid and an annoying teenager visiting Aunt Kay."

"But why wouldn't someone report him missing? How long do you think he's been dead? Doesn't he have family?"

Max sighed. "I don't know, Maggie, and with all due respect to Javier, I'm not sure I care at the moment. We need to focus on us. Our family. You, me, and the kids. Javier had some good innings. I thought he was an old man when he taught me to recognize animal tracks as a kid. Maybe he caught the flu or something after we last talked to him. He could have come out here desperate to catch up on his promises and fallen down the stairs, or had a heart attack, or a stroke. Let's let the police sort it out."

I looked back at the house and the driveway packed with emergency vehicles. I sighed and smoothed my T-shirt. I'm not sure why I'd decided to wear a white shirt on moving day. It was getting grubbier by the minute.

"We said we wanted to break out of our rut," I said, trying to find something positive in this dreadful turn of events. "We craved a new adventure. . . . I guess we got what we asked for, but I'm a little afraid to find out what happens next: the zombie apocalypse? An earthquake?

"Sharknado?" said Max. "Be careful what you wish for." We walked toward the barn and our responsibilities.

"Mom, come look!" said Brian from the dark center of the barn, beyond its open doors. "This is so cool!"

Max and I walked inside. The barn was straight out of *Charlotte's Web*: quiet, cool, a tiny bit musty, smelling of hay. Roof beams soared above our heads. A loft graced the far end of the room. Like many barns in the area, this one was a drive-through. A central two-story corridor ran the length of the building. Enormous rolling doors enclosed both ends. On each side of the main door, single-story hips jutted out, separated from the main section of the barn by a row of rough-hewn support posts.

Small windows in the upper story and on the lower side walls let in some light, but I needed to give my eyes time to adjust to the relative dimness compared to the bright sunlight outdoors. Square footage–wise, the barn might be as big or bigger than the house, but it was difficult to compare them.

Max walked to a bank of light switches that were more modern than anything inside the house. He flicked them up with two swipes of his hands and we had light.

"Mom, Mom, we can put in a swing!" Brian said. "Like the one in Zuckerman's barn!"

"We'll see, honey," I said. I wasn't the only one channeling the kids from *Charlotte's Web*.

"I don't suppose there's a barn bathroom?" I asked Max. The iced tea I'd had at lunch was reminding me that we hadn't talked to the police detective about access to facilities in the house.

"I'm not sure," said Max. "Let's look around. There was an outhouse back here when I was a kid."

"*Eww*," the boys chorused.

Max laughed. "It wasn't bad—not when it's just for family use. But Aunt Kay considered putting a bathroom and shower out here and making the barn into a rustic guesthouse. I don't know if she ever did. Let's look."

I let them explore while I wandered behind the barn.

Live oaks cast purple shadows on the golden hillside above a dry creek. Max had told us that the land beyond the creek belonged to the Mid-Peninsula Open Space District and was public land that could never be developed. He'd told us stories about backpacking there when he was a kid. From here you could access trails that would take you to the coast and back. I was tempted to let my mind venture at least that far, but I yanked my thoughts back to the business at hand.

We were going to run out of daylight in a few hours and we still didn't know where we were sleeping or eating. I hadn't a clue when our furniture would arrive. I sniffed at my shirt. We could use a change of clothes. We were dusty, tired, and in need of showers. I was desperate to find a toilet.

I looked up at the hills and watched a hawk banking into a turn and diving for food. I winced, waiting for the cry of a captured rabbit. I could grasp the whole circle-of-life concept, but wasn't keen on seeing it play out in front of me. The hawk rose with a writhing snake in its beak. It was gross, but I smiled. I hoped it was a rattlesnake. This was the second time today I'd been soothed, watching the hawk soar and float on thermals, rising above the nonsense complicating our life on the ground. And now I'd discovered that hawks hunt snakes. *That* was my kind of bird.

Max came back, put his hand on my shoulder, and watched with me as the wind rustled the grass. I put my hand over his. We both took a moment to just breathe.

"It's beautiful here," I said.

"I found the bathroom," Max said. "Light and water are both working."

"The boys?"

"Hunting for arrowheads by the creek."

"Are there arrowheads here?" I said, thinking there was no end to the enchantments this property held for my kids.

"I'm not sure," Max answered. "I found one once, but I half suspect Aunt Kay planted it. Arrowheads are about the hunting, though, not the finding."

I turned and scanned the inside of the barn. I thought about its working electricity and plumbing.

"We could sweep up this floor," I said. "Get it cleaned up enough to stay here tonight. Same plan as before, but with our sleeping bags in here instead of upstairs in the house."

I looked at the shadows of the clouds moving on the hill. "Do you think Detective Mueller will hold his questions long enough for me to find a Target? I could pick up a few towels and change of clothes? Find a pizza or burrito place and order takeout?"

"And wine? Lots of wine?"

I nodded. "A baguette for us? With cheese and grapes?" I was starting to like this plan. A lot. My phone would tell me how to find the nearest Target and how to get back home.

Max smiled and nodded. "Marshmallows and stuff too? We used to have bonfires down here when I was a kid. I can keep our little savages busy hunting up some kindling, but grab a box of firewood, just in case."

"I think we've got a plan, at least for now. We can sort out the rest after we've had food, showers, and we've got our beds organized."

I kissed Max, took a quick break in the bathroom, and walked back up the hill to the car. Belle scampered behind me. She expected to ride shotgun whenever I was in the car, but I sent her back to Max and the boys.

"Not now, girl," I said. "You go back to protect the guys. We're finding our way 'round this setback, but on a day like today, you never know where the next crisis will come from."

Two hours later, refueled with a latte I'd grabbed at the kiosk inside the Target in nearby Mountain View, I pulled my car back into the driveway and experienced a brief flicker of that coming-home feeling. Parking the car at the barn and having Belle race out to greet me made it seem even more like coming home.

But entering the barn was like . . . magic. Max and the boys had transformed it. Our sleeping bags and inflatable mattresses were lined up on the right side of the main corridor. A cloth-covered folding table and chairs graced the center of the barn. Drooping wildflowers filled a plastic soda bottle, creating a centerpiece. The whole barn was backlit by a bonfire that crackled outside the open back doors.

"Amazing!" I said to the boys and Max, who all began talking at once.

"I picked the flowers," Brian said.

"I set up the beds," David added.

Max shrugged. "About fifteen minutes after you left, a volunteer from the police department came down and asked what we needed. He felt bad that we were new to town and, instead of being greeted by the Welcome Wagon or a neighbor with cookies, we met up with a dead body and were kicked out of our house. He came back a while later with the table and chairs. He brought us some cookies, along with breakfast and lunch stuff in a cooler for tomorrow. The rest the boys scrounged from the car and the barn loft. We've had a blast."

I spun around like the lead in a Disney movie and felt every inch a pampered princess.

I set a grocery bag on the table, sank down on one of the chairs, and pulled a towel from the Target bag. "Who wants the first shower?"

Later, when we were stuffed with food, sticky with marshmallows, and Belle and the boys were tucked into bed, Max and I snuggled next to the fire. The stars twinkled and the evening felt like an odd fairy tale: disaster followed by a happy ending.

"I don't suppose the fairy godmother who brought the cookies solved the rest of our problems?" I said, refilling Max's wineglass and sighing.

"'Fraid not," Max said. "But I bought us a little time with Influx, and Detective Mueller says his team is going to work all night and should be out of here by lunchtime tomorrow."

"Did he say why they're taking this so seriously? Why they brought all the equipment and personnel? It's like they thought it was a murder or a terrorist attack."

"No, nothing like that. It still looks as though Javier fell or had a heart attack."

"Are they sure it was Javier?" I said. "Are they sure it wasn't murder? Wouldn't a murderer try to make it look like an accident? Why didn't someone miss him or call the police?"

"That's what the police are for. Let them do their jobs."

Max put his arm around me and drew me closer. "The detective seems more concerned about the broken windows, the hole in the porch, and some evidence of tampering with the electrical box. He thinks someone may have been working hard to make the house look more run-down than it should have been. He had one of his guys pull the police records. There were several vandalism reports from Javier going back as far as March. The police got a picture from the Department of Motor Vehicles and confirmed it's him. He was probably so busy trying to keep teenagers from partying in the empty house that he didn't have time to keep up with the normal chores, let alone arrange the work we requested. Poor guy." Max again brushed something from his eyes and sniffed quietly.

"Why did they have to contact the DMV? Wouldn't he have identification on him? How did he get here? There was no car or truck parked near the house, and he wouldn't have walked, would he? If he'd had the tools he needed to do his caretaking thing, he'd need a car."

"I really don't know," said Max, starting to sound a little testy. "Let me tell you what I *do* know."

I nodded and sipped my wine while Max continued the story. "The first report the police took from Javier mentioned broken windows. He called a second time to report that someone had tried to start a fire in one of the upstairs rooms. He thought it was kids, and so did the police, but they had no leads. They sent an officer to investigate and were monitoring social media, but nothing came of it, and Javier didn't report any more damage."

"But the house is a mess," I said. "Why did he stop reporting the damage? Why didn't he tell us about it?" I shivered. He'd probably hadn't wanted to worry us. We were used to gang tagging and vandalism in parts of Stockton, which was a bankrupt urban center with no money for maintenance and cleanup. Graffiti was an eyesore, annoying when the paint obscured street signs and expensive for store owners who struggled to keep their properties looking nice. But this was the first time I'd looked at vandalism as a violation of my personal space. It had never before hit this close to home.

"Maggie, I'm sure Javier thought he had plenty of time to repair the damage and didn't want to scare us away. He was excited that we were coming and that a family would be living in the house again. But it doesn't matter, now. We need to focus on getting the kids settled into school, not on all these questions the police are better suited to answer." Max sighed and tilted his head from side to side, stretching tight neck muscles. We were all sore from packing up for the move.

"Really, Maggie, think about it. The police need to figure this out, not us," he said. "Detective Mueller—he asked us to call him Jason, by the way—is going to bring coffee down in the morning and have breakfast with us. Fill us in on where they're at with the investigation. After that, he'll have someone interview us for the file, and they'll be done."

"Can they wrap things up that quickly?" I asked. "I mean, I'm thrilled that they're clearing out"—I took a giant swallow of my wine—"but a man died."

"All I know about crime-scene investigations, you could fit in an hour-long TV crime drama," Max said, pouring the last drops into his glass.

"Oh, wait," he said. "I do know something. Jason said they have a policy now of turning a crime scene over to professional cleaners when they've finished their investigation."

I tried to wrap my head around that, wondering why, and whether I'd had too much wine to figure it out.

"You know, for health reasons," Max said. "Bodily fluids, diseases—"

"Okay, okay, that's enough detail," I said, scrunching up my nose and trying not to gag. "I get it."

I watched the fire and jumped when the call of a coyote broke the silence.

Max laughed. "A coyote. Wait, you'll hear more. Like a chorus calling good night."

Minutes later, other coyotes chimed in, each one with its own unique tone coming from a different direction.

"I guess we should head to bed too," I said. I stood, stretched my sore muscles, and reached out a hand to Max. "A professional cleaning company, huh? Do you think they'd be willing to stay longer and clean up the whole house? Would they help out with some of the repairs too?"

"I'll ask. If the cleaning team won't, maybe we can find someone else to help."

"Leave that to me. I'm the professional organizer, remember? I'll find someone. Maybe several someones. I'll need them to refer to clients after I get Simplicity Itself up and running again."

We poured water on the fire and covered the coals with dirt. We checked on the boys. They were nestled in their sleeping bags with Belle sandwiched between them. As my head hit the pillow, I realized Max and I still had not addressed the issues of Bangalore and the moving van. I wondered if our decision to move had been reckless, whether we were in over our heads, and whether I'd ever get our family moved in so that I could focus on my business. I hoped I could find a way to salvage our plan to settle in quickly, especially if the police were right and there was an angry vandal out there. A vandal who seemed as determined to move us out as we were to move in.

Chapter 4

Moving and organizational overhauls are stressful. As an organizing professional, it's my job to know when to encourage clients to take a break and when to push through to the finish.

From the Notebook of Maggie McDonald
Simplicity Itself Organizing Services

Friday, August 29, Morning

I woke to the sound of Belle barking. Rubbing my face, I felt ridges where I must have slept on the zipper of my sleeping bag. I smelled hay, sneezed, and then inhaled the aroma of fresh coffee and wood smoke. I got up when I heard Brian trying to convince Max that s'mores were an appropriate breakfast food.

The night before, we'd fallen asleep in our clothes. This morning, I was happy to be fully dressed when I saw there were two strangers seated at the folding table. I was dying to brush my teeth, but my need for coffee overpowered my desire for good dental hygiene. I pulled a chair up to the table and sat.

A large person next to me handed me a cup of coffee. His bearlike paw palmed the milk carton and it hovered over my cup. I nodded. The paw poured, then set down the carton and passed me the bagel bag. Still warm. I took a large gulp of coffee, pushed the hair from my eyes, and examined the strangers. On my right, a large, bald, bearded man scooted a plate of cream cheese toward me.

"This coffee is . . . amazing," I said. I took another sip, put down my cup, and reached out my hand. "I'm Maggie McDonald."

The stranger smiled and shook my hand. "Stephen Laird, purveyor of coffee and bagels and other emergency provisions. Thank you for welcoming us into your—"

I nearly spit out my coffee, laughing as I watched the gracious man's gaze dart to all corners of the barn, as if searching for a polite word for our situation.

"—home." He settled confidently on the word. "It *is* a home, isn't it?"

I lifted my cup to Stephen Laird and to the younger man sitting across from me. I thought I'd seen him before but couldn't place him.

"Officer Paolo Bianchi, ma'am," said the second man. "I hope you don't mind that I grabbed a cup of coffee?"

Officer Bianchi looked dreadful. He was unshaven with dark circles under his eyes. Thin to the point of gauntness, he drowned in the dark-blue police windbreaker he wore over a T-shirt.

"Ahhh," I said. "I remember you. The Subaru with the kayak?"

Officer Bianchi nodded and pulled out an iPad. "I'm sorry, but I have to ask you a few questions, when you're ready."

"Give the woman a break, Paolo," Stephen said. "Finish your coffee and bagel, Mrs. McDonald. Take a shower if you need to. Paolo can wait." Stephen grabbed a chocolate-chip cookie from the plate that we'd not put away last night.

"Did you make those cookies?" I said on a hunch. "Are you our fairy godmother from last night? The police volunteer?"

Paolo's eyes widened and he choked on his coffee. Stephen smiled.

"I am, indeed," Stephen said. "I hope my contributions helped."

I nodded, my mouth too full of warm bagel to answer.

"I aim to please." Stephen pushed back his chair, picked up his paper dishes, and tossed them in a blue garbage bin labeled *recyclables*. He must have brought the bin with him too.

"I can't begin to thank you, Stephen. You've made all the difference."

He waved off my thanks and made a sharp whistle through his teeth. I heard a scrambling noise and a huge mastiff scooted out from under the table like an infantryman elbowing his way across enemy territory. The dog was as big as the table. How had I missed him? His breathing alone should have created a draft across my feet.

Stephen caught me staring and smiled as the mastiff circled him and plopped in a perfect, silent heel on his left. "He's my stealth dog," Stephen said. "Invisible until . . . well, until he's not."

I crossed the room to pet the dog, taking two swipes to rub his massive head.

"What a good boy you are, you gorgeous thing. Do you have a name?" I stroked floppy ears as big as my hand.

"Munchkin," answered Stephen.

I raised my eyebrows and rocked back on my heels to look Stephen in his blue eyes—eyes that dared me to ask the obvious question: How on earth did this beast earn the name Munchkin?

Instead I asked, "How did he come to be yours?"

"That's a story for another day." He turned and Munchkin loped after him. "He wasn't always this big," he called over his shoulder, answering the question I hadn't asked.

Inscrutable mysteries. Both of them.

I watched them head back up the hill toward the house and wondered where my family had gone. Officer Paolo Bianchi cleared his throat. I turned toward him, but not before I saw Jason leave the house and head down the hill, clapping Stephen on the shoulder and stooping to greet Munchkin.

"What can I do for you, Officer Bianchi?" I said, taking a seat, refilling my coffee cup, and taking a bite from my bagel. Sesame seeds tumbled to the table and a great glob of cream cheese landed on my T-shirt. I didn't care. The bagel was too good and, after all, I lived in a barn. I could eat like a pig if I wanted to.

"We need you to tell us what happened yesterday, ma'am," said Paolo, turning red and looking past my ear instead of looking me in the eye. "Confirm everyone's whereabouts."

Jason's shoes made crunching noises as he walked over the gravel outside. He strode into the barn. Like Bianchi, he was unshaven and exhausted, but Jason's stubble gave him the look of an edgy fashion model and fatigue made him look brooding.

"Good morning, Mrs. McDonald," he said. "Bianchi—good work, but I'll take it from here. Go home, get out of that kayaking gear, get some sleep. I'm calling the team in for a briefing at three o'clock. The day is yours until then."

Bianchi looked at his watch and winced. "Six and a half hours," he said. "I'd better get going. Thank you for your help, Mrs. McDonald."

I nodded to Bianchi, shook Jason's hand, and invited him to sit. I poured coffee and passed Jason a plate. While his manners were perfect, probably well-honed to put the public at ease, he gave food and coffee his full attention before addressing me. Eventually, he opened his mouth to speak, but I interrupted him.

"I suspect this breakfast was your idea, Detective. Thank you. It was very thoughtful. We've eaten now, though. Would your team like some of it? They're welcome to come down or I can have the boys bring it up to you at the house."

"It's Stephen Laird you have to thank," said Jason. "He has an uncanny sense of what people need in an emergency. You're new here, but the rest of us are used to seeing him at callouts, feeding people, handing warm blankets to displaced kids, comforting."

"Does the man never sleep?"

"Not much, he's—well, that's his story to tell."

Jason pulled out a dog-eared notepad and stubby pencil. He caught me looking at his note-taking tools. "I'm old school," he said. "No iPad for me. If I drop this or sit on it, it's still good. And I like to drive the bad guys nuts while they wait for me to finish writing and ask the next question."

Jason flipped the pages of the notebook. The pause in conversation gave me time to wonder whether I was being manipulated like those suspects he'd mentioned. I squirmed in my chair.

"Okay, then, Mrs. McDonald," he said.

"Maggie, please."

"Maggie. Your boys and Max tell the same story about yesterday morning. I need to hear it from you. You want to take me through it from the time you arrived?"

It didn't take long to tell, even with the other questions Jason asked about the condition of the house.

"Max is nuts about this place and tends to look at the world through a forgiving lens," I told Jason, explaining about our brief visit in February and Max's trip alone in April. "After the April inspection, Max said the house was perfect. But I don't think even Max would have described the house, as it is now, that way."

"That's what's worrying me," Jason said, leaning back in his chair and sipping his coffee. "We're finished with the basement and are going to turn the scene over to the cleaners in"—He looked at his phone—"forty-five minutes. I called in the fire department arson investigator to take a look at your electrical box."

Jason handed me two cards. "I'm giving you these as an Orchard View neighbor, not as a police officer. Those are electricians who have worked on my own house. I put the arson investigator's name and number on the back in case any electrician you hire wants to consult him. The electrical box was rigged so that, once it drew enough power—like when a family moved in—it would have caught fire."

I felt as though a mouse with icy feet had run up my spine. I shivered, though the day was growing warm. I picked up the cards for the electricians and stared at them.

"Our arson guy fixed up the box so that it's safe to use the power," Jason said. "But he recommends you do a full rewire. He's got kids the same age as yours and says that as soon as you fire up the oven or try to do laundry, you're going to be blowing fuses. But there's no longer any danger of fire."

The full impact of the dangers Jason was describing broke through my attempts at denial. "Fire?" I dropped the card and stared at him.

"The arson guy said the whole place could have gone up." Jason flipped through his notebook while I tamped down panic over the thought of my family being trapped in a flaming house because I'd done something as simple as preheating the oven.

"That sounds more serious than ordinary vandalism," I said, making fists with my hands under the table.

"We'll be investigating. Let us know if you see anything unusual."

"We've just moved in—not even moved in. How would we know what's usual?" My rising concern for my family's safety was tightening my throat and making my voice squeak.

Jason looked up from his notebook. "Okay, then, let us know if you see anything that *concerns* you. I doubt you'll see anything that our trained investigators wouldn't have spotted, though. I wouldn't worry." He pushed the chair back and slipped his pen and notebook into his jacket pocket.

Before he left, I started to ask him another question that had been bothering me. My single question morphed into many, which I asked in a tone of rising panic. "What about Javier? Do you know what happened? Why did he die here? Why did no one report him missing? Was he murdered? Are we safe? Should we change the locks?"

Jason stood and looked down at me with a patronizing expression I'd not seen him make before.

"We've confirmed what I told Max yesterday. The body was that of Javier Hernandez, a caretaker employed by your aunt's estate. He worked here three days a week. The medical examiner will make the determination on cause of death. As for your other questions? *You* concentrate on moving and let *us* focus on the investigation. It's *my* job, not yours, to ask questions and discover the answers to them."

He spoke slowly and emphasized every word. "Please let our officers handle the investigation. Orchard View does not need amateur detectives. This is *not* a television show."

He smiled to lessen the sting of his words.

"I was *curious*," I said. "God knows I have no interest in becoming Orchard View's Miss Marple or Jessica Fletcher. We just want to move into our house. And get started on school and our jobs, and"—I resisted the urge to act out my frustration like a bratty toddler—"I don't know, maybe pay our respects to Javier Hernandez, Max's only remaining link to his aunt? Mourn for someone who loved the house as much as we do?"

"We're doing our best to make sure you can do that as soon as possible." He cleared his throat and looked up the hill toward the house. "You'll see our cleaners arrive in hazmat suits. Don't let their outfits upset you. It's standard protocol, but Mr. Hernandez's body hadn't been there long enough to require much in the way of hazardous material treatment."

Eww.

I hesitated to ask whether the cleaners could be hired to clean and repair the rest of the house. Hazmat suits? That wasn't what we needed, not after today, anyway.

Jason handed me yet another card. A Realtor card.

"We don't want to sell," I said, surprised at the conviction I heard in my voice. I still hadn't had a chance to talk to Max about Bangalore and the house or my doubts concerning our decision to move. But I didn't have to talk to Max, not really. I knew what he wanted, what I wanted, and what the kids wanted.

"We're staying. Even if we have to fight off vandals ourselves."

"Finding and taking care of the vandals is *my* job, remember?" said Jason. "As is uncovering the full story behind what happened to Javier Hernandez. The card is for a friend of mine, Tess Olmos.

She's got teams of people she can call to clean up a house in a hurry and stage it for a quick sale. I'd go with her contacts for anything you need."

I drained my coffee cup. "It looks like there's nothing left for me to do but make a few calls." I knew better, of course. I'd learned my lesson yesterday. My plans to move this project forward could slip sideways at any time. I took the proffered card, but I wasn't sure how smart it would be to use the first referral I'd received. I didn't yet know whether Jason was a good investigator, let alone a good judge of quality in home-maintenance providers. I changed the subject.

"Have you seen my family? I heard them when I woke up, but I haven't seen them yet."

"They took off down the drive with your dog—Belle, is it? They looked like they were headed off to explore the neighborhood. One of the boys was carrying a stick like an expedition banner."

Jason slapped the table with his palm and left. I looked at my watch. I had time to clean up before Max got back with the kids and we planned our next step.

My cell phone rang. I glanced at the display. My mom. Much as I loved her, she was the last person I wanted to talk to at the moment. She'd been against the move, insulted because she said Max and I were leaving her and the rest of my family.

I was sure Mom was calling to see how things were going, but I knew how the phone call would progress. I'd outline the roadblocks, including the late moving van, Max's impending flight to India, the body in the basement, the vandalism, and the devastating electrical fire we'd narrowly sidestepped. There would be a painful pause in the conversation. She'd take a deep breath and suggest moving back to Stockton. In fact, she'd probably drive her van out here and start loading us into it.

That couldn't happen. For me, there was no going back.

I'd return Mom's call later.

After my shower, I chose a clean white T-shirt and underwear from the Target bag, pulled on my jeans, and shoved my feet into my sneakers. Max and the kids still weren't home, so I headed up the hill, past the house, planning to walk to the end of the driveway to check the mailbox and to see if I could spot my family returning from their walk.

The herd of emergency vehicles had thinned. The jumpsuited pair with the generator was shoving their gear into the back of the same SUV it had emerged from almost twenty-four hours earlier. I thanked them and continued down the rutted drive toward the mailbox.

Pleased to see that someone had kept the mailbox clear of weeds and overhanging branches, I peered inside and plucked out a flyer advertising lawn services. I'd normally recycle something like that without reading it, but today, in a new place, it was mail. And it added to the growing feeling that I was at home.

The sound of raspy breathing made me look up. A tall, lean, blond man walked toward me down steep Briones Hill Road. He held the leashes of three wheezing Pekinese dogs, all of which began yapping once they saw me. Their high-pitched barks made me feel as if all the marbles in my head were loose and banging into one another.

The man's dress shoes slipped a bit on the gravel at the edge of the road. His neatly pressed pants, shirt, and jacket were huge leaps up, style-wise, from my jeans and sneakers. His hair, and the hair on the Pekes, made them all look like they'd stepped from a salon. I ran my hand through my still damp hair, thinking maybe it was time for a cut and highlights. My light-brown hair, dusted with what I liked to call tinsel, had a tendency to look drab and scruffy without routine maintenance.

I put out my hand and said hello. The man ignored both overtures. He looked me over, head to toe.

"Mrs. McDonald?" he said.

"Yes, yes I am," I said, pleased that someone in the neighborhood seemed to have known we were coming. "I'm Maggie McDonald." I stepped forward and held out my hand again. He ignored it.

"Quite a lot of noise here last night. This is a quiet neighborhood. I hope we won't be disturbed by sirens on a regular basis now that you have moved in."

"Umm . . ." I had no idea how to respond to his comments, which were oddly unfriendly. I'd expected more of a *Welcome to the neighborhood, I'll bring cookies over later, do you need to use a phone?* kind of greeting.

But the man shifted tacks and held out his hand. "I'm Dennis DeSoto. We heard you were coming this weekend. I noticed no moving van has arrived. Are you staying or cleaning the house to sell?"

"Good morning, Mr. DeSoto," I raised my voice to be heard over the yapping Pekes. "We're staying, but still waiting for our furniture to arrive."

DeSoto made a face. "That house has become an eyesore since old Mrs. Kay McDonald left. It's dangerous. You might as well tear it down and start over. Build something fresh and modern. And I hope you'll be paying more attention to the landscaping."

I surprised myself by leaping to the defense of our house. "Oh, it's not that bad," I said. "It's a classic beauty that needs some tender loving care. We'll settle in quickly, I'm sure. My boys will be headed to Orchard View Middle School and Orchard View High School next week."

"I hope you've pre-enrolled them," Dennis said, making a little pout with his lips. "It's difficult to find room for students at this late date."

"For the public schools? Don't they have to take everyone?"

"Everyone who lives within the district will find a spot, yes. But you'll need to show a deed or a gas bill to prove you live inside the boundaries. We've got the best schools in the state. All the parents want their kids to go here. You'd be surprised what people from other areas will do to sneak their kids in. You can find the details on the website outlining what paperwork we require."

"We?"

"Oh, yes. *We.* I'm on the school board and am very involved in fund-raising and other important programs. I've got three children at Monte Viejo Elementary and a son at the middle school, where I'm the PTA treasurer. My oldest, Dante, is at the high school."

"That's great. You've got kids the same age as mine. Maybe they'll have a chance to meet before school starts."

"My children are consumed by athletic camps," he said. "I doubt they'll have time."

"*O-kay.*" I dragged out the syllables as I tried to find a way to end the conversation. "Well, thanks. Nice to meet you." I used my best manners. I was new here and it was too soon to be making enemies. But that didn't stop me from bestowing an irreverent nickname on the self-involved fool. Henceforth, whenever he annoyed me, I'd refer to him as Mr. Snooty.

Mr. Snooty patted the pockets of his jacket while the Pekes sniffed at my ankles and left slobber on my sneakers. "I hope there is still room for your boy in the middle school. If not, you'll have to cart him across town to the other junior high."

"No buses?"

Mr. Snooty looked shocked. "Buses? We haven't had buses since the 1970s. We *drive* our kids to school.

"Look," he added, looking at me as if I were a hopeless case. "Here's my card. Let me know if you have questions as you settle in."

I was feeling storm-tossed trying to keep up with the shifts in Mr. Snooty's demeanor. We actually *had* preregistered the kids for both schools, but I hadn't been able to interject that fact into the conversation. Mr. Snooty seemed happy to assume we'd dropped the ball on those details, but Max and I were serious about our kids' education and determined to leave nothing to chance. And what was with the business cards? Did everyone around here carry cards when they walked the dogs? If that was the case, I was out of my depth. When I walked Belle, I carried poop bags.

Mr. Snooty flapped the card in my face until I took it from him. "I'm a Realtor. If you decide you want to sell, let me know."

I put the card in the back pocket of my jeans and looked up the road. It climbed quickly up the steep hill.

"Thanks so much," I said with feigned cheeriness. "My family is off on a walk and I'm hoping to catch up with them. Maybe we'll see more of you after school starts."

Mr. Snooty waved and I headed up the hill. I turned back once and saw him peering up our driveway with his hand on the mailbox. He crouched and knelt at the base of the post. I wondered if he was the one who'd weeded the area. Nah. I could already tell he wasn't the type. He was probably picking up after one of his dogs.

I turned my back on Mr. Snooty and I looked up toward a cleft in the mountains that separated Orchard View from the Pacific Coast. Max had told me that a thick bank of fog—the "marine layer" that served as natural air-conditioning for the San Francisco Bay Area—spilled over the top of the mountain in the late afternoon. Now, in mid-morning, it was receding as the sun heated the valley.

I caught up with my family at the top of the hill. Belle hopped around me and the boys regaled me with stories of the deer, rabbits, hares, and quail they'd seen. We walked a short way down the other side of the hill, hoping to see more wildlife, but after about fifteen minutes the boys said they were hungry. We headed back to the house together, making plans for the afternoon.

We were a hundred yards from the mailbox when it exploded with an ear-shattering *boom*.

Chapter 5

When you're not sure how to tackle a cleaning or organizational problem, ask. Most people are delighted to share their expertise.

From the Notebook of Maggie McDonald
Simplicity Itself Organizing Services

Friday, August 28, Afternoon

Belle lunged, pulled the leash from Brian's hand, and ran to glue herself to my side to protect me and receive reassurance. I knelt, held her shivering body, and felt comforted myself.

The boys ran to the smoking mailbox before I could stop them. Max dialed 9-1-1. David pushed the hanging metal door closed with the corner of his T-shirt. I'd expected shrapnel and a splintered redwood post, but the damage seemed minimal despite the enormous boom.

"Cool!" David said.

"Someone might have been hurt," I said. "What if we'd been standing next to it?"

"I think anyone standing right next to the explosion would have been more scared than hurt," Max said, opening and closing the mailbox door, demonstrating that it still worked. He snuffed out a smoldering spark with his foot. David whacked at the weeds with a stick, looking for other signs of fire. Brian had gone up to the house to hunt for a bucket or a hose long enough to reach the mailbox. It had been a long, hot, dry summer all over California and we were conscious of how easy it would be to start a wildfire.

Our ears were still ringing ten minutes later when Officer Paolo

Bianchi pulled his Subaru to the side of the road. This afternoon he had a sailboard strapped to the roof of the car. I wondered whether he sailed in the gale-force winds and tricky currents of San Francisco Bay or if he preferred someplace calmer.

He jumped from the car and tripped, grabbing the door for balance. Ducking, he reached into the car for his iPad. He pushed his sunglasses back on his head, greeted us, and replaced the glasses to peer at the mailbox.

"A cherry bomb," he said. His fingers danced over the internal keyboard of the pad as he took notes. "Kids. They picture this giant explosion and think they'll film it and it will be the next viral video. Instead, there's a *boom*, the door blows open, and that's it."

"The sound was loud enough for us," Max said.

"They may have lit more than one bomb," Bianchi said, peering into the box, plucking out the charred remains of explosives and placing them in an official-looking evidence envelope. "You know how to get the soot off?"

I nodded. "Swipe it with dish detergent and hose it down. If that doesn't get it all, start over and scrub a bit with a nail brush or try a solution of TSP—trisodium phosphate. Where's the nearest hardware store?"

"Head to the end of this road. Turn downhill at each intersection until you reach Foothill Expressway. Turn left and follow the signs to downtown. The hardware is on First Street."

"You think kids did this?" I said.

Bianchi nodded.

"Why's that? Have you had a rash of explosions like this? We didn't see or hear any kids." Once I'd started questioning him, it was hard to stop.

The young officer looked at me. His face turned pink. He opened his mouth and closed it. I wondered why someone who seemed so uncomfortable talking to people would chose a career that required interacting with the public.

"Umm," he said, staring at the ground. "Maybe they had a remote? Like you use to ignite model rocket motors?" He walked behind the mailbox and pushed aside the grass. "Here," he said, picking up a wire and following it until it disappeared among the overgrown shrubs that clogged the hillside between the house and the road.

"We'll get the crime-scene guys back out here and let them see if they can pick up any evidence the kids might have left."

"Wouldn't kids be kind of giddy if they were planning something like this?" I asked. "We didn't see or hear anyone while we were walking down the hill." I had two kids and I knew how noisy they could be, particularly when they were trying to be quiet.

Bianchi looked uncomfortable. Max came to his rescue.

"Maggie, let Officer Bianchi do his job," Max said. "Let him ask the questions. He can check and see if there are records of other exploding mailboxes, I'm sure."

"The only person I saw out here today was Dennis DeSoto," I said, handing the officer the card Mr. Snooty had given me. "He was fussing around the mailbox about twenty minutes before it blew up. Maybe he saw someone."

"Thank you, ma'am," he said, taking the card. "Please call me Paolo. And please ask your boys to keep an eye on social media for videos posted by kids bragging about blowing things up."

I nodded, although I wasn't sure how much good that would do. We hadn't lived here long enough for David and Brian to acquire local friends. I thanked Paolo for his time, especially since he'd been up all night working on the other investigation—the one involving the body in our basement.

Max and I waved goodbye to Paolo and walked back up the driveway. I'd have been happier with a swift apprehension of the brats who'd done this—and would have loved to see them covered with soot and soap, scrubbing our mailbox. But Max and Jason Mueller were right. Tracking down troublemakers was a job for the police, not for a professional organizer or a family that had as much on its plate as we did.

"The police," Max said, interrupting my thoughts. "Our new best friends."

The rest of the day and the weekend passed in a flurry of trips to the hardware store for household-repair items and to the mall to buy Max a wardrobe and luggage appropriate for India. The hazardous-waste cleanup team came and went, but between the lingering smell of death and the harsh chemicals they'd used to sanitize the basement, we decided to stay in the barn until our furniture arrived. A few more days with the windows open would help the house air out. I hoped it would also help me shed the creepy feelings I had every time I thought of a man lying dead in our basement.

I was also fighting my dread of Max's departure, though I tried to remain upbeat for his sake. I knew he felt guilty leaving us before we'd moved into the house, but we'd given up everything in Stockton to make this move, and we needed Max's job to be a success. He was still the new guy, and it was too soon for him to be saying he wouldn't do what the company asked.

I scratched at an itchy spot on my leg and shook off my negative feelings. I needed to focus on the good stuff that would happen this week. The moving van would arrive. The boys would start their new schools and we'd all start following a more predictable routine. I sighed. And one day soon, I'd be able to start my plans to launch Simplicity Itself 2.0, the Silicon Valley version.

Looking back on the weekend, I was glad I hadn't been able to see the future.

Chapter 6

When you're stuck waiting, consider the time a gift.
Make lists. Clean your purse. Clear your head.

From the Notebook of Maggie McDonald
Simplicity Itself Organizing Services

Tuesday, September 2, Morning

I woke up early Tuesday morning, now fully adjusted to camping on the barn floor. It was the first day of school. I glanced at my phone, looking for a text or email from Max to say he'd arrived safely in Bangalore.

I'd never felt so far from him. This separation, coming so soon after we'd made a move that we'd hoped would give us more time together, was going to be difficult. I needed to make the best of it, though. It was time to get on with my day. The boys and I could write him long emails tonight detailing the events of the first day of school.

I showered and donned my jeans, T-shirt, and grubby white sneakers. There were advantages to a limited wardrobe. I didn't have to waste time deciding what to wear.

I woke up the kids. David jumped in the shower while Brian started his breakfast. I could tell Brian was nervous about starting a new school because he was quiet. Normally, he chattered through breakfast, barely pausing to take time to chew.

"Hey, Mom," David said. He joined us dressed in a towel he'd wound around his waist. Drying his hair with another towel, he sat at the table and poured cereal into a bowl. There'd be time to lecture him on proper mealtime attire another day. Technically, we were still camping.

"Roll up your sleeping bags," I said. "We're back in the house tonight."

"Unless we find another body," Brian said, grinning. The cheeky little devil dodged the dish towel I threw at him.

Both boys dressed in record time and climbed in the car with Belle while I grabbed my phone, grocery bags, and shopping list. With no working refrigerator, I was afraid to stock more than a day's worth of food.

After dropping David at the high school, Brian and I headed to the middle school, where I parked in the shade. Brian gave Belle a quick pat, made the American Sign Language symbol for *I love you*—our family code—and dashed out the door.

I let Belle out the back of the car, attached her leash, and gave her a quick stop-and-sniff moment at a nearby patch of grass. Belle finished her own morning-hygiene routine and tugged on the leash.

"We'll walk later, Belle," I said as I opened the rear hatch. She hopped in. I pulled out my tinted lip balm. Normally, I'd dress up a bit for the first day of school, but this year, grubby jeans and sneakers were my only option. I rolled down the windows to let cool air in for Belle, squared my shoulders, and marched off to the first PTA meeting of the year.

I squirmed on an uncomfortable metal chair and listened to the "Let's Get School Off to a Good Start" meeting. I'd attended dozens of these back-to-school lectures, but this was the first time I'd been to one outdoors. Late summer and early fall in Stockton were too hot for outdoor meetings.

"Thank you for being here to support your students," said Principal Harrier from her podium. "I'm sure we're going to have a wonderful year. I'd like to introduce our new teachers . . ."

Blah-blah-blah. The meeting was the standard drill and I barely listened. By this time in my career as a mom, I could have given one of these presentations myself. My attention wandered off, but I dragged it back to Miss Harrier. I'd met her in February when we'd come to Orchard View to peek in the windows of the house before we had the keys. We'd made appointments ahead of time with both schools to preregister the boys and get their paperwork in order. At the high school, the meeting took all of fifteen minutes, including a tour of the campus.

In contrast, the middle-school meeting came to a halt when Miss Harrier realized the transfer of the property had not been finalized and we didn't yet live in the district. I'd convinced her to register Brian anyway, on the basis of the preliminary paperwork I'd brought with me. I'd promised to deliver documentation from Pacific Gas and Electric on the first day of school. Why the gas company had the final word on who went to school where, I had no idea. Bureaucracy seldom makes sense.

I'd tried to drop off the form before school this morning, but the office had been packed with fidgety adolescents held in check by a diminutive woman dressed in canary yellow from head to toe. I'd decided to wait until she'd solved the kids' problems before I bothered her with my paperwork.

Miss Harrier droned on. "I run a tight ship," she said, slapping the leather cover of her iPad. "The rules are posted. Everyone has a copy. Every student and parent will sign forms stating they have read the rules and will be responsible for them. No excuses will be accepted. That holds true for homework, attendance, and for all forms."

This woman should run a military academy. I looked at the other parents and wondered if I could become friends with anyone. I'd already seen and avoided my snooty neighbor who had been shaking hands and passing out his cards this morning. What was it with the people in this town and their business cards? And what was making me so negative? Maybe the fact that Max wasn't here.

I gave myself a mental slap and tried to focus on something other than self-pity.

Directly in front of me was a woman who looked like she'd stepped from the pages of a fashion magazine. Her hair was sleek, shining, and dark—almost as dark as her black business jacket and tight, straight skirt. She'd alleviated the black with a Chinese red scarf artfully draped over a white silk blouse. Her heels were black stilettos with red soles. I didn't know the name of those shoes, but I knew they cost about as much as I'd spend on a trip to the vet with Belle and the cats. The suit screamed money and high fashion. I checked her off the potential friend list right away.

I sighed and slumped in my chair.

"There are cookies and coffee on the tables in the back. Please stop and pick up your packets of all the necessary forms," concluded Miss Harrier.

Chairs clattered as parents gathered their belongings. A group of helpful dads folded chairs and stacked them on carts. I allowed myself another unattractive moment of self-pity, thinking that ordinarily, Max would have been there to join the other dads.

Miss Harrier slapped her hand against her iPad—a sound I was learning to hate. She barked for attention with a voice that would have done a drill sergeant proud. The crowd quieted, though a metal chair clanged when it fell to the pavement.

"I neglected to announce earlier that we are grateful to an anonymous donor"—she looked at my neighbor, Mr. Snooty DeSoto, who turned and smiled at the crowd—"for a contribution of record-breaking generosity to complete our all-season track. We appreciate *all* the donations we've received, but we are truly overwhelmed by this show of parental support."

Someone behind me snorted and I turned to find a plump, frizzy-haired woman wearing a flowing purple skirt with a mint-green T-shirt and Birkenstock sandals. "Anonymous, my foot," she said, elbowing the dominatrix woman in black who'd been sitting in front of me.

"You've got that right," said the dominatrix. "Darling Dennis DeSoto does it again. Showing us how much more dedicated he is than anyone else, but maintaining his sham humility by making the donation 'anonymous'." She did the air-quote thing with the first two manicured fingers of each hand. "But he made sure everyone knew who that anonymous donor was. Typical. How soon do you think we can clear out of here? I've got things to do."

Maybe I'd misjudged them. The snooty Dennis DeSoto couldn't be *all* bad if he'd made a huge donation to the school. He'd put his money where his mouth was, at least. The plump earth mother and the dominatrix both had a little bit of the irreverent sarcasm I liked to see in someone who might one day become a friend.

Harrier slapped her iPad again. "This donation is particularly welcome in light of the fact that the district has reported a financial setback that may impede our academic program."

A murmur of concern rose from the crowd, but it stopped when Harrier slapped her iPad for attention. I entertained the snarky thought that Harrier had the skills to launch a career as a flamenco dancer.

"An accounting discrepancy was discovered in this summer's audit of foundation accounts. The foundation board has frozen funds pending an investigation and that will delay our receipt of the money that helps us provide programs no longer supported by the State of California. Those who are interested in learning more may wish to attend the board meeting in October."

October seemed a long way off to begin resolving an important funding issue, but I didn't say anything. I was too new and too unfamiliar with local issues to have an educated opinion. The parents moved into tight little groups, waving their arms and speaking in voices that rose nearly to the point of shouting. Harrier's tone implied a temporary setback or slight trimming of funds. But from the noise of the crowd, I guessed that either cutbacks were new to Orchard View or the parents didn't believe the budget trimming would be as minor as Harrier had suggested. In Stockton, I would have buttonholed one of my best friends, the head of the PTA whose cousin was on the school board, and had the complete story within minutes. I couldn't do that here. Not yet.

These parents were angry, focused on potential budget cuts, and not interested in meeting new parents like me. Someday maybe, but not today. I picked up my dictionary-sized stack of forms, dropped a copy of the gas company's letter in the office, and got back to the car just after Belle started to bark.

I dropped the forms in the back of the van and grabbed Belle's leash. "Let's make a good impression, girl," I whispered. "Try to hold it until we get off school grounds." I didn't want the parent group's first impression of us to be the image of my dog desecrating the plush school lawn.

"You know that's my parking space, right?"

I looked up, confused. A woman wearing pressed khakis, pink ballet flats, and a matching pink sweater stood behind my car, scowling.

"Excuse me?" I said. The woman scanned my clothes and my dusty car. Her expression told me we'd not made a good first impression.

"You're in my parking space. I had to park clear over on the other side of the campus. I always park here."

"I'm sorry," I said. "This is my first day. I'm Maggie McDonald. My son started seventh grade today. We're new." I reached out my hand to shake hers. She ignored it. Maybe people here didn't shake hands? I was starting to feel like I might have landed on another planet. Was she kidding about the parking spot or were there really assigned places? I was too new to know.

"Pauline Windsor," said the woman, looking at her phone. "My daughter Rebecca is student council president."

"Nice to meet you, Pauline."

Pauline waved her hand and hiked back to her car, which was parked only a few rows over. I shrugged and set off with Belle, who was much easier to read than the Orchard View humans.

I looked around the neighborhood as we followed a concrete sidewalk past manicured lawns, trimmed bushes, and cheerful fall flowers. The houses were California ranch-style, built in the fifties and sixties. I thought about how easy it would be to fix up Aunt Kay's house and put it on the market. Her house and land had been appraised at more than fifteen million dollars. Land was scarce in Silicon Valley and prices for even the small tract homes and lots were creeping toward three million.

In addition, if we sold Aunt Kay's house and bought a smaller one within walking distance of both schools, we'd save big on property taxes. We'd have the remainder of the money from the sale to finance the boys' college expenses and build our retirement nest egg. It was a tempting thought, but didn't allow for Max's emotional attachment to Aunt Kay's house. Nor for the fact that even though we had only been there for a short time, the boys and I had become almost as attached to the house as Max was.

From across the street, I heard another dog barking—the deep woof of a large dog.

Belle strained at her leash, pulling me in the direction of the woof. I looked both ways and crossed the street. It didn't matter where we walked, as long as I remembered how to get back to the car. Belle pulled, forcing our speed up to a trot. I gave the leash a little tug, reminded her to heel, and pulled a treat from the pocket of my jeans. Her tongue lifted it from my palm.

Two houses up from where we'd crossed, a black BMW was parked in front of a well-landscaped house. I slowed my step. Behind the BMW, on the passenger side, stood the dominatrix from school, waving her arms and calling to me.

"Oh, I'm *so* glad to see you," the dominatrix said. "Please, would you mind helping me a moment?"

Help her? She seemed like the type of woman who had every hair in place, every wrinkle ironed out, and every appointment entered in the latest version of the iPhone. Why would she need *my* help?

I shrugged. I needed all the luck I could get at this point and I figured the best way to make the Fates happy and maximize my good fortune was to help someone else. Even someone I wasn't anxious to meet and who might throw my schedule off enough that my latte would have to wait.

I pasted a smile on my face as I approached.

"Sure," I said. "How can I help? I saw you at school, didn't I?"

"My son Teddy is starting eighth grade. Are you new? I've not seen you before. I'm Tess Olmos."

The name sounded familiar, but I couldn't remember where I'd heard it. I stood on the driver's side of the car. I'd expected her to walk toward me and hold out her hand after introducing herself, but something about this whole scenario was off. She sounded friendly, but she hadn't moved. Should I approach her? Did she have personal-space issues?

"I'm Maggie McDonald," I said. "My son Brian is in seventh grade and I've got a freshman at the high school."

"Boy or girl?" asked Tess. "Umm . . . would you mind coming closer? I really need your help, but I don't want to shout it out to the whole neighborhood."

"Boy. David." I walked around the car and burst out laughing, then covered my mouth with my hand. I'd just met this woman and the first thing I did was laugh at her? She'd think I was a barbarian with no manners and she'd be right.

"It's not funny," Tess said. "Oh hell, of course it is." She started laughing too.

The fancy kick pleat of her skirt was stuck in the passenger door. I was guessing the car was locked. Her keys had fallen out of reach, along with her purse.

"Can you grab the keys and unlock me?" Tess said. "I'm not sure how this happened. If I'd caught the jacket in the door, I could have taken it off. I was about to try stripping off the skirt, but every time I reached for the zipper, a car went by. I'm so glad you showed up."

I grabbed the keys and her purse and unlocked the door.

Tess smoothed her skirt and threw her arms around me. "Thank you *sooo* much. Today was not the day I wanted to get naked in my front yard. You *have* to come in and let me give you coffee, at least."

I started to decline. "No, we've got to get back. I've got the movers coming and this one needs a walk and the groceries—"

"Stop right now," Tess ordered. I obeyed. The dominatrix was back. "Stop. You must come in. I make the best coffee and I've got cookies. You need energy for moving. I should know. I'm a real-estate agent. I'll give you a snack to give your boys. Nothing says *home* like after-school cookies."

Trying to disagree with Tess would be as useful as tackling a bulldozer. I didn't like confrontation and I wasn't going to fight a battle I wasn't sure I wanted to win. Coffee and cookies actually sounded wonderful.

"Look," Tess continued, pointing at Belle. "Take your gorgeous girl around to the backyard. My Mozart is there. That's him barking. He's a German shepherd, but he's a marshmallow. They can play while we get to know each other. I'm so glad you came by when you did. My lucky day. Go on, now. I'll head into the house and let you in the back door."

I wondered why she didn't invite me in through the front door. I shrugged. People are weird. She took great care with her appearance. Maybe she didn't think dogs belonged in the house.

I followed a path lined with African iris and lobelia around the side of the house, through a redwood gate, and into the backyard. A German shepherd bounded to greet us, tail wagging. I let Belle off her leash. The pair sniffed each other and then they were off, chasing one another like puppies.

Steps led to a redwood deck that extended across the back of the house and looked like a picture in an upscale garden catalog. Comfy-looking red cushions covered black wrought-iron armchairs and ottomans. The look had the welcoming feel I hoped we'd someday achieve in our new house.

I peered through the window, but it was dark inside the house and I couldn't see a thing. I tried the knob just as the back door opened. I stumbled into the room and was helped up by a woman who had to be Tess's twin sister.

She looked like Tess but without the edgy black and red power outfit. This woman's hair was pulled back in a scruffy ponytail. She wore a gray sweatshirt splotched with white paint and jeans that appeared to be a size or two too large. On her feet were a battered pair of Ugg boots on which I was sure I'd spotted a lump of dried cookie dough.

"Tess?"

"Shh." She laughed and pulled me into a kitchen that smelled of the cookies. "This is the at-home Tess. I shed those killer heels and that silly power suit the minute I walk through the door."

I must have looked skeptical, because she pulled me through the house and threw open the door to a room near the front door. The size of a small bedroom, it looked like a Hollywood dressing room with racks of classic black and red suits and snowy white blouses. A lighted counter held scads of cosmetics. A robe lay crumpled on the floor of the adjacent bathroom.

My astonishment showed and Tess laughed—a gentle, burbling laugh that was at odds with the woman I'd seen at the school.

"I keep my business stuff in here. It used to be the guest room. Mozart and the cats aren't allowed in here—it saves time not to have to swipe off dog and cat hair. I can get changed in a heartbeat if anyone needs me for work. For everyone except my friends I wear these dominatrix clothes. They help me get deals signed quickly."

I shook my head and smiled. "Um . . . I have to admit that *dominatrix* is exactly the word I chose to describe you when you were sitting in front of me this morning."

Tess laughed and tugged me back toward the kitchen. "Isn't that Miss Harrier awful? I swear she'll be the death of me. If a form isn't filled out exactly right she'll rip it up and send it home. The parents want to kill her. And now with the budget cuts . . ." Tess shook her head.

She pulled cobalt-blue mugs and plates from the cabinet and continued talking as she pointed me toward a chair at a round table covered with a red-checked tablecloth. "Swear-to-God, the only reason she's still alive is that kids are in middle school for such a short period. By the time parents are ready to throttle her, their kids have moved on to high school."

Tess measured ground coffee into a paper filter and poured boiling water over it. I found the lack of a computerized coffee machine refreshing. Much as I thrived on fancy coffee, I was glad to know there were people in this town who didn't need the trendiest appliances.

Tess handed me a steaming cup and pushed a pitcher of cream toward me. I poured the cream until the coffee turned the color of a paper grocery bag, then lifted the mug to my lips. It smelled heavenly. I sipped and Tess passed me the plate of cookies. Oatmeal. Old-fashioned. Homey.

"Now, tell me where you're from and where you're living," Tess said. "Is there anything you need? You said the movers were coming. What time? We'll watch the clock. You must be swamped. Are you working?"

I looked at the clock. It was five past ten. I still had plenty of time. I glanced out the window, watching the dogs tugging on opposite ends of a knotted rope, growling, but with their tails wagging. I sighed. A contented sigh. I was having fun watching them and getting to know both of Tess's personalities.

"Let me help you with the moving, Maggie. No one sells houses just after school starts, and I've got plenty of time right now. Is your electricity on? Do you need the laundry done? Do you need any help unpacking? Is your Internet up?"

I laughed. "I don't even know what I need yet. I mean . . . I've got a list. . . ." I pulled my notebook out of my purse, a small battered backpack that had once been blue and white, but was now more gray and faded denim. "I'm a professional organizer. Lists are my thing. Being prepared for anything and easing people through transitions is what I do." I shook my head and laughed as I smoothed out the page. "I'm starting to think I need to hire my own organizer."

My phone rang.

"Excuse me," I said to Tess, as I rummaged in my backpack. "It might be the movers.

"Hello? This is Maggie."

"Mrs. McDonald, this is Roberto, from Stockton Movers? I've got bad news."

My heart sank. This reprieve in Tess's kitchen had lifted my spirits and made me forget that nothing about this move had gone as expected.

"We got the team together this morning and they were on schedule until they got to the windmills."

"Okay," I said, waiting for the bad news. I knew where he meant. Thousands of space-age windmills dotted the hills that separated the San Joaquin Valley from the San Francisco Bay Area. The windmills harvested power as gusts roared through the narrowed pass, but wind speeds at the top of the hill had been known to flip heavy big rigs. I imagined the worst—all our worldly belongings being run over by speeding motorists.

"The brakes locked up as they headed down the grade," Roberto said. "The team pulled the truck over. The crew and your furniture are fine, but we're going to have to send a new cab out to pull the trailer. We just can't risk it with the bad brakes."

"No, you're right," I said. "I'm glad no one was hurt. But . . . um . . . Roberto? When will you deliver our furniture?"

"Not for another forty-eight hours, I'm afraid, ma'am. We sent all the other cabs out with teams this morning. We have to wait until one comes back with an empty trailer so we can swap it out for your load."

I could have argued with him. Pleaded. I could have reminded him that everything we owned was on that trailer, that it was taking longer to get it from Stockton to Orchard View than it would have taken to move it across the country. But I knew he was doing his best. Arguing would waste time and make us both more miserable than we already were.

I sighed. "Roberto? Thanks for letting me know. Thursday will be fine. Should I expect you at noon? . . . That's right. Twenty-one eleven Briones Hill Road, off Monte Viejo."

I hung up the phone, made a face, shrugged, and snatched a cookie from the plate.

"Tess?" I asked my new best friend. "Did you mean it when you offered to help with my laundry?"

Before Tess could answer, my phone rang a second time. I glanced at the number, but didn't recognize it.

"Mom? Can you come back to school?" Brian sniffed. "I'm in trouble and the principal wants to talk to you." Brian's voice and his fear were broadcast loudly through the phone, shattering whatever peace remained in Tess's kitchen.

"I'll be right there, Brian. Hang tough. We'll sort it out."

Tess grabbed her keys. "Leave Belle here with Mozart. I'll drive you."

Chapter 7

The organized person will save time by getting to
know the most influential and important people in any
organization: the front office staff, the custodian, and
any security personnel.

From the Notebook of Maggie McDonald
Simplicity Itself Organizing Services

Tuesday, September 2, Midmorning

I ran from Tess's BMW toward the school. The woman I'd seen in
the office earlier met me outside the front door.

"Mrs. McDonald?" Now that she was out from behind the front
counter, I could see that she was, indeed, covered head to toe in canary
yellow. Her feet sported yellow high-tops. A yellow bow secured her
ponytail. Shorter than five feet tall, she looked like a diminutive Big
Bird.

"It's Maggie," I said. "Is Brian okay?"

"Brian is just inside. He's fine, Maggie. I'm April Chen, the assistant principal. I wanted to fill you in before you see Brian or Miss
Harrier."

"What happened?"

"I talked to Brian. You requested that he be put in either eighth-
grade math or in the seventh-grade algebra class? And in band?"

"That's right."

"Brian went to his first-period class this morning. He figured
someone made a mistake with his schedule because band wasn't on
it. He asked the other kids what to do and they told him they'd show
him to the band room."

April held up her hand to keep me from going inside. "You have to hear this, Maggie. Before you see Brian and Miss Harrier, you have to know he didn't do anything wrong."

"But, he said—"

"Five minutes with Horrible Harrier, and any kid would confess to having started the Civil War, but don't tell anyone I said that. If I ran the zoo, things would be different around here."

I swallowed hard and nodded. April looked over her shoulder toward Miss Harrier's office and continued: "The music teacher didn't have Brian on her class list, so she called the office to correct Brian's schedule, asking to have him placed in her band class instead of theater. She told me that he wanted to move into advanced seventh-grade math in place of basic math skills."

"Basic math skills? What's that?"

"What it sounds like," April said.

"That can't be right."

"That's what Brian said."

"Did he have an attitude or something?"

April laughed. "I asked him that. He said that this was his first day and way too early in the year to be showing attitude. I like your kid, Maggie. He's a good one. I wanted you to hear that before—"

Miss Harrier flung the office door open so hard it banged against the front of the building. Her face was scrunched up, as if she'd swallowed a lemon. She stood with the posture of a drill sergeant and the tension of a volcano about to erupt.

"April, thank you. I'll take it from here. Follow me please, Mrs. McDonald." Harrier stomped back into the school office and nodded to Brian, who looked miserable and small, slumped in the chair outside her personal domain. "Brian, join us if you please, *now*."

I clenched my teeth and my fists to keep my thoughts from turning into words, or worse, actions. I normally steered clear of conflict, but where my kids were concerned, all bets were off. There was really no need for Harrier's stern "now." Brian was right outside her office, for heaven's sake. If he'd dawdled—and he was a world-class dawdler, like most twelve-year-old boys—it would have taken him two seconds instead of one to reach her desk.

Miss Harrier invited us to sit in the scratchy upholstered chairs in front of her desk. She plucked two business cards from a wooden file on her desk and put one in front of each of us. Neither Brian nor I picked them up.

Harrier shuffled papers on her desk and turned on her iPad.

"Looking at our school roster over the weekend," she said, peering at me over the top of her black-framed reading glasses, "I realized that we had limited room in some of our classes and I had to make adjustments to a few of the students' schedules. Apparently, Brian thinks he can dictate his own schedule."

"Are you saying you can't accommodate him in band?"

"There are seventy-five students in that class, Mrs. McDonald. It is oversubscribed."

It was a concert band class. What difference would it make if the enrollment was seventy-six students instead of seventy-five? And why, if students needed to be cut from the class, did Brian need to be one of them? There were always students who were taking band only because their parents were making them. Those kids would almost certainly volunteer to be dropped from the class. I turned to Brian.

"Did you introduce yourself to the teacher?" I said. "Did you ask if she had room in her class for you?" My kids had grown up on a university campus. Their grandparents and dad were professors. The unwritten etiquette of academia was in their blood.

Brian looked at his hands and nodded. "She was happy to hear I play French horn." He looked up at me. "Mom, I have to take band."

Miss Harrier *tsk*ed. "You see, Mrs. McDonald, this is the attitude with which I have a problem. Orchard View Middle School students do *not* dictate to their parents, teachers, and administrators. At this age we expect them to understand that they cannot have everything their own way."

I took a deep breath and thought before I spoke. Brian needed to play music the same way he needed to breathe and I knew that band was a great way for him to meet friends. He was going to take band. But I'd hear the rest of the story from Miss Harrier, first.

Silence and tension built within the room that was so quiet and stuffy that we were all startled when the air-conditioning fan kicked on and the metal vent made the annoying buzzing rattle that is universal to all public schools. All it would take to prevent that sound would be to tighten the screws on the cover to the ventilation shaft, I thought. But Miss Harrier seemed more interested in putting the screws to my son.

"What's happening with his math class?" I said, jerking my attention back to the matter at hand. In February, when Max and I had met with Miss Harrier, she'd agreed that Brian's test scores would place him in an upper-level class. It seemed like a straightforward decision. Could Miss Harrier be one of those people who was still, in the twenty-first century, quick to agree with a man and argue with a woman? I didn't see how the principal of a public school could operate that way.

"Mrs. McDonald, all our math classes are fast-paced and instruction is individualized. I'm sure—"

Her use of educational jargon triggered new levels of anger in me—I'd been exposed to too much of it at the university and had found it often signaled that the speaker was feeling more pompous than they had a right to feel.

"Miss Harrier, Brian grew up on a university campus and we've had trouble keeping up with his hunger for math. If we'd known that your classes could not accommodate him, we would have suggested he take math at the high school or the junior college."

Miss Harrier shook her head. "I assure you, Mrs. McDonald, we are used to ambitious parents pushing their children, thinking they can dictate . . ." She sighed. "We are one of the top schools in California, but we are also a public school with limited funding."

In the back of my mind, I half-wondered if this was a shakedown for a donation. It was a ridiculous, paranoid thought, but once again, Miss Harrier was talking about funding. I wanted to ask about the foundation, and why the missing money created such a huge problem. Surely the school could manage on state funding? But I was here for Brian, not to solve California's financial crisis. Maybe Miss Harrier was in shock over budget cuts and overreacting? Maybe she was having a bad day dealing with angry parents and frustrated teachers and was taking it out on us?

April tapped on the door, opened it, and handed Miss Harrier pink message slips. "Excuse me," April said, showing great deference. "I did some checking. I have a solution that I think will work for everyone. With your approval, of course, Miss Harrier." April raised her eyebrows, apparently requesting permission from the principal to continue. Miss Harrier nodded. April outlined her plan.

"The band teacher and the advanced-math teacher say they have room in their classes. If we change Brian's PE class, both those classes will fit his schedule. I'll be happy to make changes in the computer as soon as you've decided how you want to move forward."

April backed out of the room and closed the door.

Brian and I looked at Miss Harrier. April had left the ball firmly in her court, but there was only one logical play. The muscles in Miss Harrier's face tightened. She put her hand on her iPad and clicked her pen.

"I see," she said. "Brian, it appears that things have worked out well for you today." She smiled, but it looked more like a grimace. "I hope you will thank the teachers who have been so flexible. Please return to the band room. You can pick up your new schedule from April after the bell rings."

Brian stood and moved his chair so that it was precisely parallel to the front of the desk. "Thank you, Miss Harrier," he said. He squeezed my shoulder. "See you after school, Mom. Thanks for coming." He left the room and closed the door behind him.

I watched him go and turned to Miss Harrier. "Thank you," I said. "I'm glad it worked out." I shook her hand and left before she could change her mind.

Brian and I had achieved what we'd needed to and I'd leave it at that. But I had an odd feeling that I was missing something important, or that there'd been a subtext to the meeting that I was supposed to have picked up on, but hadn't.

Outside the office, Brian ran toward me. "I'm sorry I had to call you on the first day of school, Mom. I'm sorry I got into trouble."

"You did absolutely the best thing by calling me. I'm happy to come. Any time." I put my hand on his shoulder. "Grown-ups need to know when to ask for help, Brian. They need friends who are on their side. They need to know what they want, be persistent, and be gracious when they succeed. They need to learn that some things are worth fighting for. You did every one of those things." I rumpled his hair—something he had told me he didn't like, but that I still did from time to time, though I was trying to stop. "Ready to go back to class?"

Brian nodded and bounced off to the band room without glancing back.

I met Tess at her car. While we'd won this round with Miss Harrier, I was quite sure we'd not heard the last from her. She was angry and frustrated and I hoped she wouldn't take that out on Brian.

"It's going to be a long year at the middle school, Tess. It's going to be a very long year."

Chapter 8

When life grows hectic, don't be afraid to hire help.
And don't overlook the fact that "hiring help" is a
broad-based term. Paying more for appliances from a
store that delivers on time, every time, is an efficient
choice. Buying ready-to-go meals from the supermarket
can be like hiring a part-time cook. Be creative and be
gentle with yourself.

From the Notebook of Maggie McDonald
Simplicity Itself Organizing Services

Tuesday, September 2, Approximately eleven o'clock.

"I think it's too soon for a drink," Tess said. "But would a latte help?"

Much as I wanted to spend the day sipping fancy coffee with Tess and watching the dogs play, I needed to get back to the house.

"Can I have a rain check? I need to pick up Belle and go home." My voice cracked and I cursed inwardly as I fought off tears I did not want to shed in front of Tess. Our friendship was too new for tears.

Tess pulled a giant tissue box from the backseat and handed it to me. "Spill," she said. "Words, tears, whatever you need to, but spill. This has got to be about more than a delayed moving van and a cranky principal. What's going on?"

I successfully fought off the tears, but caved and told Tess everything—the dead man in our basement, camping in the barn, the house that wasn't in anywhere near the condition we'd expected, the dangerous electrical box, the exploding mailbox, and the worst thing:

that Max wasn't here with me, and wouldn't be around to help for at least a couple of weeks.

Tess frowned, then her face lit up. "I've got it. We'll both go to my house. You grab Belle and get home. I'll pick up coffee and sandwiches and bring them up to you. Briones Hill Road you said, right? Twenty-one eleven? That's the old Wilson Craftsman. I've been dying to get in there for years. I'd kill for the listing too, but if I were you, I wouldn't sell it for the world."

Tess pulled into her driveway, turned off the car, looked at me, and smiled. "After you show me around, I'll grab your laundry. I'll have it clean and dry by school pickup time, so your kids don't have to go to school naked while you wait for the moving van."

I hugged Tess. Then I got in my own car, thinking that one of the things I liked about her was that she and April were the only people I'd met in Orchard View who had not tried to give me their business cards.

Back at the house, I phoned an electrician and arranged for him to give me a quote on bringing our wiring up to code, so we could plug in all of our devices without burning down the house.

Max had donated Aunt Kay's power-hungry 1970s-era appliances to a nonprofit who'd picked them up on Labor Day. I hoped I'd have time tomorrow to order some inexpensive, energy-efficient replacements that could be delivered immediately. I had a list I'd developed with a vendor in Stockton who had given my clients great prices. I hoped to make similar arrangements here.

I headed upstairs to check on Holmes and Watson. Despite the craziness over the weekend, both cats seemed much more comfortable and even the grumpy Holmes was weaving himself around my feet, threatening to trip me. I scratched him behind the ears and he rubbed his cheek against my leg.

"Think you're about ready to come out of the closet, Mr. Holmes? How 'bout if I leave the door open and give you a little more room to explore?"

Watson bounded off an upper shelf and raced around the bedroom as soon as I opened the door. She chased an invisible monster from one corner to the next. After a few laps around the room, she jumped up on a window seat to lick her paws in a thin patch of late-morning sun.

Sun. Solar panels. We wanted to think about putting solar panels on the south-facing barn roof. Bills for heating a house this old were going to be enormous, even with our plan to repair or replace the windows and add insulation. There was so much to do. Refinishing the floors and getting rid of the dark curtains, painting, repairing the gutters and roof, re-graveling the drive, trimming trees, and . . . and . . . and . . .

Belle barked, announcing Tess's arrival.

"It's open," I called from the bedroom window. "I'll be right down."

I gave Watson a quick scratch behind the ears and told her to look after her brother. I shut the bedroom door and dashed downstairs to greet Tess.

Tess stood in the kitchen with a grocery bag and two large cups of designer coffee. She turned to greet me, still wearing her "at-home Tess" garb.

"I brought milk, but you have no refrigerator."

"It's on my list, along with about a hundred other items." I pointed to her clothes. "I thought you didn't leave the house like that?"

"Mostly. But no one notices me when I dress like this. They're so used to seeing the taller, trimmer, better-dressed Tess, they ignore me. It's the hide-in-plain sight phenomenon, I guess, and a corollary to the rule that says people see what they expect to see."

Tess shrugged and put the groceries on the counter. She handed me a coffee cup and sat on the bottom step of the back stairs.

"This place is amazing. I can't believe you get to live here," she said.

"I'm starting to feel the same way, but it's been a rough couple of days."

Tess nodded and scanned the kitchen's pressed tin ceiling.

"I've got a list of some of the projects that need doing," I said. "Would you mind taking a look and telling me the best way to get them done? I could do this in a flash in Stockton, but I'm out of my depth here. I started a list of contacts as soon as I knew we were moving, but I'm guessing you already know the best people through your own business."

She stood up and walked through the pantry to the dining room. "I think I can do better than that, Maggie. Can you and the boys stand to live in the barn a few more days?"

I blushed. Living in a barn was losing its charm for me.

Tess turned toward me and smiled. "*If* you can stay in the barn, and put off the movers for a day or two, I can get a team in here to clean and wax the paneling and refinish the floors—even paint if you want. Adelia will give you a fair price and her team does quality work."

Tess looked from the heavy oak mantle and window seats to the simple but elegant molding, and then at the built-in cabinets and window seat on the landing halfway up the front stairs. Her face lit with a slow smile.

"One of the wonderful things about a job like this is how quickly it will go from looking run-down to becoming a showplace."

I frowned. *Showplace* was the term Aunt Kay's lawyer had used for the house, and Tess's use of the same word brought back a wave of the disappointment and frustration I'd felt when we'd arrived. The last thing I wanted was a house where my family and friends were afraid to track in a little dirt or put their feet up.

Tess interpreted my frown immediately. As a Realtor, empathy was probably an important part of her job.

"Oh, not a *show*place," she said. "But gleaming in a way that will let you enjoy its best features. The architect designed this house for a family with comfort in mind. You're going to love it here, Maggie." Tess twirled with enthusiasm, spilling coffee on her sweatshirt and the floor.

She sat on the bottom step, held out her hand and snapped her fingers.

"Let's have a look at that list of yours. I'll make a bunch of calls and get things moving."

Tess made calls that I was afraid had started a tsunami, but it felt great to have someone else in charge for a moment and be tugged along in her confident wake. She grabbed a black leather bag, pulled out a measuring tape, and started shouting out numbers for me to copy into her red leather notebook.

I scribbled down the numbers as fast as I could. She made me read them back to her while she double-checked them.

Later, with her book full of measurements and her arms full of our dirty laundry, Tess loaded up her car. Before she left, she barked out more orders. "Adelia and her team will be here within thirty minutes. Supervise them as little as possible and make the rest of your phone calls. Adelia will update you on the schedule after they get here."

"How much is this costing me?" I asked. It sounded like magic and I had no idea what the going price was for sorcery in Silicon Valley.

"Adelia will give you an estimate when she arrives, but I guarantee you wouldn't be able to do it yourself for much less than she'll charge you. And it would certainly take you much longer." She winked and said, "Trust me."

"Yeah, right," I said. "We'll see." But I was kidding. Much of what Tess was doing for me was similar to what I often did for my own clients. I felt a twinge of guilty pleasure at putting myself in the capable hands of someone whose expertise and professionalism rivaled my own.

Tess laughed, climbed in her car, and rolled down the window. "Let's get coffee in the morning and take the dogs to the park. I'll show you around town."

I nodded and waved. She rolled up the window and flogged her fancy BMW down the bumpy drive.

I grabbed my sandwich and the rest of my coffee, took them to the front porch, and sat in the shade. The coffee was lukewarm, but just as tasty as it had been with that first sip. Belle flopped next to me and fell asleep, exhausted from her romp with Mozart. I checked my watch and my notes on school-dismissal times. I didn't understand why Silicon Valley people complained about traffic and air quality but could find no money for school buses. I shrugged. I couldn't fix that problem today.

Today, I needed to move the cats to the barn bathroom before Adelia and her army arrived, but I had time to tap out a short email to Max before I picked up the kids.

I closed my eyes and tried to imagine what Max might be doing right now. Sleeping, if I had the time zones right.

I tried to recapture the image Tess had given me of our house with gleaming floors, polished wood, and fully repaired shining windows. The magic had left with Tess. My imagination was good, but not that good.

To: Max.McDonald2111@gmail.com

From: SimplicityItselfOrganizing@gmail.com

Miss you! Kids got off to school this morning. There was a mix-up with Brian's schedule, but we got it sorted out. Movers won't be here until late in the week. It's a long story. Met a new friend with great contacts to help with fixing up the house. Sounds like it might cost a fortune but it will be good to get the floors done before the furniture comes. I'll get a better idea of her rates and what she can do and we can decide how much more we want her to tackle. I'll write again tonight with news on the boys' first day. Let me know how things are going in India and where you're living, etc. Bri wants to know if you ride an elephant to work.

Love, Maggie

To: SimplicityItselfOrganizing@gmail.com

From: Max.McDonald2111@gmail.com

Hang tough. Do you need me to come home? If so, I'll jump on the first plane out of here. You know that, right? The job's important, but you and the kids are more important. Can't wait to get your emails about how school went. Details, please! Tell the boys to email me. Tell Brian I've seen a sacred cow, but no elephants yet.

It's odd getting to know my co-workers in Santa Clara from 8,000 miles away. Bangalore is exotic in spots, but inside the hotel and at Influx, you wouldn't know you were away from Silicon Valley. The guy I report to here is great, but he was in a terrible car accident this morning. It may extend my stay here, since there is really no one else they can leave in charge. I know that's not what you wanted to hear. I'm hoping to visit him tonight and will talk more to Jim in Santa Clara in the morning, after which I should be able to give you a more definite return date. If you need me, I'll start home in a heartbeat.

Have the police learned anything more about the man in the basement?

Love, Max

Chapter 9

If you're spending all your time in the car, make the car
work for you. Stock water and healthy snacks. Load a
plastic bin with homework helpers: papers, pencils,
calculator, scissors, markers, and tape. Children
waiting for siblings can use the time to recharge
and do homework.

From the Notebook of Maggie McDonald
Simplicity Itself Organizing Services

Tuesday, September 2, Early afternoon

An hour later, Adelia's team arrived and began sanding the floors
with four giant machines. Tess must have warned Adelia about
the sketchy electricity because each sander connected to one of two
generators with a long orange cord. The sound was deafening. The
tripping danger was huge.

Another team washed the windows on the outside. Adelia had more
helpers pulling weeds, sweeping up leaves, and cleaning the gutters. A
fourth team replaced the broken windows, cut new boards to fix the
damaged planks on the front porch, and repaired the sagging screens.

At the rate they were moving, they'd have the house remodeled
by the time I picked up the boys. The house filled with happy energy
as they shouted and teased each other over the sound of the sanders,
driving out some of the sadness from Mr. Hernandez's death. That
thought led to the fact that I still hadn't heard whether the medical
examiner had ruled his death a murder, an accident, or an unfortunate
natural death.

* * *

Twenty minutes later, I pulled up in front of the high school to wait for David. I was early, so I called the housing inspector both Jason and Tess had recommended. After so many unpleasant surprises, I wanted to make sure that Max and I knew everything the house needed before we got too far ahead of ourselves. Making the house comfortable and safe was one thing. Going into debt over renovations that could wait was another. The inspector agreed to meet me on Saturday at noon.

I'd just ended the call when David climbed into the passenger seat. Belle licked his face as though he'd been gone a year. I handed him a bottle of water and a granola bar.

I checked over my shoulder to avoid running over any kids or absentminded parents, pulled out of my parking spot, and headed to the middle school to repeat the pickup process there.

"How was it?" I asked David, whose backpack bulged with books and other lumps and bumps I couldn't identify. "Do you have much homework?"

"Some, but it's not too bad. Is all our stuff unloaded from the moving van? Our first P.E. unit is swimming and I need to find my board shorts." David reached into his backpack. He grabbed some forms and shoved them in my face. I pushed his arm back so I could see the road, then showed him the dish tub I'd put on the floor between the two front seats to hold the forms I needed to review and sign for the kids and the house.

"I need them signed right away, Mom," David said. "I want to take marching band zero period. I'll have to be here at quarter to seven every morning. We'll have all-day practices on Saturdays. Afternoon practices on Tuesday and Thursday. Maybe some trumpet sectionals."

"Wow, when did this happen?" I wondered how David, who could have qualified for the Olympic Sleeping Team, was going to drag himself out of bed early enough to be showered, breakfasted, dressed, and at school by 6:45 each morning. And how would he stay awake in his classes?

"In concert band. The other kids asked me to join."

"It's a huge commitment," I said. "I don't want you dropping out because you change your mind and want to sleep in."

David rolled his eyes. "I know this speech, Mom. I'll stick with it. It's music with other musicians. It's trumpet. Sign the papers."

I pulled up in front of the middle school and chose a space in a far corner of the parking lot—away from the spot Pauline Windsor had laid claim to. I'd have to ask Tess about that. Were there really assigned spots, or was Pauline one of the odd parents with entitlement issues who crop up in every school?

"Here, Mom. Sign the papers," said David.

I took the papers and looked them over. There was a long list of expenses for shoes, uniform cleaning, buses, gloves, and T-shirts, but it didn't look too bad. David still had the trumpet he'd played since fifth grade, so we could skip the instrument rental or purchase costs. Those predawn hours could be a problem, though. I didn't think I'd have time to drop off David and go home to pick up Brian and get him to school before the first bell. If David joined marching band, we'd all be forced into the same predawn schedule. Decisions involving the whole family were the sort of thing I'd ordinarily discuss with Max, but this issue was too big to explain with email, and I didn't want Max to feel guilty. If he were here, one of us could take David and one of us could take Brian. The schedule wouldn't be an issue.

"Mom, sign the papers." David waved a pen in my face.

"David, stop," I said, snatching the pen from his hand and tossing it in the dish tub. "I hear that you want to do marching band. I hear that you're committed, but this decision will have a huge impact on our family and I need to think about it."

"I signed you up to make brownies for Saturday."

"David . . ." I sighed. "Honey, that's exactly what I'm talking about. Marching band demands a lot of students *and* their families. We don't have a working oven and you signed me up to bring brownies?"

David started to protest, but I cut him off. "I'm willing to buy brownies, so that's not a problem, but there will be other requests for parent help, and I'm up to my ears with the move and renovations, and getting Simplicity Itself off the ground again. If it's important to you, we'll find a way to make it work, but it's not the slam-dunk decision you seem to think it is. Do you think you can find a carpool to help out?"

I flipped through the papers in the tub. I was going to have nightmares about drowning in paper. Paper that turned into bats and house-wrecking vandals, no doubt.

"You said something about a bathing suit," I said. "When do you need it?"

David shrugged. "Right away. We started P.E. today, Mom. It shouldn't take me too long to find it, though. I know what box it's in."

"That's good, honey, but the movers can't get here until Thursday and I'm hoping to push them back to Friday or even Saturday. You won't have your swimsuit until Monday."

"Seriously?"

"If we have to buy a new swimsuit, we'll do that," I said. "But if you know you won't have pool time until Monday, that would save us a trip to the store."

"Let me ask my friends," David said, picking up his phone and typing. "I got some numbers at lunch."

I smiled, delighted that David had new friends already. "If you want to invite any of them over . . ." I began.

"How 'bout we wait until we have a fridge," David answered, rolling his eyes. "Look, there's Bri. Looks like he's had a good day too."

Brian was in the middle of a knot of boys carrying instrument cases, shoving each other, and laughing. I'd fought for band for him this morning, knowing it was one of the fastest ways for him to make friends. Now David was asking me to do the same thing for him.

A rapid-fire series of *pings* erupted from David's cell phone. He bent over it, thumbs flying as he texted back.

"Board shorts can wait until Monday," he said, still typing. "I've got a ride home from practice on Saturday."

One advantage of having so many things go wrong this week was that I'd learned I needed to become better at accepting help and asking for it, especially from the kids. I needed to remember that anything could be fixed and that I couldn't manage everything on my own. I was making new friends and breaking new ground, just like the kids. So was Max. What we were going through wasn't *all* bad. It was, in fact, exactly the change Max and I had been looking for. *Be careful what you wish for* was another one of Aunt Kay's favorite sayings.

I signed David's band form and handed it to him. "As long as you can be flexible and promise to help as much as you can when you're not in band, we'll make it work."

David shoved the form in his backpack and beamed at me.

Brian flung open the car door. "The coolest thing happened after lunch," he said, climbing in, dropping his backpack on the floor and buckling his seat belt.

"Right after lunch, a porta-potty exploded—the one at the construction site next to school. What a stink! There was sh- well, you know, *stuff*, everywhere. Harrier was furious, but all us kids couldn't stop laughing. The fire department came to clean it up."

"But what happened? How?" I started.

I handed Brian his water and granola bar and started the car. "Do they know who did it?"

"That's all anyone talked about the rest of the day," Brian said. "But no one was about to rat anyone out. The police talked to a few kids, but I don't know if they found out anything."

Two explosions, one in our mailbox and another at the school. That was too much of a coincidence for me. I needed to call Jason and see if he thought there was a connection. And I needed to ask Tess about it too. She would know if there were usual suspects at the middle school. I had to remember to ask her about the funding issues too. But that could wait until we walked the dogs tomorrow.

I told the boys we'd be sleeping in the barn for at least another night. They didn't seem to mind. Apparently, camping still held charms for them that were lost on me. But the prospect of gleaming floors sustained me. All I wanted was to settle my family into the house and the town. I felt as though I'd been trying to do that for days and not getting any closer to my goal. Now, the goal was in sight, at least in terms of the house. But I couldn't help feeling unsettled. And it wasn't because we were new to town and living in the barn. With the sabotage at our house and the school, a man dead by accident or misadventure, and the mysterious school-funding issues, I feared Orchard View might not be the rural escape Max and I had hoped it would be.

Chapter 10

When any plan, including a plan to reorder your life, is
going badly, it's important to: Identify the problem.
Consult someone. Make a plan. Repeat as necessary.
Exercise and fresh air often help and seldom hurt.

From the Notebook of Maggie McDonald
Simplicity Itself Organizing Services

Wednesday, September 3, Morning

Wednesday morning, I pulled up in front of the middle school,
planning to drop Brian before meeting Tess for our trip to the
park. But three police cars with lights flashing were parked in the red
zone. More lights flashed near the front office door.

Something was wrong. I parked the car and walked toward the
school buildings with Brian. April, dressed all in red today, stood
atop a broad concrete bollard. Waving her arms as if she were direct-
ing aircraft toward a gate, she instructed students to walk to their
classes and asked parents to depart quickly. No one listened. Groups
of chattering parents and students pointed toward the office door.

"We might as well join them," I told Brian. "At least until we figure out what's going on."

It didn't take long to get the gist. Someone, maybe the same
delinquent who'd blown up the portable toilet, had moved beyond
malicious mischief. On the wall next to the front door, three squirrel
carcasses were nailed in a triangle with their bushy tails hanging
down and their heads lolling. My stomach turned. I'm not a squirrel
fan, but the scene was gruesome, violent, and held all the horror of a
medieval torture chamber.

"Eww," said Brian, echoing my thoughts. "I'm going to the band room." I squeezed his shoulder and watched him go.

A uniformed officer removed the bodies from the wall with gloved hands. A jumpsuit-clad tech with what looked like fingerprinting paraphernalia stood by hoping, I assumed, to pick up prints from the wall. *Good luck with that.* When I'd dropped Brian off on the first day, I'd seen a group of kids trying to see how high they could jump and slap that same wall. The surface would be full of fingerprints left by the innocent.

I sighed and walked to the car. Shoving Belle out of the driver's seat, I turned the key and drove to meet Tess.

Tess had pulled a black pickup truck out of the garage for the trip to the park. The dogs climbed into the back of the cab. I sat in the front and fastened my seat belt while Tess told me the plan for the day.

"First, I'm showing you stuff," she said. "I brought coffee and we'll talk about school while the dogs play. Until then, focus. Here's your intro to Silicon Valley." She wore black-and-red business wear this morning, which seemed an odd choice for the dog park, but I didn't ask her about it. I had other things on my mind.

Tess drove down Shoreline Boulevard, pointing out the public pool, the train station, and movie theaters where she said we'd spend lots of weekend evenings delivering the boys and their friends to blockbuster films. And then we hit Google and traffic ground to a halt. Crosswalks and sidewalks were filled with casually dressed Googlers, most of whom looked like high-school kids carrying black backpacks. Some walked, but many rode bicycles painted like preschool toys: red, yellow, blue, and green.

"They ride them between buildings," Tess said. "Leave one in the rack when you go in, pick up another on the way out. There's no mistaking them, so no one steals them. Or maybe Google has enough money to replace them if someone steals them, I'm not sure."

Tess turned left at the next corner and slowed to turn left again into a drop-off circle. She slowed and pointed to the lawn between her car and the nearest building.

I felt as though I'd fallen into a game of Candy Land. Giant dessert-shaped statues including a cupcake, gingerbread man, and what looked like a bright green robot filled with jelly beans were plopped on the lawn, scattered randomly as though a giant had been bringing treats to a picnic and spilled his lunch. Tourists stood next to the installations, posing for photographs with sugary treats that towered over their heads.

"The statues represent various phases of the Android operating system," Tess explained. "The jelly-bean robot made big news a while back when its head popped off during a heat wave."

"I know how he must have felt," I said, laughing.

Mozart woofed, reminding us to move on to the dog park. Tess drove back to the main road, where we passed buildings belonging to other high-tech icons and a giant tentlike structure that Tess told me was a concert venue.

We passed a kiosk marking the entrance to a park complex that included a golf course, sailing lake, and walking trails.

"It's built on an old garbage dump," Tess said. "There's a great place to have lunch out there, but we'll do that another time. We can't go any farther with the dogs than the dog park."

It seemed too bad to me. It looked like a great place for dogs to play. But the dog park was nice too, with dog-height drinking fountains and fences for safety. Inside the fenced area, we let Belle and Mozart off their leashes, and they took off. I sat on a bench while Tess poured us cups of coffee from her thermos.

Mozart and Belle ran from one end of the park to the other sniffing and exploring—checking pee-mail, Max called it.

"What a great day," I said. "But what a gruesome way to start out. Did you see those squirrels at school?"

"What squirrels?"

I stared at her as if she'd lost her mind. How was it possible that Tess, who was clued into every little thing that happened in Orchard View, hadn't heard about the squirrels?

"What?" she said. "Teddy walks to school. I wasn't there this morning. What happened?"

"Three squirrels, crucified in a triangle on the wall next to the office." I shuddered. "Gruesome."

"Were they nailed up alive? That's sick. Really sick."

"First the portable toilet, now the squirrels . . ." I said, thinking out loud. "And a bunch of vandalism at our house. Are they connected? Is trashing other people's property normal around here?"

"Of course not," said Tess, sounding offended. "We get kids taking a baseball bat to mailboxes from time to time, some graffiti, but this stuff is . . . bizarre."

"And what's the story on the funding crisis? Parents were freaking out yesterday. Harrier downplayed it when she announced it, like it was just a small accounting wrinkle that needed to be ironed out. But when Brian and I met her later, she implied that classes might be cut."

"I've got friends on the board of the foundation—" Tess began.

"Wait, back up. What *is* the foundation?"

Tess sighed and put down her coffee cup.

"Oh, lord," she said. "California school funding is as complicated as it gets, particularly as it relates to districts like Orchard View. It takes an advanced degree in accounting and probably another in political science to completely understand it, but I can give you a summary."

She stood as if she thought better on her feet. "Way back when, our schools were well-funded and among the best in the country. In the 1970s, three separate cases based on school financing went to the California Supreme Court. The court ordered changes to create equity among school districts. Local taxes went to the state and were redistributed on a per-student basis. Theoretically, every student and every school received the same funding, no matter where they lived."

I nodded. "Got it. Stockton gets some extra funding because of at-risk kids, but I'm with you so far."

"After that, two things happened. First, districts like ours that had previously enjoyed excess funds were alarmed to see world-class science labs, libraries, and arts programs on the chopping block. Second, additional add-on efforts over the years—a Band-Aid approach to increasing funding for needy districts—left us, and districts like us, among the poorest districts in the state. We don't qualify for any of the aid programs that benefit communities like Stockton."

"But your test scores are through the roof," I said. "Max and I checked before we decided to move."

"Part of that is demographics. In affluent areas, you tend to have well-educated parents who work hard to support their kids' education. In poorer districts, where parents are working two or three jobs to keep food on the table, there's no time left for reading aloud or any of the other things that help kids do well in school."

Tess looked at her watch, scanned the park for the dogs, and pushed her hair from her forehead. She sighed, sat, and continued explaining. "The rest comes down to things like parcel taxes and the foundation.

They're politically controversial, because some people see them as ways to circumvent funding laws. In Orchard View, we have voter-approved parcel taxes—extra property taxes—that go directly to our schools. That helps, but not enough to fully fund science and the arts. Back in the 1980s, parents created the Orchard View Education Foundation to augment school funding."

"And those are the funds that disappeared?"

"No, to make matters even *more* confusing, there are two separate foundations, and most people refer to them both as 'foundation funds'. As far as I know, the Orchard View Education Foundation is rock-solid. The second one is a private family foundation that donates funds for what used to be part of the standard curriculum, but are now considered 'enrichment programs.' Courses like theater and music—I think it also pays for a portion of the science program. It's run by the DeSoto family with funds from apartment projects that go back to the postwar building boom."

"*Dennis* DeSoto?"

"Same family, different brother. It's a big family. Ten kids, I think. Umberto, the oldest, runs the DeSoto Family Foundation. Apparently, a routine audit uncovered discrepancies that triggered further investigations, and the foundation's board froze the funds. There are a bunch of local, state, and federal agencies taking a look, and it's really hard for civilians like us to know exactly what's happening. But, because the DeSoto Foundation annually donates about two million dollars to the schools, the investigation has left the schools with big budget holes."

"But everyone says the funds disappeared."

"That may be true. The rumor mill is often surprisingly accurate. But I don't know if we'll ever know exactly what triggered the freeze on the accounts. The bottom line is that, for now, funding has dried up and that means budget cuts. No one knows how much, because the scandal might make people unwilling to donate to the Orchard View Education Foundation or even the PTA."

"But why? It sounds like all these different funding mechanisms are completely separate."

"They are, on paper at least. Absolutely. But a lot of people volunteer at more than one and donate to more than one. And, unlike you, most people—even those who've lived here all their lives—won't think to ask the right questions."

"What a mess."

Both dogs lay panting in the shade of the park's lone tree—an ancient California oak with spreading branches. I walked to the drinking fountain and pushed the button to let water into the dog-level bowl. Belle and Mozart came running. I raised my voice so Tess could hear me over the sounds of water splashing and dogs slurping.

"Okay, never mind the DeSoto Foundation for now, but would it make sense to get a group of parents together to brainstorm ways to stop the vandalism? Maybe walk our dogs on the grounds in a revolving schedule to patrol the school at night? Compare notes on what our kids have heard?"

"Brilliant," said Tess, jumping up and brushing off her skirt. My jeans were covered with dust from the park and my sneakers were speckled with mud from the puddles the dogs were making around the water fountain. Tess was spotless.

"I've got to get back for a showing," she said, gathering up her thermos and our cups. "Let's talk about this in the car."

Belle and Mozart were reluctant to leave, but jumped into the car, planting their muddy paws on the front seats before curling up quickly in the tiny backseat of Tess's pickup. She grabbed a pile of ragged towels and wiped mud off of her own cushion before passing the towels to me.

Driving back up Shoreline toward home, Tess and I worked out the details. I borrowed her phone and texted everyone she told me to. I was new and didn't have enough social clout to get parents to adjust their schedules to come to an afternoon meeting. But Tess did.

I thought we'd have the meeting at school, but Tess didn't want to risk alienating Harrier before we had a plan. I texted someone named Elaine Cumberfield as Tess dictated a message asking if we could meet at her house across the street from the school. With Elaine's approval, we texted some other people and asked them to attend a two o'clock meeting to discuss strategies for stopping the vandalism. Tess had me text Stephen Laird in case he wanted to attend.

"What about Jason or someone else from the police? Is there a school liaison officer?" I asked.

"Stephen will take care of that."

"Stephen the police volunteer?" I raised my eyebrows, curious about Stephen's connection to the police department.

"Stephen is everywhere and he's a bit more than a volunteer,"

Tess said. "He was with the military police in the Marines, and helps the police in all sorts of ways, particularly in public-liaison roles like this one. It's a bit unusual, I guess, but we're a small town. The police will be fine with this meeting. Trust me."

Tess winked and I laughed. I had to trust someone. It might as well be her. I wasn't sure about Jason approving our efforts, however. He'd told me to stay out of the investigation into Javier Hernandez's death and the vandalism at our house. Would he consider this meeting part of his investigation? I certainly thought the crimes were connected, but I didn't know what Jason would think.

Tess pointed out Elaine Cumberfield's house as we drove by. It had a white mailbox adorned with the carved wooden head, feet, and tail of a West Highland white terrier. It was clever and cute—just shy of cutesy.

"I'll meet you there a little before two," I told Tess as we climbed out of the pickup. "Do you want me to bring snacks or anything?"

Tess shook her head. "Elaine loves to feed people. Wait until you taste her gingerbread cookies."

By the time I had Belle back in my car, Tess had put Mozart in her backyard and hidden her pickup in her garage. She brushed her windblown hair into a neat French twist and stood a little taller. Her ability to change her appearance and persona so quickly and completely unnerved me. But I did trust her and appreciated her help.

I checked the clock on my phone. I had time to drive to the house and check in with Adelia and the electrician. I'd ordered appliances from a shop Tess had recommended. I hoped their claim that their installers were always on time was accurate. They were due at noon. Considering they needed to deliver and install a refrigerator, dishwasher, range, washer, and dryer, if they were any later than noon, I wouldn't have time to make the meeting that had been my own idea.

To: Max.McDonald2111@gmail.com

From: SimplicityItselfOrganizing@gmail.com

Both boys like school so far. I hope you got the emails they sent. It makes no sense, but I don't trust the Internet to reliably deliver emails across 8,000 miles. David signed up for marching band. It will mean long hours for all of us, since he needs to be at school every morning before 7 am. Can you believe our little snooze monster is voluntarily getting up that early? He hasn't complained yet. Neither has Brian. And no, I don't think you should come home from India to drive David to school! I hope things are going well. Are you getting to know people?

There was some vandalism at the school—super-creepy stuff. Three squirrels were nailed to the front office wall. A bunch of us are meeting to set up parent patrols and compare theories on who might be behind things. I wonder if it's the same person who was trashing our place before we moved in. I'll let you know what I find out.

Floors look great. Adelia, the woman who's in charge of the crew, is a cross between Mary Poppins and a five-star general. I know you hate working with contractors, but I think even you would love Adelia.

You won't recognize the place when you get back. Has that date been firmed up? Let me know, and we'll pick you up at the airport—in the middle of the night if necessary. We all miss you. Even the cats.

Love, Maggie.

To: SimplicityItselfOrganizing@gmail.com

From: Max.McDonald2111@gmail.com

Squirrels? Nailed to the wall? That sounds like the work of a seriously disturbed individual. If it IS the same person who was damaging the house, PLEASE be careful. Can you get the police to patrol the neighborhood at night? Are they making any progress into the investigation into Javier Hernandez's death?

If you feel unsafe at all, move to a hotel. And let me know, so I can come home.

I'm glad the house repairs are going well. Go ahead and hire this Adelia person to do whatever you need. If you need to transfer funds from Aunt Kay's estate account, go ahead. That's what the money's for—upkeep on the house. We didn't anticipate this trip to India and I feel bad that I can't help out. I'm glad the electrician could get started so soon. We definitely want to get moving as soon as possible on safety-related fixes.

You're doing a fantastic job and making me feel almost superfluous. Almost.

The managing director here is going to be fine, although he's uncomfortable at the moment. He broke both legs and cracked his pelvis, so he won't be mobile for several weeks. Looks like the easiest solution for the company is to have me stay and take care of things until he's up and around again. I'm learning tons and loving the work. I'd like to stay IF that works for you and the boys. Let me know if you need me to come home. Our family needs beat Influx's needs, hands down.

Love, Max

Chapter 11

Meetings should be tightly focused with definite start
and end times. Encourage members to hold one meeting,
rather than engaging in side conversations on sub-issues
that can be distracting and time-consuming.

From the Notebook of Maggie McDonald
Simplicity Itself Organizing Services

Wednesday, September 3, Afternoon

Adelia and her team had the work well in hand when I stopped by the house to check on their progress. The floors and paneling they'd finished gleamed in contrast to the sections they'd not yet reached. As Tess had predicted, the appliances arrived on time. The electrician had nearly completed his work and agreed to stay in case anything went wrong once the new units were plugged in and running. Energy-efficient engineering can only take you so far. Major appliances will still make the electric meter spin, no matter how earth-friendly they are.

I had no qualms about leaving Adelia in charge. With her on the job, there was little left for me to do. I was in the way. I drove to school in plenty of time for the meeting, parked in the shade, and left the windows open a few inches so Belle could catch the breeze. I filled her car water dish from my water bottle and spread out her cooling pad. She settled in for a snooze and I walked across the street.

An elderly woman who could have been the model for the Good Witch of the North opened the door. She was accompanied by a West Highland white terrier who'd apparently been the model for the mailbox I'd noticed when Tess pointed out the house earlier.

"Elaine Cumberfield," she said, holding the Westie back with her foot while she shook my hand. "You must be Maggie McDonald. Please come in. May I introduce Mackie? I will put him in the bedroom if you're not a dog fan."

I knelt and rubbed Mackie behind the ears. "Nice to meet you, Mr. Mackie," I said. "I'm Maggie McDonald. I feel certain we must have a common ancestor." Mackie's ears stood at attention and he tilted his fuzzy white face, listening politely.

Elaine laughed and pulled a long gray sweater closer around her, overlapping it in the front. "So, you *are* a dog fan," she said. She leaned in closer to me and whispered, "I knew that. Stephen told me about your Belle. I just didn't think it would be polite to indicate straight off the bat that we'd been talking behind your back."

I liked Elaine, her dog, and her house, immediately. She wore a long lavender print skirt and white Keds that were heading toward a soft gray—the sneaker version of patina. A purple knit shirt and the gray sweater completed her outfit. Her house was done up in shades of navy and periwinkle blue with a focus on comfort. From the wear on the arms of the sofa, and the faded marks of a growth chart on the doorframe, I could tell she'd lived here a long time and raised a family. Pictures of young women with small children dotted the hall table, but I didn't have time to examine them closely.

"We're in the living room, dear," Elaine said. "Let me get you a hot drink. Are you coffee or tea?"

"Coffee, please."

Stephen Laird stood as we walked in. He was the only person I recognized other than Tess and April Chen, the assistant principal from the middle school.

"Good afternoon, Mrs. McDonald," Stephen said. "Do you remember meeting me at your house over the weekend?"

"Of course," I said, shaking Stephen's hand and smiling. "You brought bagels and coffee and your wonderful dog, Munchkin. Please, call me Maggie."

"You've met Elaine, April, and Tess?" Stephen moved his upturned hand in an arc, indicating the women I'd already met. "At the window is Flora Meadow. On my left here is Pauline Windsor."

Tess sat in a navy corduroy club chair next to the fireplace. She wore her power suit, but had kicked off her heels and tucked her feet beneath her. Across from her sat Pauline Windsor. Like everyone else in the room, Pauline had looked up and smiled when I walked in, but I was wary. I wished I'd remembered to ask Tess about her. I was dying to figure out what I'd been missing when Pauline accused me of hijacking her personal parking spot.

April sat on the floor next to the coffee table. The woman Stephen had introduced as Flora Meadow perched on the window seat beneath a bay window. She picked dead leaves from a lush geranium and crumpled them in her palm. She looked like a younger, stouter, and more nervous version of Elaine.

Stephen passed me a plate of gingerbread men, while Elaine handed me a steaming mug of coffee.

"I guessed you take cream," she said. "If you prefer black, I'll pour it out." I assured her it was perfect and took a sip to prove it. Real cream.

Elaine sat in an overstuffed Victorian rocker looking as if she'd escaped from a Brontë novel. Her hair was meant to be pulled back in a bun, but renegade hairs created a friendly cloud around her head.

Stephen patted a seat on the couch next to him. "Have a seat, please, Maggie."

"We're still waiting for Dennis DeSoto," Elaine said. "But why don't we tell Maggie about ourselves before we begin."

She turned to me and smiled. "I'm Elaine. I've lived in this house for fifty-five years, ever since I started teaching history at Orchard View the year it opened. My husband was the first principal. I took a few years off while our three girls were young, but later on I taught and became principal after my husband died."

Stephen interrupted her. "Elaine's in on this meeting, Maggie, because she keeps a close eye on the school."

"And I'm Flora Meadow," said the woman from the window seat, fingering the crystal medallion she wore around her neck. "I'm the PTA secretary, a parent, and an herbalist."

I had no idea what an herbalist did, but from the crystal and the fairies embroidered on the bottom of Flora's forest-green skirt, I figured it was some sort of Northern California New Age thing. I had a vague impression of having seen her among the parents on the first day of school.

Flora must have been used to explaining her profession. "I work with herbs and roots to devise natural treatments to support balanced body systems and maximize health," she said, rattling the description off as if it were all one word.

"Now is not the time for a commercial break, Flora dear," Elaine said. Flora looked offended and shrunk in on herself like a startled snail retreating into its shell.

The front door crashed open. Dennis DeSoto had arrived. "Ah, good to see you're all here," he said. "I can't stay, but April, I wanted to let you know that Demi has everything in hand in the office, so you can stay here as long as you need to. I must run. I have an important meeting."

Dennis scanned the room and scowled when his eyes met mine.

I had no idea why he'd taken such a dislike to me. But he was odd himself, so I decided not to worry about his opinion.

"Thank you, Dennis," said Elaine. "Please don't let us keep you from your *important* meeting."

Dennis disappeared as quickly as he'd arrived.

"Who's Demi?" I said.

April grabbed a gingerbread man from the plate on the coffee table and bit off his head. "Her name is Elisabeth," April said. "She's married to that jerk. Dennis just *calls* her Demi. All their kids have names starting with D, and Dennis thought hers should match." She glared at the headless gingerbread man and amputated his foot. "Elisabeth is kind, smart, and attractive. I can't figure out why she stays with him. A man that self-centered *cannot* be good in bed."

Tess snorted. I tried to hide my smile with my coffee cup.

"You should switch to decaf," said Flora. "Chamomile tea can be calming too." She picked up her cup with a shaking hand and smelled the coffee. "Is this Starbucks or from the independent coffee shop, Elaine?"

"I'm afraid it's Maxwell House, Flora. Would you like some tea?"

Flora replaced her cup in the saucer without taking a sip. She muttered something under her breath about fair-trade practices and how no one took these things seriously except her.

Stephen cleared his throat, and everyone's attention shifted to him.

"Let me tell you what I know about what happened at the school last night," Stephen said. "And then we can talk about how we'll proceed." He looked at his watch. "It's five past two now, and I'd like to get us all out of here before school ends at three.

"Police investigators suggest the porta-potty explosion and the squirrels were done by the same kid or group of kids. My contact did not tell me, specifically, what the connection is."

I half raised my hand and Stephen nodded to me.

"Does that mean the vandalism at my house may be connected too?"

"What vandalism?" Pauline said.

I started to answer, but Stephen jumped in. "Maggie and her family moved in less than a week ago, but have experienced a spate of property damage."

"I thought we were here to discuss protecting the school," Pauline said. "Not to cater to individual homeowners."

"You're right, Pauline," Stephen said. "Maggie is here not only because it was her idea to brainstorm ideas to protect the school, but also because the problems at her house may have some connection to the school issues. Her experiences may help us catch whoever is behind this."

Pauline looked away.

Stephen continued: "Maggie suggested we encourage dog walkers to exercise their pets on the campus, and ask parents to find out what their children have heard from other students. The police are in favor of both ideas, but suggest that dog walkers patrol in groups, keep their dogs on leashes, their cell phones handy, and, of course, clean up after their pets."

"Miss Harrier will have a problem with that," said Pauline. "She's always been at odds with the dog owners who use the field before and after school."

Stephen smiled. "Munchkin and I have been the target of her wrath, and you're right, there's no love lost between her and the dogs. She's worried about liability and overwhelming poor April here with requests for help from kids who've stepped in a mess the dogs left behind."

April wrinkled her nose.

"The police will step up vehicle patrols through the night and do a walk-through in the late evenings." Stephen paused and looked at Elaine. "We'll be relying on you and the other neighbors to report anything you see or hear that's unusual." He tilted his head and rubbed his earlobe. "Remember, stopping vandalism is necessary for several reasons." He ticked them off on his fingers. "We want to catch minors, address any issues they have, and scare the pants off them before they have to be tried as adults. We want to keep the school in good shape for the students. And, let's face it, vandalized schools don't give voters a good impression. The school parcel tax is up for renewal next year, and we'll need every vote to get it passed."

Elaine chimed in: "And no school has extra staff or funds to be doing unnecessary maintenance." Everyone made noises of agreement.

Tess spoke up. "You each have different spheres of influence, so talk up this effort among your friends and neighbors. Refer any questions you can't answer to Stephen, April, or me. April, if Miss Harrier has any issues, have her call Stephen or Jason Mueller. But please assure her that the police are in favor of our plan, although we can refine it if there are any problems. I'll draft up a letter if you like, for Harrier's signature. To tell the school community what we're doing?"

April nodded. "That would be great. She'll want to edit it, so if you can get it to me on a thumb drive, I'll tell her it's a draft that you need her help with."

Pauline spoke up. "I'll put together a roster for the dog walkers, so we can make sure we've got coverage on evenings, nights, and weekends." She pulled out her phone and her fingers moved quickly, apparently making notes. "Elaine, I know you like the hour before school. What about the rest of you? Stephen?"

"Munchkin and I have another assignment at the moment, but let me know if you can't get anyone for the wee hours: two-to-four, or midnight-to-two. I'll find someone."

Pauline nodded. "I'll let you know. If students are our vandals, I don't think they'd be out that late, but you never know."

Tess leaned forward in her chair. "Mozart, Teddy, and I will take after dinner. Say, seven-to-eight?"

Pauline looked at me, fingers poised over the phone. "And you? Maggie, was it? What time would you like? I know you have that golden retriever."

I hesitated. The kids and I had no routine yet. I had no idea what would work. And with Max gone, I needed to be home in the evenings with Brian and David. They were both old enough to be left alone for short periods, but I wasn't ready to let them fend for themselves on a regular basis.

Stephen broke in on the conversation. "Pauline, let's leave Maggie off the list for now. She's just moved and has a lot on her plate." He held up his hand as Pauline began to protest. "Even if she saw someone destroying school property, it would be difficult for her to identify the person. She doesn't know anyone yet, besides us."

Pauline sniffed.

Stephen's understanding of my predicament left me in an expansive mood, so I threw Pauline a bone. "I've been active in my children's schools, Pauline," I said. "I intend to volunteer both here and at the high school after we get settled. Our moving van still hasn't arrived, though." I smiled and was expecting an empathetic smile over the perils of moving, but she ignored me.

Stephen consulted his watch. "Two-forty-five. If no one has any other suggestions or questions, I can let you loose to corral your kids."

Pauline left quickly. Everyone else welcomed me to the community and made the proper social noises of sympathy over our vandalism trouble. Flora urged me to get involved in the PTA and recommended some soothing herbal tea. "Most folks around here don't understand how stressful Orchard View can be, especially when things aren't going well. I'm sorry for all your troubles, Maggie."

I thanked her, after which Flora left to meet a client for an aromatherapy consultation, while April returned to school. Elaine didn't have a dishwasher, so the rest of us washed, dried, and put away her dishes, chatting as we did so.

"I'm very sorry you've run into so much trouble in less than a week, Maggie," Elaine said. "Orchard View is a great town. I hope you and your family will be happy here."

"I hope so too," I said. I thanked her for hosting the meeting, gave Mackie a quick scratch behind the ears, and turned to leave.

I was almost out of earshot when I heard her whisper to Stephen, "What about . . . ?"

Could they be talking about me behind my back? I frowned and squirmed inwardly with that uncomfortable thought, but then I rejected it. One of the things I'd instantly liked about the group was how straightforward they all seemed. But Elaine's whispered comment served to confirm my feeling that there was a great deal more going on in Orchard View than any newcomer could fathom.

Chapter 12

If your schedule leans toward early mornings, develop a
repertoire of handheld breakfasts you can eat in the car.
Take time the night before to lay out your clothes and
everything else you'll need for the next day.

From the Notebook of Maggie McDonald
Simplicity Itself Organizing Services

Saturday, September 6, Morning

The remainder of the week passed in a flurry of chores, homework, and home repairs. Tess and I had spoken on the phone, but
neither one of us could find a spare hour to meet for coffee. Friday
afternoon, the moving van arrived with an extra team to speed up the
unloading. After school, the boys and I made our beds, unpacked our
clothes, and took warm showers that washed away much of the tension that had built over the course of the week. We ate pizza in our
pj's and crashed early, serenaded by the coyote choir.

On Saturday morning, David and I were getting organized to
leave for band practice when a sleepy-looking Brian drifted down the
stairs in a T-shirt and boxers. Belle followed. I let her out and passed
Brian a spoon, bowl, box of cereal, and a carton of milk.

"Thanks, Mom," Brian mumbled around a crunchy mouthful of
Cheerios. "Is it still okay if I stay here alone this morning?"

"If you want to," I said, not sure whether he was asking to stay or
if he wanted me to force him to go with me. Brian wanted to be independent, but staying alone in a house, particularly one in which a
man had recently died, might be a little creepy.

"Umm . . ."

"You don't have to," I reminded him. "I'd be happy to have your company. And I don't have many errands. The building inspector will be by later, but I should be home by then."

"I'll stay here and go back to sleep." Brian yawned. I put out my hand to rumple the little-boy curls, but pulled my hand back, remembering just in time how much he didn't like it.

David came down the back stairs two at a time.

"Hey, squirt," he said to Brian, laughing as Brian responded by sticking out his Cheerio-covered tongue. "I thought you were going to sleep in?"

"Someone," said Brian, glaring at his brother, "was bellowing marching-band tunes in the shower this morning. Woke me up."

It was time to go.

"Got everything, David?" I said. "Let's get a move on." I grabbed my keys and backpack, let Belle in from the porch, and told her to stay with Brian. She curled up under the table at his feet.

"Brian, can you feed her when you've finished breakfast? Just put your dishes in the sink."

Brian nodded. He reached for the milk carton and knocked it over. Belle scrambled to clean the evidence off the floor. I tossed Brian a dish towel and a sympathetic glance, and David and I took off for the car, band, and errands.

We navigated the curves on Monte Viejo Road through the morning fog. It wasn't raining, but I had the wipers on. Every few feet, a big drop of condensation slid off the end of a branch and plopped onto the windshield.

The vast temperature swings typical of a California fall were one of the most difficult things about David's schedule. By afternoon, it would be warm enough for shorts, T-shirts, and iced tea. First thing in the morning, however, we shivered in jeans and fleece hoodies, and we each had an insulated travel mug for the predawn trips to school: hot, rich coffee for me, creamy milk chocolate for Brian, and hot chocolate with a splash of coffee for David. Hot drinks and peanut-butter toast were our favorite portable band-morning breakfast so far, but we would need to vary our repertoire as the season wore on.

I tapped my fingers on the steering wheel and tried to remember the items on my to-do list. David was quiet, and I looked over once or twice to make sure he hadn't fallen asleep.

When I dropped him at school, David told me practice finished at 3:30 p.m. and he was getting a lift home from another band parent.

"Hang on!" I said as he was closing the car door. "Who is this parent?"

David rolled his eyes. "I told you I had a ride for today, remember? On the first day of school? When I wanted you to sign my band form? You wanted me to set up a carpool to help out, so I did."

I shook my head. "But I don't know her. . . ." I started to reply, but my cheeky kid was a step ahead of me.

"It is as I have feared," he said in a fake accent. "My mother has indeed gone mad."

He switched to his normal tone of voice. "Look, Mom, I'll text you her number and you can call her. But I met her yesterday and she seemed okay. No horns. No knives. No chainsaws. I promise if she's a bad driver I'll ask to get out and I'll call you. I'm fourteen, Mom. I know this stuff."

I might have scolded him for using a disrespectful tone, but instead, I laughed. "Okay, kiddo," I said, "but remember that there is a very fine line between a smart kid and a smart-ass. Remember to stay on the right side of that line."

He shut the door and strode off, waving. The car behind me honked and the driver gestured for me to move on. I sighed and moved forward. Being the parent of a young teen was tough. Just when I wanted to pull him close, David pushed me away. And when I thought he should be more independent, he tended to cling. I wished Max were here to consult with. Before I left the parking lot, my phone *ping*ed with what I assumed was the contact information David had promised me. I'd try to meet the mom for coffee, but if that didn't work, a phone call would have to do. But if she sounded like a flake, didn't answer, slurred her words, or sent my mom antennae aquiver in any way, I'd be at school to pick up David.

By noon, most of my errands were done. I'd phoned the mom who'd be driving David home. She lived less than a quarter mile from us and we agreed to meet for coffee the next day. She confirmed that she'd met David the day before when she was checking uniform measurements, and thought he was a charming child. Her son also played trumpet. She hoped I wouldn't mind if she drove David home and that I might be willing to carpool from time to time.

I thanked her and said I looked forward to meeting her. I refrained from mentioning that I also wanted to confirm that she wasn't a chainsaw-wielding psychopath.

I'd forgotten to get gas until I was almost home and didn't have time to turn around and still get back in time to meet the building inspector. I typed a reminder on my phone. The gas gauge was on empty, but I hoped I still had a little fuel in reserve.

I called to Brian as I walked into the kitchen. No answer. No Belle running to greet me. I walked to the table to look for a note and deposit my grocery bags before going back to the car for more. I nearly slipped on the tiles and banged my elbow hard on the table as I tried to avoid dropping the eggs.

The kitchen looked like something out of an old *I Love Lucy* episode. A thin sheen of soapy water covered the floor and bubbles oozed from the running dishwasher. I sighed and leaned my head on my hand, wincing as my bruised elbow hit the table.

Poor Brian. It looked like he'd tried to help by starting the dishwasher, but made the classic mistake of using laundry detergent or regular dish soap in place of the powder formulated for dishwashing machines.

I turned off the washer and grabbed towels from the drawer next to the sink. I threw them on the floor, kicked off my shoes, and pulled a mop from the rack Adelia had installed behind the basement door.

I'd barely started mopping when I heard Belle and Brian on the back porch. They burst into the kitchen and Belle kept going, sliding across the kitchen trailing her leash and snapping at the bubbles floating in the air. Brian just stood in the doorway, staring.

"What happened?" he asked.

"Oh, honey, can you grab those soaking towels and put them in the sink? And bring me some dry bath towels from the linen closet upstairs?"

"But what happened?"

"Did you start the dishwasher after breakfast? And grab the wrong soap?"

"No way. You told me to put my dishes in the sink!"

"It was great of you to want to help. It's a common mistake, mixing up the soap."

"Mom, I didn't do this!"

"It's okay, Brian."

"*But I didn't do it!*"

I stopped mopping and looked at Brian. I believed him.

"But then . . . who did?" I asked.

"Adelia?"

"She had a family thing today. She's not coming until late this afternoon. Could you have forgotten to lock up?"

"With bad guys blowing up the mailbox? No way."

"But no one else has a key. . . ."

We stared at each other. I thought about the implications. Obviously, someone else *did* have a key. But what kind of a vandal starts up a dishwasher? Had it been someone trying to help who'd made a mistake? Or someone trying to do more damage to our house and make it *look* like a mistake? Either way, it was creepy to think of someone being in the house without an invitation.

"I think it's time to change the locks, Mom," Brian said. "Maybe this afternoon?"

"Good idea. Do you want to look up a locksmith on your phone or should we see if someone on Adelia's team can do it?"

Brian pulled out his phone. "Can I see if there's someone who can come out before Adelia gets here?"

I nodded. Brian called and after checking with me, arranged for the locksmith to come out within the next hour.

I finished mopping and fixed lunch. The locksmith came on time, fixed us up with new keys, made copies on the grinder in his truck, and was gone. Brian and I agreed that the new keys made us feel even safer than we'd thought they would.

The building inspector came and suggested we plan to: Redo the roof, gutters, and downspouts. Replace the windows. Add to the insulation. And have the place tented for termites. In general, though, his report was far better than I'd feared and uncovered few surprises.

Adelia came and her team helped me get all the furniture in place on the now-gleaming floors. By four thirty they'd come and gone, and I was wondering where David was and whether I should phone him.

David had said practice would finish at three thirty, but I didn't know yet whether marching practices tended to run late, or if the kids stayed and chatted afterwards. I decided to wait a few more minutes before phoning him to check up. I walked to the living room, sank into the down cushions of our denim sofa, and admired all that Adelia and her team had accomplished.

Boxes still needed unpacking and lamps needed to be matched up with their shades and plugged in, but the heavy pieces were in place. Adelia had surprised me earlier by unrolling one of the most beautiful Persian rugs I'd ever seen. It had belonged to Aunt Kay and had been stored in the basement, still wrapped in brown paper from its last cleaning. The rich blues, greens, golds, and reds pulled the room together, merging our faded denim sofas with the rich wood of the Craftsman house.

I was about to call David when I heard a car door slam. David trudged up the drive looking worn-out from his long day of practice.

"Daniel's mom said to tell you she'll see you for coffee tomorrow," David said. "She would have stopped to say hi, but practice ran late and she needs to pick up Daniel's little brother from soccer."

He kicked off his shoes, walked into the living room, and tossed his backpack and trumpet on a window seat. "I'm starving. How long 'til dinner?"

"It will be a while, but you can make a sandwich now if you want. The sandwich fixings are in their usual spot in the fridge."

David made and gobbled two sandwiches and a huge glass of milk, regaling me with tales of marching-band practice in between bites.

In the same way that I was building a home for us here, within the daunting, fast-paced confusion of Silicon Valley, David was building himself a comfortable home within the confines of Orchard View High School.

David said he planned to take a shower and start on homework. Brian was practicing his French horn. I decided to gas up the car in case I forgot later, despite the reminder note on my phone. Belle stayed with the boys. With the locks changed and both boys home together with Belle, I figured they were probably safe from the dishwasher-starting prowler. I shook my head over that. A prowler was a prowler. It was creepy thinking someone had been in our house uninvited. But a prowler who did housework? Was that even more creepy or something I could get used to? I shrugged, hoping that it wouldn't happen again and I'd never have to find a real answer to that question.

I'd stopped at the closest gas station when a familiar Subaru pulled up to the pump next to me. Its roof rack held a silver road bike that looked to be pretty high-end, though I didn't know much about the nuances of cycling and its equipment. A lean man wearing a green Lycra cycling outfit unfolded from the front seat, smiling as if he knew me.

"Paolo Bianchi, ma'am, remember me?" he said, holding out his hand. "Officer Paolo Bianchi."

My hand smelled like gasoline from the pump, but I made a show of wiping it on my jeans before I shook his hand.

"Of course I remember you," I said. "I was confused by the switch in the sports gear on top of your car."

Paolo laughed. "The guys at the station are always on my case," he said. "I'm new to the force and they say they've learned more about me from what's on top of my car than from talking to me."

I smiled, happy to have a friendly face to talk to while I waited for my tank to fill. "Has there been any progress in the investigation?"

Paolo frowned and looked uncomfortable. I thought about filling the silence by telling him about the dishwasher incident, but it was just too weird. I wasn't sure he'd believe we'd had an intruder. Wasn't it more logical to assume that Brian or I had reached for the soap powder and grabbed the wrong box by mistake? And that we'd later forgotten we'd started the dishwasher? It's easy for anyone to forget having done a routine task like pushing the *start* button on a kitchen appliance.

But Paolo spoke up and I lost the chance.

"Jason . . . er . . . Detective Mueller asked me to call you about that, as a matter of fact."

"Go on," I said. I was used to encouraging young men to talk. Right now, Paolo Bianchi didn't seem much older than David.

"Detective Mueller is concerned about the vandalism."

"He mentioned that last week."

"Yes, but there's more. The detective called a guy from San Jose State who has been doing a study on teenage vandalism. He's got this theory that while it's all destructive, most of it comes down to teenaged angst and the kids grow out of it."

"Boys will be boys?" I'd always hated that expression and thought it was a cop-out—a way for adults to avoid the hard work of teaching boys to act like responsible young men.

"Some of it," Paolo said. "Like tagging, knocking over garbage cans, and trashing mailboxes."

"He's saying we should ignore that?"

"No, no, he's saying we should catch them as young as possible, throw the book at them, and turn them around before they rack up an arrest record."

I nodded. Paolo's bundle of mixed metaphors was a good match for my own thoughts on the subject.

Paolo continued. "He's saying that some of the other things that get lumped in with hooliganism—arson, destroying property—*those* come from a whole different level of rage. And, instead of growing out of it, the kids' behavior is likely to escalate."

Paolo took a deep breath. The pump *ping*ed at me and I unhooked the nozzle from the car and replaced it on the pump. I pushed the button for my receipt and replaced the gas cap.

"That's what's worrying Detective Mueller, Mrs. McDonald. That criminologist? He was able to figure out a lot from pictures of the vandalism at your house. He looked at the damage Mr. Hernandez reported months ago: broken windows, sprinklers turned on and left to run all night, garbage cans emptied all over the lawn. He compared those to the more recent destruction: the fire upstairs, the damage to the floor boards of the front porch, the booby-trapped electrical box. The San Jose State guy thinks you've got an angry kid or young adult who is targeting your house, and his rage is escalating."

"Does this expert know about the exploding mailbox or the damage at the middle school?"

Paolo shook his head. "We haven't had a chance to check in with him since those things happened. I need to update him. It's on my list of things to do."

I had to like a young man who seemed to treasure lists as much as I did.

Paolo bit his lip and shifted from one foot to the other.

"Was there something else you wanted to tell me?" I asked.

Paolo looked at me, glanced away, and said nothing. He was making me nervous. I bit my lip and searched his face, hoping that whatever he was hesitating to tell me wouldn't put my family at greater risk.

Chapter 13

Need a quick dinner idea? Try breakfast for dinner.
Nothing is quite as comforting or as easy to prepare
as breakfast food.

From the Notebook of Maggie McDonald
Simplicity Itself Organizing Services

Saturday, September 6, Evening

Paolo avoided eye contact and sighed. "Detective Mueller asked me to warn you. He wants you to be sure to lock up, turn the outside lights on, and keep your animals inside."

"The animals? This guy would hurt our animals? Isn't that a whole other level of crime? One that's more indicative of a serial-killer wannabe?"

Paolo blushed and then turned to take the gas nozzle out of his Subaru. "I'm not sure of the research on that. The detective just wants you to be careful, ma'am."

After he'd finished printing his receipt and stuffed it in his back pocket, he looked at me through the strands of his reddish-brown hair. "Mrs. McDonald. I didn't mean to scare you." He pushed the hair from his eyes and tucked it behind his ear. "I joined the force because I wanted to do computer forensics. I'm real good with computers, but I'm not so great with people. I can't seem to get a handle on when to talk and when to be quiet. Or how much to tell people and what to keep to myself. I'm always getting it wrong. Mrs. McDonald, if you see the detective, can you tell him I asked you to be careful? Don't let on I told you that other stuff?"

I assured Paolo that I would keep his secret, and that I was grateful for the information. It helped me get a better sense of what the boys and I needed to do to stay safe.

His scrunched-up shoulders relaxed. "We've got a car making rounds through your neighborhood."

"What are the chances you'll catch him that way?"

"Slim to none," Paolo admitted. "Though one of our patrols did spot a guy running from near your house into one of the wooded front yards of the houses across the way a few days ago. Our hope is that the kid who is responsible will see our patrols and figure he doesn't have time to do any damage."

I looked at my watch. "I'm sorry, Paolo, but I've got to run. Thanks for warning me. I'll tell the boys to be careful. Thank Jason for me. I'll tell him you did a great job filling me in."

"Thanks, Mrs. McDonald."

"Tell the patrols they're welcome to stop in any time if they want a cup of coffee, or the restroom—everything in the house is working now."

I jumped in the car and checked *get gas* off my list.

By the time I got back, the boys had finished homework and instrument practice and helped me whip up our favorite comfort meal—breakfast for dinner. David was nearly asleep at the table.

After dinner, while the boys got ready for bed, I slumped on the couch and sipped a glass of chardonnay. I held the glass up to the light and looked at the room through the golden liquid. It was only nine o'-clock, but I was beat. And missing Max. It was time to check on the kids and head to bed.

I put the glass in the kitchen sink and locked the doors. I headed upstairs with the cats padding after me. David was fast asleep with the lights on and Belle snoring at his feet. I switched off the light, closed the door, and moved on to Brian's room.

My youngest was rereading the third Harry Potter book. Watson jumped on the bed and stood on the open pages. "Someone thinks it's time for you to go to bed," I said.

Brian rubbed Watson behind the ears, while Holmes wove himself around my ankles. "Is it okay to feel a little sad?" Brian said. "I miss Dad."

"Of course," I said. "He feels the same way. Do you want to send him an email?"

"Maybe in the morning."

I picked up Holmes and placed him at the foot of the bed, where he began his nightly bath. Brian shoved Watson off his book. He closed it and put it next to him on the bed. I moved it to the night table, knowing that it would otherwise end up on the floor. Brian was an active sleeper.

I kissed my fingers and touched his forehead, turned out the light, and headed for my own room. I'd expected to lie awake missing Max, but I barely had time to pull the quilt over me before I too was asleep.

What felt like minutes later, I woke up startled and afraid. Belle was barking and scratching at David's door. I shoved Holmes off my chest, grabbed the throw at the foot of the bed, and raced into the hall, bumping into the doorframe while still shoving my feet into my sneakers. David opened his bedroom door, rubbing his eyes. Belle shot from the room and down the stairs, skidding when she made the turn at the landing. Her bark echoed through the house.

Brian somehow managed to sleep through the commotion. David and I followed Belle at a run and watched as she ran from window seat to window seat, clawing the windows so hard I feared she'd break them.

David was pale and had a white-knuckled grip on the baseball bat he held in his right hand. I scooped up my phone from the charger on the front-hall table and speed-dialed Jason.

Belle seldom barked, except in greeting or to let us know she was in when she wanted out, or out when she wanted in. Her frantic barking and snarling was something I'd never heard before. It made my heart pound and my scalp prickle.

Jason's phone was answered by a dispatcher. She kept me on the line while she alerted the patrols in the area and contacted the detective. "Sit tight, ma'am," she said. "Stay inside. Do you want me to remain on the line until help arrives?"

"Thanks, but no," I said. "I think I hear the sirens, now." I hung up the phone.

"You hear sirens?" David whispered.

"No," I said. "But I'm going to take a look around."

David clipped Belle's leash to her collar and she strained at it, tugging us toward the back door. I grabbed a flashlight from the counter. Max had prepared an army of them, lined up in formation, when we were dealing with the sketchy electricity. Flashlights were an obsession for Max, probably stemming from a long-forgotten childhood experience with a power outage or earthquake or nightmares. In any case, he felt most prepared for emergencies when we had lots of working flashlights with fresh bulbs and batteries. He'd recently replaced most of our oldest ones with new high-powered LED lights that were brighter, smaller, and lighter.

We teased him about his addiction, but I was grateful for his preparations. I handed a flashlight to David and chose the largest one for myself. It could double as a club. I pushed open the back door, cringing as it screeched, announcing our presence to anyone who might be hiding in the yard. We turned on our flashlights and headed down the dew-slick steps.

"Do you have any idea what time it is?" I asked David.

He shook his head and waved his flashlight around the backyard and down toward the barn. We jumped at the sound of something crashing through the bushes, but it sounded like we'd startled a large rodent or raccoon rather than a two-legged intruder.

"Check the barn or the front?" David whispered. Belle was pulling us toward the front yard and wheezing as she strained against the leash. I pointed with the flashlight and we crept around the side of the house, following Belle.

Before we reached the front, a patrol car with lights flashing but the sirens off came up the drive, followed by an unmarked SUV. Jason and Stephen jumped from the SUV, while a uniformed officer I didn't recognize opened the door of the patrol car and turned on a flashlight that was both larger and brighter than mine. Stephen opened the back door of the SUV and Munchkin jumped down.

"I'll take a look around," Stephen said, holding Munchkin's leash and heading down the drive, swinging his light in large arcs ahead of him.

"Is anyone hurt?" Jason asked.

I shook my head. "Thanks for coming."

"No problem. Let's get you both inside where it's warmer and you can tell me what happened."

Without keys, the only way back into the house was through the kitchen. We retraced our steps. I made coffee and pulled out the cookie jar that still held a few of the oatmeal cookies Tess had made. I shivered and pulled the throw around my shoulders. Even oatmeal cookies wouldn't help us feel secure at home tonight.

While the coffeemaker gurgled, David and I told Jason what little we knew. We'd nearly finished when Stephen and Munchkin returned.

"I asked the officer to move the car down to the street with the lights on," Stephen said.

His demeanor confused me. He seemed to have more clout with the police than I would have expected for a volunteer. But I had neither the time nor the inclination to clarify the situation tonight.

"Someone tried to force the lock on the barn," Stephen added. "I wired the handles together. It looks secure enough for tonight, but the lock will need to be replaced."

"I'll call the locksmith in the morning," I said. "He changed the locks on the house earlier today . . . or was it yesterday?" I looked at the clock on the stove, which showed it was minutes until midnight. It seemed much later.

"You changed the locks?" Jason said. "Was that a precaution or did something happen?"

I ran through the odd events with the dishwasher, emphasizing that both Brian and I were sure that someone had been in the house. We didn't know why or how they'd intruded, but we were certain neither of us had turned on the dishwasher.

"I believe you," Jason said. "It's a new dishwasher, right? I need to get out the manual for the first week I own any appliance. You'd both remember turning it on because you would have needed to think about it more than usual."

I felt my shoulders release some of the tension that had them hunched up almost to my ears.

"Getting the locks changed immediately was a good idea," Jason said. "Next time, though, let me know if anything happens that you can't explain. Your instincts are good. If anything worries you or the kids or Belle, I want to know."

I stood and poured coffee into mugs. I handed one to Stephen and another to Jason, and put a carton of milk and a five-pound bag of sugar on the table. We were making progress with the move, but I hadn't yet unpacked a sugar bowl or cream pitcher. David stirred hot-chocolate mix into a cup of hot water.

Stephen palmed his coffee mug. "Munchkin and I are going to take a look out front."

They hadn't been gone more than ten seconds when Stephen called from the front room. "Jase? I've got something here you're going to want to take a look at."

Jason leapt from his chair, spilling his coffee. He dashed through the pantry and dining room to join Stephen at the front of the house. David and I followed.

With a tight rein on Munchkin's leash, Stephen pointed his flashlight beam toward the welcome mat outside the open front door. Munchkin bared his teeth and growled. I didn't blame him. In the center of the circle of light cast by the flashlight was a small gray squirrel pinned to the porch with a four-inch nail. The nail looked exactly like those that had pierced the bodies of the squirrels at the middle school.

Chapter 14

Sometimes listening is the greatest gift. I learn so much
from my clients' stories.

From the Notebook of Maggie McDonald
Simplicity Itself Organizing Services

Sunday, September 7, Early morning

Jason moved between me and the impaled squirrel, backing David
and me into the house while he dialed his phone.

"I want a patrol team walking the road in front of the house until
dawn," he barked into the phone. "At six, I want them going door-to-
door asking questions. Put our best guys on it. If anyone in this neighborhood saw anything or knows anything, we need to know too."

We reconvened in the kitchen. Jason topped off our coffee and
started a new pot. He took a sip and placed a hand on David's shoulder. He looked at Stephen and Munchkin.

"Are you two okay to stay here for what's left of the night?" he
said.

Stephen nodded. If anyone had asked me later, I would have
sworn Munchkin did too.

"That's not necessary . . ." I began, but Jason interrupted me.

"No arguments, Maggie," Jason said. "This is serious stuff. This
vandal is escalating and we need to know you're safe. We have to
catch him before he does anything worse."

I opened my mouth to argue, but Jason cut me off.

"Stop," he said. "Stephen is staying here. He's Marine Corps retired, Special Operations Command. He does this sort of thing for us

often. He'll take good care of you so that I can focus on the investigation and catch this guy before he actually injures someone."

"Maggie, David, go on up to bed," Stephen said. "And take Belle with you if she'll go. Munchkin and I will hold the fort down here. Mind if I build a fire?"

"That's fine." I put my arm around David and we trudged up the stairs. I looked over my shoulder at Stephen, but he flapped his hand at me, urging me up the steps.

"Go on," he said. "I'll be fine. So will you."

At the door to his room, David stopped. "Mom, do you think we should stay in Brian's room so we can tell him what's going on as soon as he wakes up?"

I took that to mean that David would feel safer if we were all together. I felt the same way. We grabbed our sleeping bags from the top of the attic stairs where they were still waiting to be put away and moved them into Brian's room. Brian stirred but didn't wake.

"Mom, are you going to tell Dad what's going on?" David asked, whispering.

I nodded. "Right now, actually. Is there anything you want me to tell him?"

David shook his head. "Just that I hope he comes home soon."

I smiled, nodded, and held up my phone. David was asleep before I'd scrunched into my sleeping bag, trying to find a comfortable position on the floor. I sat leaning against the wall and opened the email app on my phone. I hesitated before I started typing. Should I ask Max to come home? It would make all of us feel more secure. But was it necessary? Surely the police would catch the vandal quickly and tonight's excitement would be forgotten—probably before Max's plane landed in San Francisco. I sighed and started typing.

To: Max.McDonald2111@gmail.com

From: SimplicityItselfOrganizing@gmail.com

Hey Hon,

First, let me tell you that we're all safe, happy, and doing well after our first week with the new routine.

Second, I'm not excited about you being gone at all, let alone a few more weeks, but I'm glad you're able to help out the manager

who was hit by a car. That poor man! He must be in terrible pain. What's his name? I can't go on calling him "Man hit by car."

Third, I need to fill you in on some weird stuff that's going on. Before I do, though, please know that it's all under control—over and done with. If you left India right this minute, by the time you arrived it would probably be nearly forgotten. So, no worries, OK?

Saturday morning, when I took David to marching band and ran some errands, Brian was home with Belle. They were out exploring and while they were gone, someone came into the house and started the dishwasher. Weird, right? Unfortunately, they used laundry soap or something, and when I came home, the floor was covered with suds. We got it wiped up quickly and there was no damage, but it felt creepy to know someone was in the house— even someone who felt like doing dishes and didn't take anything. Brian and I solved that problem by getting the locks changed. The locksmith was great and fixed us up with new keys in a little over an hour.

We all went to bed pretty early. David loves marching band, but it's taking a lot out of him. He comes home, does homework, eats like a horse, and falls asleep. Remember when the kids were little and would fall asleep with their heads in their plates? We may be in for a reenactment of that period in our lives.

Sometime before midnight, Belle started freaking out and woke David and me up. Something was clearly wrong, so I called 911. Detective Jason Mueller came back, along with Stephen Laird— the big bald guy with the mastiff. At first they couldn't find anything wrong, but later Stephen found a squirrel nailed to the front porch. (I think the squirrel was dead before it was nailed to the porch. I don't know why that matters so much, but it does. It would be worse to think it had suffered.)

The police are taking it seriously, along with the dishwashing intruder. Jason asked Stephen and Munchkin (the mastiff) to stay here tonight. At first I didn't want them to but Jason insisted. He says that Stephen is some sort of super-stealthy attack-trained Marine (retired), so we're in good hands. I think Munchkin could chomp the arm off anyone who wanted to hurt any of us.

So, please don't worry. But let me know if your schedule gets pinned down any better and you have an ETA for landing in San Francisco. Just being able to write this all down has helped.

We all love you and miss you!!

Maggie

To: SimplicityItselfOrganizing@gmail.com

From: Max.McDonald2111@gmail.com

What?! I need to come home. This all sounds crazy and super-dangerous. I'm glad Stephen was able to stay, but the person protecting you all should be me.

I'll look into flights home and send you my itinerary. No arguments.

Love, Max

. . . and BE CAREFUL!!

To: Max.McDonald2111@gmail.com

From: SimplicityItselfOrganizing@gmail.com

I keep forgetting that the middle of the night here is mid-morning there. Do I have that right? I hate time zones. And yes, I hate that my dear beloved husband is a gazillion miles away and can't give me a hug and say "There, there, everything will be OK."

At this point, though, that's really all you could do. It's been super-quiet here after all the excitement. I'm working off a tiny bit of an adrenaline rush, but the kids are all snoozing and even Belle is sound asleep.

Would it help if you could hear our voices? Do you want to phone? I think you said that 8 pm here is a good time there for you to call. We'll all be here tomorrow night if you want to phone in.

Would it help if I had Jason Mueller email you?

I absolutely promise I'll email if there's anything to worry about. Please don't worry.

Love, Maggie

To: SimplicityItselfOrganizing@gmail.com

From: Max.McDonald2111@gmail.com

OK. I'll stay put. But telling me not to worry about you and the boys is crazy. Please ask Jason to email me with an update. It's not that I don't believe you or trust you, but it would feel good to hear "nothing to worry about" from a detached third party. I guess if I freak out every time you tell me something has happened, you'll stop giving me an honest update. I know that's not what I want.

Do you think one day when we're old we'll be able to look back and consider this a great adventure and laugh about it? I hope so. But, please remember that in order for that to happen, you need to stay safe! Be careful! You, Brian, and David are the most valuable things in the world to me. Nothing is worth endangering any of you.

And, yes, I'll call at 8 pm your time on Sunday. I need to hear your voice.

Love,

Max

I put down my phone and listened to the kids, both of whom were fast asleep. I climbed out of my sleeping bag, grabbed my throw—which was serving as my bathrobe—and snuck back down the stairs. A cheerful fire burned in the fireplace, highlighting the tiles with the knights on them. Stephen must have heard me, because he turned toward me as I stepped off the last step.

"Do you need anything?" I asked Stephen. "More coffee?"

"Tea would be great," he said. "I'll make it. What kind?"

"Mint, please," I said, "With caffeine and honey." We had a full cupboard devoted to tea: black, green, caffeinated, decaffeinated, and herbal. Stephen stood, threw another log on the fire, and moved to the kitchen without making a sound. *Special Operations.*

After he brought me a steamy cup of perfectly brewed tea, we sat in silence watching the fire. Munchkin snored under the big square coffee table, which bore the scars of family games and crafts.

"Can't sleep?" Stephen said.

"Nope. Not sure whether it's nerves or a desire to catch the twisted little brat in the act."

"Catching twisted little brats in the act is what I'm here for . . . and Munchkin too."

Munchkin, hearing his name through his dreams, thumped his tail and went on snoring.

"He'll be a big help," I said.

"Oh, he's a good soldier. Sleeps when he can, but is never more than a second away from full alert."

"How'd you two meet?" I said. "Last week, in the barn, you promised you'd tell me one day."

"It's a long story . . ."

"Tell me." We needed to pass the time and I needed to know this man better if he was going to be spending the night on my couch.

Stephen took a deep sip of his tea and passed his hand over his bald head. He sighed, leaned back against the couch cushions, and began.

"Jason mentioned I was Special Ops?" he said.

I nodded.

"I was in Afghanistan, heading up an expeditionary force of bomb-sniffing dogs and handlers. We'd been there about six months. The dogs, the handlers . . . we were a tight group. We found more improvised explosive devices—you know, IEDs—and saved more lives than any robotic unit ever has. Eventually, the insurgents figured out it was our unit that was throwing a wrench in their plans."

A log shifted in the fire and sparks flew up the chimney. Stephen got up, grabbed the poker, and rearranged the logs.

"Was Munchkin one of those dogs?"

Stephen laughed. "The way he eats? He'd have broken the Defense budget beyond repair. No, we met up after . . ." He paused and picked at nonexistent lint on his jeans.

"You don't have to tell me," I said, not wanting to probe a painful wound.

"No, it's okay. They say it helps to tell." He fiddled with what looked like a wedding ring on his left hand.

"Make a long story short, my dog and I headed out, clearing a path for the patrol behind us. My dog, Paxon, cut his foot and I stopped to bandage it. While I was doing that . . . well, I was the only one who made it out."

"Paxon?"

"The whole patrol. It started with a *thud*. One big *thud*—not even a sound, but more like a feeling under your feet, like someone picked up the whole world and dropped it on its ass, leaving your stomach somewhere up around your chin until it falls with the same *thud* and knocks you flat. I have no idea what happened. Paxon hadn't alerted me to anything. Near's I can figure, some brand-new baby grunt forgot he was in a war, stepped off the trail and onto a mine.

"Paxon recovered sooner than I did and he took off, running in circles, sniffing and whining, looking for our buddies. A sniper picked him off. I dove behind a rock and called for air support, but by the time they arrived, the snipers had killed everyone." Stephen sighed, slumped, and touched the side of his head. "I got off with a head wound and a shattered leg."

I didn't say anything. Dozens of sentences half-formed in my head, but they all sounded lame. I couldn't begin to imagine this man's pain or the sacrifices he'd made. He looked up from his tea, rubbing Munchkin's paw with his foot. I couldn't tell whether he wanted comfort, understanding, or silence. *When in doubt, go with the truth.*

"Stephen, I'm afraid to say or do anything that would make your pain any worse." He stared into the darkness beyond the fire, expressionless, saying nothing. "I can't even begin to understand the depth of your sacrifice . . . or theirs. Thank you for trusting me with your story. I'm honored."

We both let the silence linger. Stephen sipped at his tea, then peered into the mug, looking surprised that it was empty.

"My turn," I said. "What are you drinking?"

Stephen handed me his mug. "Tea. Earl Grey. Hot."

I shared a smug smile with him, recognizing a fellow *Star Trek* fanatic, and took his mug. "One Captain Picard special, coming up."

Restocked with tea, I took my place on the sofa opposite Stephen and tucked my feet under me. He was supposed to be telling the story of how he and Munchkin met. We hadn't gotten to Munchkin yet, but there was no way I was going to ask Stephen to continue. That decision was up to him. But his story had captivated me and made me completely forget the stupid brat who was terrorizing my family.

Stephen crossed, uncrossed, and recrossed his legs.

"I don't remember much after that," he said "Not for a long time. Just bits and pieces of medevac helicopters, a base hospital, then Landstuhl and Walter Reed.

"They had me at the veterans hospital in Palo Alto, trying to fig- ure out whether I'd get to keep my leg and helping me walk again after the surgeries. I stayed on, helping other vets and working with retired Marine dogs. You know they used to euthanize them?"

I leaned back into the cushions of the couch, away from Stephen, and covered my mouth with my hand, shocked that anyone could kill a healthy dog, let alone one trained to give up his or her life to save American soldiers.

"They don't anymore. They discharge them and send them home like any soldier. The dogs end up working for other government agencies or for the private sector or they get adopted. I work with the dogs and canine handlers who are struggling with post-traumatic stress. No one knows the best way to treat that—in dogs or in peo- ple—so we're figuring it out together. Matching up dogs who've lost their handlers with handlers who've lost their dogs—finding ways for them to use their skills at home.

"One day, I'm taking one of the dogs for exercise. Getting him used to the sounds of suburbia, you know. Nice spring day. Wind is blowing. Fruit trees in bloom."

Stephen's story had shifted into present tense. His hands became fists and his jaw tensed. I could tell he was reliving the story as if it were happening right here, right now.

"And some numb-nut tosses a firework into a Dumpster." Tears began to flow, unchecked, down his cheeks. "Why would anyone do that, anywhere? But especially in a place where there are people hurting, wounded, fighting for their health and sanity after too many explosions." He shook his head and continued.

"I pick up the dog and run. I'm surprised I'm running, since I'm not even walking well at that point, but I need to get out of there, so I run. The dog is shaking and I'm shaking. We have no idea where we are or where we're going. We're just trying to get away." Stephen picked up his tea, hands shaking.

I pushed a box of tissues across the coffee table toward him. He ignored it.

"They found us later, behind the stairs of a loading dock, still shaking and whining. The two of us. What a pair."

I still had no idea where Munchkin figured into this story, but I couldn't interrupt Stephen. I was awestruck that he would share such a personal story with me. Maybe that's why, I thought. Maybe the fact that I was a virtual stranger made it easier. Either way, it was good for me to remember that there were greater dangers than degenerate squirrel-impaling vandals.

Stephen sipped his tea and continued. "He and I were discharged after that and we recovered together. Quinn was his name. A great dog. Yellow lab. We didn't sleep much, either of us, but walking helped, so we'd go out together walking, late at night. Got to know the night people, the street people. Lots of them are veterans. It's real quiet around here at night. No traffic. A different world."

Staring far into the distance, Stephen continued his story. "One night, we're passing behind the big grocery on Grant Road, steering clear of the Dumpsters and the loading dock. But we hear a whining noise. Crying. Real pathetic. It's coming from the Dumpster. Neither one of us wants to get anywhere near it. But the crying goes on and we have to do something. We make it our mission, like we've got orders or something. We get closer and Quinn starts sniffing, whining, and pulling on the leash. He sticks his nose under the Dumpster. I kneel down, wishing I had a flashlight, when Quinn pulls out his head. He's got what looks like a dirty old sock in his mouth. He drops it at my feet like a tennis ball."

"Munchkin?" I said.

"In the flesh, what there was of him. I don't think he was more than a week old. I stuffed him inside my shirt, fleas and all. He was freezing and I wasn't sure he'd make it. But between us, Quinn and I got him warm and clean, and filled his little tummy with some warmed-up milk from the fridge. He fit in my hand with room to spare."

"Hence the name."

"Right. It turned out that milk was the wrong thing to give him, but first thing the next day Quinn and I got puppy-rearing protocols from a Marine veterinarian at the VA. I fed Munchkin puppy formula every two hours and Quinn cleaned him up like he was the pup's mom. The rest is history." Stephen rubbed Munchkin's belly, but there wasn't enough room under the coffee table for Munchkin to do more than shift his weight and sigh in doggy contentment.

"But what happened to Quinn?"

"Quinn was old before his time. He'd seen too much, hurt too much, missed too many good soldiers. One night, before Munchkin was full-grown, I woke up to hear Munchkin crying like the first day we found him. Quinn was gone."

After a few moments of silence and respect for the fallen, Stephen looked up. "Quinn left me in good hands, though. Munchkin and I make a good team."

I could only agree. With the fire dying and the sky starting to lighten up, it was either time to catch a little bit more sleep or to get started on breakfast. I chose food. "Would you and Munchkin like some eggs?" I whispered.

Stephen nodded, picked up his tea mug, slipped his feet into his shoes, and stood. Munchkin wriggled out from under the coffee table. "We'll take you up on that. I'll check in with the police and then Munchkin and I will do a quick patrol around the property and make sure everything's okay out there."

I winced at the reminder of the murdered squirrel on the porch. After hearing Stephen's story, I wasn't about to complain about any of the discomfort or confusion in my own life. Nothing I'd experienced could compare. So much pain. So much suffering. And Stephen was one man. There were thousands of young men and women who could tell any number of stories, equally heartbreaking. I felt intimidated by the honor Stephen had done me, trusting me. Oh, I knew he still had secrets he hadn't shared. Everyone did. And it seemed as though Orchard View was full of them.

But I knew now why Stephen walked around at night, which was probably why he turned up at so many crime scenes where people needed help. And maybe the fact that he was Special Operations was the reason Jason seemed to trust him to manage parts of his investigations—and had him stay with us last night. I was missing something, though. Lots of things.

I went to the kitchen to put the mugs in the sink and whip up eggs, toast, and coffee. It was going to be a long day. I knew where the day was starting—here in my comforting kitchen with my family, my new friend, and my dog, all of whom were protective and loyal. But I was pretty sure I had no idea where we were headed from here, or where we'd end up.

Chapter 15

There's a time in every project when the goal seems un-
reachable. Chaos and confusion reign. But to go back is
unimaginable. Get more boxes, take a break, and begin
again. The only solution is to press forward.

From the Notebook of Maggie McDonald
Simplicity Itself Organizing Services

Sunday, September 7, About six o'clock

I decided to make muffins to go with the eggs. I was compensating
with carbs, but it felt good to have a plan and to move forward
with a project that was straightforward. The smell of muffins would
be comforting.

I was gathering the dry ingredients when I heard Stephen and
Munchkin climbing the porch stairs. They came through the back
door and Munchkin snuffled my hand before curling up under the
table.

"Everything looks fine outside," Stephen said as he poured a cup
of coffee. "No sign of anything or anyone at all unexpected." He but-
tered the muffin tins without being asked while I stirred the batter.

"How can this guy come and go like that?" I said. "With no trace?"

"Got me," said Stephen. "But Jason just pulled up with his sidekick Officer Bianchi and we'll see if they found out anything."

If I'd known I'd be entertaining so many people for breakfast, I'd
have taken the time to add another leaf to extend the kitchen table.
By the time the food was ready, we'd moved to the long table in the
dining room. I was glad I'd decided to make the muffins, which dis-

appeared along with the coffee, eggs, toast, bananas, orange juice, and everything else remotely breakfast-like I had in the house.

When we were down to crumbs and coffee, the boys took off to the barn to examine the damage to the lock and hunt for more clues. Stephen, Jason, and Paolo lingered over coffee and filled me in.

"Any word from the patrols?" Stephen said.

Paolo Bianchi shook his head. "They canvassed the entire neighborhood," he said. "And, Detective? You might need to do some damage control. Nearly every one of the neighbors promised to have a word with the chief, or the mayor, or their legislative representative, or all three. A predawn Sunday-morning knock on the door wasn't popular with anyone."

"I figured," said Jason. "But at least they were home. Did anyone see anything? Know anything?"

Paolo shook his head. "We got nothing. Some folks said they'd keep an eye out."

"Okay, then." Jason tapped his wedding ring on the table. He hadn't mentioned he was married. I wondered when I'd get to meet his wife. I wondered what she thought of the odd hours he kept. Being married to a police officer had to be even more difficult than being married to a software-engineering manager who was living in Bangalore.

"Maggie," Jason said, "you should be fine during the day, but we'll keep the patrols going. If you call in, they can be here within minutes." He looked at Stephen, who nodded. "Stephen and Munchkin will stay here at night until we know more."

I started to protest, thinking we were asking too much of Stephen's generous nature. He shook his head. "Look, Maggie," he said, "I've got some things to do at the VA hospital today. There are some guys I need to visit, but after that I'm free and happy to help. Let me."

I gave in. "Thanks, Stephen." It wasn't easy for me to be dependent on others, especially people I'd known for such a short time. But I was learning that I couldn't do everything alone, and Stephen was becoming a friend—a friend of our entire family. And friends were for leaning on. I could do this.

After that, the day passed in a blur. The police cleared away the squirrel and Adelia's team patched up the porch. Stephen promised to swing by the hardware store and pick up the items we needed to repair the lock on the barn.

I was exhausted, but if I kept moving I was fine. I did laundry, ran the vacuum, and put away the sleeping bags. It wasn't until mid-afternoon, when I was starting to think about dinner, that I realized we'd eaten nearly everything edible in the house. I needed food for dinner, for the kids' lunches, and for breakfast in the morning.

Grabbing my list, I went to track down the boys and tell them my plan. I found them in the attic, where they were unrolling a rope ladder meant as a fire escape. I knew in a heartbeat their plan was to check it out, "escaping" from the attic down into the garden.

It wasn't that bad an idea. Hadn't the fire marshal at the university told us to practice our escape plans? I looked the rope over. As far as I could tell, it was sound. Brian tried it out, then David. They wanted me to try too, but I passed, figuring that the extra incentive of flames chasing me in a real fire would be all I'd need to fling myself from the roof. Here, in broad daylight, with no flames in sight, I couldn't make myself do it. I was chicken, but my cowardice—or maybe *caution* was a better word—made the boys feel brave in contrast.

We wrapped up the rope and I reminded the boys that they still had homework and chores to do. I scribbled their meal and snack suggestions on my grocery list and asked if they wanted to join me. Neither one did, so I took Belle with me and headed down the stairs and toward the car.

"Mom, Mom," Brian called after me, clattering down the stairs and catching up with me in the kitchen. "There's a problem!"

"What's up, Bri?" I asked with one hand on the doorknob.

"I need a form. A permission slip. We're going to the symphony on Monday."

"What form?" I began, but Brian's problem was beginning to dawn on me. He'd need a form for the trip. One of the dozens of forms Principal Harrier had handed out the week before, slapping her iPad and repeating, "No excuses. No exceptions."

Oh, boy.

"Do you know which form it is? What it looks like?" I was pretty sure the forms were still in the backseat of my car where they'd sat, untouched, since I'd stashed them there on the first day of school. Finding one form in that stack wouldn't be easy.

Brian shook his head. "It doesn't matter. It needs to be submitted the day before. We should have turned it in on Friday."

I wasn't certain, but I thought that our new friendship with Assistant Principal April Chen might enable us to get around the rule, but I didn't want to put April in a tight spot and I didn't want to run afoul of Horrible Harrier either. Yikes.

Brian sat on the bottom step of the back stairs, looking miserable.

I bit my lip and looked at my dejected little guy. I wracked my brain as I rinsed dishes and put them in the dishwasher, hoping that moving around would help me invent a solution.

"Are the forms online?" I said. "Can we print one out?"

"David's been having trouble with the printer setup. But Mom, the form was due on *Friday.*"

I knew what I wanted to say, but hesitated because I wasn't sure whether I would be teaching him the right lesson. Would I be showing him how to circumvent the rules? When in doubt, lead with the truth.

"Brian, I don't condone things like splitting hairs or gaming the system. When you know what a rule intends, you should follow it. You should do the right thing. But . . . Miss Harrier is a stickler for details and precision. Maybe we can be precise too."

I sat next to Brian on the bottom step.

"Do you know *exactly* what her rule says?" I asked. "Does the form need to be handed in and time-stamped on Friday, or twenty-four hours ahead of time, or does it say *the day before?* Or do they just need it before school starts on Monday morning?"

I thought for a minute. "And who gets to school first? April or Miss Harrier?"

Brian's face brightened as he figured out what I was getting at. "You mean, drop it off tonight and Harrier won't know it wasn't there on Friday afternoon?"

"Exactly," I said. "It won't meet the letter of the law, but it might just solve the problem."

"Maybe . . ." agreed Brian. ". . . with a little help from April."

We shared a conspiratorial smile.

"Run up and see if you can get David to beat the printer into submission and make it spit out your form. I'll fill it out, sign it, and drop it through the mail slot at school on my way to the grocery store."

By the time David and Brian had printed out the form, it was seven o'clock. I asked the boys to stay on top of their chores and get ready for school while I was gone. Belle and I jumped in the car and drove the winding road down the hill. The sun had dropped behind the mountains of the Coast Range and thick fog rolled in, dimming the lingering sunlight and muting the colors and definition of the landscape. I gripped the steering wheel and peered at the street signs, many of which were obscured by overhanging branches. The drive to the middle school was becoming second nature, but not in the dark. And not when I'd been up most of the night before.

Afraid I'd forget something, I tapped my index finger on the steering wheel, reminding myself of my goals for this trip. Drop off the stupid form; buy milk, cereal, lunch stuff, and something quick for dinner.

Oh, and I needed to get it done before an escalating reprobate decided to take a torch to our house. Arson wasn't quite one step up from sacrificing a squirrel on our porch, but I wasn't sure what the developmental steps of a psychopath entailed, and I didn't want to think about it.

I sighed and pulled the car to the curb in the red zone in front of the school office. I shivered as I approached the office, and then stopped dead. *Max!* I'd forgotten I'd promised Max that we'd be around for his phone call at 8:00 p.m. I looked at my watch: 7:15. I had time, as long as I kept moving and was super-efficient at the grocery store. A gust of wind sent leaves and litter skittering across the small plaza in front of the building and threatened to tear the form from my hand.

The mail slot through which I'd hoped to drop Brian's form was installed in the solid-wood portion of the door below the glass and the locking push bar. I crouched to slide the form through it, leaning against the glass as my knees protested. I leaned and then stumbled, losing my balance as the door rattled in its frame. It wasn't locked. I pulled it open and added Brian's form to the pile of other papers that littered the mat.

Oh, good. We weren't the only family submitting forms at the last minute. The door shouldn't have been unlocked, though. Why was the light on in Miss Harrier's office? And why was her polished leather briefcase sitting on the front counter?

"Hello?" Something was wrong and I wasn't sure I wanted to find out what it was.

"Hello?" I tried to breathe shallowly and silently as I tiptoed forward . . . and froze.

Chapter 16

Keep first-aid kits in your kitchen, workshop, and cars.
Any injury that can't be handled with a well-stocked
first-aid kit requires the attention of a professional.

From the Notebook of Maggie McDonald
Simplicity Itself Organizing Services

Sunday, September 7, 7:15 p.m.

I found Miss Harrier sprawled between her desk and the door, half
leaning against a metal file cabinet. The cabinet, scarred by years
of use, boasted a new indignity. A smear of blood extended from the
corner of the cabinet to the top of Harrier's head.

"Oh my God, Miss Harrier." I knelt at her side and lifted her
hand.

Her hand was still warm, but too cold for a living body, even one
in shock from a terrible injury. I dropped her hand and stood back. I
wiped my own hand on my jeans. Maybe I was trying to wipe off
death or distance myself from whatever violence had occurred here,
but I stopped myself as soon as I realized what I was doing.

Miss Harrier was dead. I had probably transferred some of her
DNA to my hand when I'd touched her. She and her DNA deserved
respect.

I looked around the room, trying to decide what to do. A coffee
cup lay on its side on the desk, and I stepped over Miss Harrier, planning to right the cup and keep the coffee from staining the papers. I
was too late. A puddle of coffee had spread across the desk. It
dripped from the desk and was soaking the carpet. Just like Harrier's
blood.

Miss Harrier would have known what to do, but I needed help. I reached for the phone on her desk to call the police before I remembered that I probably shouldn't touch anything. I reached into my back pocket for my cell phone and dialed 9-1-1.

The phone rang, and as I was waiting for dispatch to pick up, I saw the pills. Dozens of small white five-sided pills that looked like tiny little houses were spread over the carpet and desk. I sniffed. The room smelled faintly of alcohol.

"Orchard View police station. How can I help?"

I couldn't answer. As the reality of the situation finally sank in, I was too shocked to carry on a conversation. Had Miss Harrier committed suicide? Was she a drinker? Or had someone killed her?

"Hello? Do you need help? Who is calling? Where is your emergency?"

"Orchard View Mi . . . middle School." I forced the words out, but then dropped the phone and sank into Miss Harrier's office chair. I looked at the ceiling, and the door, and the clock—anywhere but at Miss Harrier's body. My hands were sweating, but I shivered and hugged my arms to my chest. I wanted to flee, but I had an odd sense that I should stay with her and that I shouldn't leave her alone.

The man in our house had died alone in the dark, in the cold, in our basement. Miss Harrier had died alone and if she'd committed suicide she must have felt more alone than I could possibly imagine. But she didn't need to be alone now. I could stay with her. I *would* stay with her. First though, I needed to finish the call.

I took a deep breath and picked up the phone. "Hello?"

The same voice responded. "Orchard View police station. How can I help?" I briefly wondered whether she'd stayed on the line, or if I'd dialed again without knowing.

I took a deep breath to compose myself and said, "This is Maggie McDonald. I'm at Orchard View Middle School, in the office. The principal is dead."

"Thank you, Ms. McDonald. I've dispatched ambulance, fire, and police officers to the scene. Are you safe?"

"Yes, I think so," I said, thinking for the first time that there might well be a murderer or a violent, destructive criminal still in the building or on the school campus.

"Would you like me to remain on the line?"

"Yes, please," I said.

"My name is Susan Diaz, and I'll stay here with you, Ms. Mc-Donald, until the police arrive. Can you tell me what you see?"

I didn't say anything. I stared at Miss Harrier. I wanted to run away, but I needed to stay with her. Susan Diaz, who shared a first name with Miss Harrier, wanted to stay with me. It was a human thing—needing that connection—or needing to offer it, needing to feel it. But so was wanting to flee.

I tried to focus on something else, and resorted to thinking about how I might organize Miss Harrier's office for greater efficiency. That led me to think whether there was anything here that was significantly different from the way I'd last seen her office.

There wasn't really anything I could do to improve upon her system, which used homemade, labeled, fabric-covered boxes to corral office supplies, forms, mail, and material to be reviewed. Charging cords for her electronics were coiled beneath the desk with their business ends attached to clips made for the purpose and secured to the desk so she would be able to conveniently use the devices while they were charging.

"Ms. McDonald, are you still there?"

I'd taken a step toward the door when I heard sirens and could see flashing lights reflected on the ceiling of the main office.

"I'll hang up now, Susan," I said. "The police are here."

I could imagine chaos outside. It was probably much like what had happened a little over a week ago at the house. I stayed where I was.

"Maggie?" Jason called from the door.

"In here . . ."

He stood in the doorway of Miss Harrier's office and holstered his gun.

He held out his arms in an ambiguous gesture. He could have been offering a hug or indicating a path toward the exit.

Belle barked frantically from the car, adding to the confusion.

"Can I?" I said, pointing in the direction of my car. And then I remembered: I was parked in the red zone right in front of the office door—the space reserved for the emergency vehicles that were now filling the parking lot.

"Should I move my car?"

"You're fine where you are," said Jason. "Get in your car and stay there. We're not sure what we're dealing with. I'll fill you in as soon as I can."

"The boys . . ." I needed to get home. "Max is going to call. I was making a quick stop here and then heading to the grocery store. There's no food in the house."

Jason pulled out his phone and hit one button. "Stephen, how far are you from the McDonalds' house? We've got a problem here at the middle school and Maggie's with me."

I couldn't hear Stephen's response, but Jason mouthed, "Fifteen minutes."

"Can you stop and get something for the boys' dinner, breakfast tomorrow morning, and lunches?" Jason asked.

Jason's face wrinkled as if he were working hard to remember everything he needed to say. "Get them started making their lunches for tomorrow. Maggie says Max—Mr. McDonald—is going to call them."

He held the phone away from his face and asked, "What time, Maggie?"

"Eight o'clock."

"Head to the house first, Stephen. If you're there when Max calls, please tell him everything's fine, but that Maggie will call him in about an hour."

Jason paused to listen. He lowered his voice and said something else that I couldn't hear. I scrunched up my forehead and frowned. I hated the fact that we needed Stephen's help, yet again, and I had no choice but to accept it.

I shoved my hands in the pockets of my hoodie and turned my back on Jason, aware that the thoughts in my head were beginning to sound like those of a pouty little kid. It wasn't that I didn't appreciate their help, I did. But I was growing more afraid about everything that had been happening around us and I felt increasingly helpless. The boys and I, and Max too, were in debt to Stephen, big-time. Maybe my concern about returning social debts was the least of my problems, but it was the one that, right now, was easiest to focus on. My concern felt petty, though. I knew Stephen would take good care of the boys and I was truly grateful.

Jason put his phone away and gave me a little push toward my car. "Go reassure Belle. I'll be with you in a minute."

I walked away and Jason called to me. "Maggie? Don't worry. We get it. When it's over you can have us over for dinner and we'll wipe the slate clean. No favors owed."

There was a lot more than met the eye in that sentence, I thought, but it was too much to sort out now. In the state of shock I was in, everything was starting to seem like too much.

At the car, I opened the door and hugged Belle, sinking my face into her soft fur. I attached the leash to her collar and felt anchored by her presence. We walked together to find Jason again. He led me to a bench in front of the school.

"Maggie, I need to ask," Jason said. "What were you doing here tonight? Why were you inside the office on a weekend?"

I looked across the parking lot at the houses on the other side of the street with their tidy lawns. Houses in which people were going about their business getting ready for the week ahead. Houses in which no one had been interviewed by the police three times in the past few days.

I looked at Jason. "I'm sorry, what did you ask me? I don't suppose there's any chance she's still alive?"

"No," Jason said. "I'm afraid not. I expect she'll be pronounced dead at the scene and taken to the county medical-examiner's office."

The rest of the evening passed with repetitious questions asked by varying members of Jason's team. I phoned the kids to make sure that Stephen had fed them and they were getting their backpacks and lunches ready for the morning.

They were full of excitement after talking to Max. Everything seemed to be under control. I assured the boys I'd call their dad, said I'd be home as soon as I could, and hung up the phone.

I sat on the bench and dialed Max's cell phone, hoping the call would go through. When we'd emailed each other to set up this evening's phone call, I'd expected him to call our home phone from his office. Now, when I needed to reach him, I wasn't sure how to do that or how much it would cost. But this was an emergency and poor Max must have been frantic.

After much clicking, silence, and more clicking, Max answered. It was a terrible connection with a frustrating delay, but I was able to tell him I was fine, and explain that the principal had died.

"Should I come home? Stephen told me you'd found another body," he said. His voice dissolved into crackling.

"Honey, I can only hear static," I said. "I'll hang up and send you an email as soon as I can. I love you. It's great to hear your voice." I could only hope that he was able to hear me. I sighed and hugged Belle, who was leaning on me as if she weighed twice her sixty-five pounds.

"Let's go find Jason," I told Belle. "Maybe he'll tell us we can take off."

We found Jason near the office, talking on his phone. From the side of the conversation I could hear, I guessed he was talking to an administrator at the school district's main office.

After he'd ended the call and agreed that I could leave, I asked him the question I knew would be the first thing Brian would ask me. "Will the kids have school in the morning? Or will your team still be here?"

"We'll keep the office closed," Jason said. "But the plan is to have counselors and school liaison officers on site to talk to any of the kids or teachers who might have something to tell us or just need to talk. We'll hold a joint assembly with the school district first thing in the morning and move forward from there."

I pulled into the driveway and parked the car close to the house.

Stephen opened the back door and held it as Belle and I climbed the steps. I was glad the table wasn't any further from the door or I might have fallen before sinking into a kitchen chair. Stephen brought me a sandwich, a glass of wine, and a large glass of water, which I drank first. *This must be what it's like to have a butler.*

"The boys are okay?" I asked.

"We made spaghetti and salad. We packed their sandwiches for tomorrow and threw in some apples and cookies. They've showered and are ready for bed with their backpacks packed."

I squinted at the wall clock. It was well after their normal ten o'clock bedtime.

Brian ran down the stairs. I turned.

"Is it true that Harrier is dead?" he asked. "Kids are talking about it on Facebook. Was she killed? Does that mean we don't have school in the morning?"

"Yes, she's dead," I said. I winced, hearing the words, but there really was no way to soften the news.

"Did you see her? Did someone kill her? Why?"

"No one knows yet how or why she died. There are all sorts of emergency personnel at the school working to find out, and I'm sure they'll tell the students as much as they can once they have information they're able to share. You *are* going to school in the morning, although your field trip may be cancelled. The district and the police are planning an assembly and getting back to business as quickly as possible."

I looked at the clock again. "It's past ten, kiddo. It's been a crazy night, but you and David need to be in bed. I'll be up in a minute to check on you and head to bed myself. Stephen and Munchkin are going to keep watch for us."

"I can't believe you found her. Were you scared? Did you talk to Dad?" Brian said.

"I'll be up in a minute and we can talk then. Go get ready for bed. And turn off the computer." Brian stomped up the stairs.

"I'm sorry you had to find her," Stephen said. "How did she die?"

"I have no idea. There were pills, the smell of alcohol, and some blood." I picked up my wineglass. My exhaustion was catching up with me, as was the idea that Miss Harrier was dead. I didn't like her. Life at the school might be easier now that she was gone. But admitting, even to myself, that one small part of me might be glad that she was gone gave me a lump in my throat that made it difficult to swallow. I put the glass down.

Stephen sat down next to me at the table. "The medical examiner will do an autopsy. We'll know more, then."

I stood and leaned against the counter. "She could have had a heart attack, an aneurism, or even a stroke. The tension around her was contagious. She gave off a sort of imperceptible hum, like a high-voltage wire. She was a heart attack waiting to happen."

"True," said Stephen. "But it's also true that she had enemies."

I shuddered. "Murder in a book or on a TV show is completely different from thinking about who could actually do such a thing. I considered throttling her myself a time or two and I'd barely known her a week—but I never would have done it."

"Jason will want to interview you as soon as possible. Brian too."

"What? You've got to be kidding. Brian? *No. Flipping. Way.*" I flung my glass in the sink, shattering it. "She was a passive-aggressive martinet. If we hadn't had April's help, she would have made Brian's life miserable. We stood up to her while she was alive and I will not let her torment us now that she's dead. Brian and I had absolutely nothing to do with her death." I crossed my arms over my chest and stared at Stephen, fuming. Belle leaned hard against my leg until I scratched her ears and calmed myself in the process.

"Whoa," said Stephen, his voice both soft and calm. "Just listen, please. I agree with everything you said. So does Jason, as far as I know. We can get him on the phone if you need to confirm that."

I boosted myself up to sit on the counter, putting distance between Stephen and me.

"Can you get to the point? I need to say good night to the boys."

"Jason needs to talk to you to rule you out of the investigation. He needs a form in the file. You're not naive, Maggie. This can't be the first time you've encountered bureaucracy."

"How do you know what Jason thinks? I just left him there at the school."

"He called after you left," Stephen said. "He wants to talk to you and Brian about your last meeting with Miss Harrier. Not about what you said, but about what you saw. He's sealed her office and left everything as it was when you found her, except the body, of course. He wants you and Brian to note anything that's changed since you were there. He's asking April and everyone else who was in there recently to do the same thing."

I flushed, embarrassed. "Sorry, Stephen," I said. "I should know by now that we can trust you."

Stephen sniffed. "I'm a Marine. I can take it."

I stood and moved to the sink to clean up the mess my wineglass had made.

"Leave it. I'll do it."

I wrinkled my forehead, confused by his kindness. How did this man manage to be on the spot whenever the police or crime victims needed him? *It's like he's Batman or something.*

Stephen continued. "Jason will talk to you and Brian at school tomorrow while everyone else is at the assembly."

I nodded. Jason was the lead detective on the case. If he said he wanted us somewhere at a certain time we had to be there.

Tired or not, though, I needed to do more.

"Stephen, what would you think about getting that group together again? Tess, Pauline, April, Elaine, and Flora? We could look at Miss Harrier's death the same way we looked at the vandalism."

"Good idea," Stephen said. "Go to bed. I'll text Tess and the rest of the gang and see if we can meet at Elaine's in the morning."

I trudged up the stairs, still exhausted and anxious. I was glad Stephen was here, but resented the fact that forces outside my control meant that we *needed* him here.

Max and I had moved to Orchard View assuming it would be a safe, healthy place for our kids to transition to adulthood. Instead, we'd faced more violence in ten days than we ever had in Stockton, which ranked as one of the top-ten cities in California for violent crime.

I would do everything I could to change the situation. But I couldn't do it alone. I needed to reach out to the people around me. People I was growing to like, but knew little about. And I needed to trust them. Trusting strangers and standing up to conflict had never been among my superpowers. But I was going to dig deep, find those skills, develop them, and use them.

Maybe the people at the meeting tomorrow would be fighting for the safety of the town or the school or puzzling out the mysteries as an intellectual exercise. I was fighting for my kids, my family, and my home. And I was going to win.

To: Max.McDonald2111@gmail.com

From: SimplicityItselfOrganizing@gmail.com

I'm so sorry I couldn't talk before! And then all that static. We live in one of the technology capitals of the world, and you're in another, and we can't talk on the phone? What's up with that?

In all seriousness, though, you must be freaking out. But don't! We're all fine, safe, healthy, and happy . . . except for missing you.

The kids loved talking to you. Do you think you can get home in time for one of David's marching band competitions?

I don't know how much Stephen Laird told you about tonight. I stopped by the school to drop off a permission slip for Brian and found Miss Harrier dead in her office. It looked almost like an overdose but not quite. If it had been a *Masterpiece Mystery* episode we would both have guessed the scene had been staged by the murderer.

But this is real life. Even if it wasn't a murder, it's sad to think that our kid's principal had a drug problem or committed suicide or accidently overdosed.

I'm trying not to worry about it and let the police handle it. I hope you can do that too. Remember, none of us died. We're all fit and healthy.

I hope the "man in the hospital" is doing well and healing quickly so you can come home.

Love, Maggie.

To: SimplicityItselfOrganizing@gmail.com

From: Max.McDonald2111@gmail.com

Another dead body . . . and a ninja Marine . . . what comes next? I'm trying to keep my imagination from answering that question.

I talked to everyone here about phone calls and whether there was a better way to assure a static-free line. Everyone just shrugged. Calls are generally reliable, but sometimes you get a bad line. It's just luck, and ours was bad.

I need to run to a meeting, but remember I love you all and miss you, and am working to come home as soon as I can. M-I-T-H is doing well. His name is Veejay. He seems to be in less pain every day.

Love, Max

Chapter 17

Why do I take so many photographs and notes? Because
memory is unreliable.

*From the Notebook of Maggie McDonald
Simplicity Itself Organizing Services*

Monday, September 8, Morning

Grapevine communications at middle schools travel with uncanny
speed and accuracy. By the time the first bell rang at Orchard
View Middle School on Monday morning, every child and almost
every parent seemed to know the details of Miss Harrier's death.

In the minutes before school started, they waited outside the multipurpose room in chattering groups like clusters of carnivorous
crows aching for more details and pecking at the information they
had. It was disturbing. Disturbingly human.

Brian and I skirted the crowd and headed directly to the office.
Paolo Bianchi stopped us on the way.

"Morning, Mrs. McDonald," Paolo said. "Detective Mueller is
waiting for you inside the main office."

"Do you know any more about what happened?" I scanned the
parking lot for Paolo's Subaru, wondering what sports equipment
might be strapped to the top this morning.

"No, ma'am. And if we did, I couldn't tell you. But take a look at
the officers hanging 'round the crowd. They're hoping to find some
folks who might know something about what happened here last
night."

I looked over the crowd. Much as I wanted to believe that Miss
Harrier's death was a horrible accident or suicide, my subconscious

kept reminding me that I couldn't rule out murder. Miss Harrier seemed to want to win every battle. Wouldn't committing suicide be admitting to the world that she'd lost a fight? But if murder was a possibility, this crowd almost certainly hid the murderer. I shuddered.

"Go on in," Paolo said. "He's waiting for you."

I pulled open the office door and held it for Brian. Jason spotted us from the doorway of Miss Harrier's office and waved us over.

"Morning, Brian, Maggie," he said. "This won't take long. We need you to tell us whether anything looks different from what you saw in your last meeting with Miss Harrier. Neither of you is a suspect."

We entered the office and Jason shut the door behind us. "Close your eyes and listen. See if any odd smells jump out at you. Try to remember what things looked like last week."

I closed my eyes and listened to the ticking clock, the mumbling voices from outside, and the hum of the ventilating system. I smelled pencil shavings, copy-machine toner, stale coffee, and something else. It could have been the pervasive locker-room scent of unwashed students, or the lingering aroma of death. Either way, it didn't offer any clues. I looked at the desk, battered and sad, and the swivel chair with a dent in the cushion worn by the bottoms of too many principals grilling too many students. The wastebasket still held crumpled papers. The corners of the industrial carpet were still dusty.

I pulled out my phone. "Can I take pictures and look at them later?"

Jason shook his head. "The chance of them leaking out is too great, no matter how careful you are. Just do your best."

"Last night, I thought I smelled alcohol," I said. "I don't smell it now."

"Rubbing alcohol or liquor?" Jason said, scribbling in his notebook with a stubby pencil.

"Can I check out the desk?" asked Brian.

Jason nodded. "Don't touch anything, but look all you want. Maggie, was that liquor you smelled?"

"Yes."

Brian stared at Miss Harrier's keyboard and her screen saver—an unimaginative bouncing ball that revealed nothing about her. There were no family photos and no calendar. Where earlier it had looked organized, it now looked sterile to me—more impersonal than a department-store display. There was nothing in this room that said *Miss Harrier was here and she was a unique and special individual.*

"Anything?" Jason said. I shook my head.

Brian stooped and looked under the desk. From my vantage point, all I could see was a mass of power supplies and cords lying in disturbingly neat coils.

"What are you looking for?" I said.

Brian stood and bit his bottom lip. "I'm not sure. I think there's something missing. You'd expect things to be different, though, wouldn't you, after a few days? She would have moved things around."

Jason nodded. "That's right, Brian. I didn't really expect that either you or your mom would be able to see anything that April and our crime team hadn't spotted, but it was worth a try. If you think of what it is that might be missing, give me a call." He handed Brian his card. I couldn't tell whether providing the business card was something Jason did as part of his routine in approaching all potential witnesses or if the detective was making a conscious effort to treat Brian like an adult and an important part of his investigation. Either way, Brian looked at it and stood a little taller—influenced, I was sure, by Jason's gesture of respect. He shoved the card in the back pocket of his jeans. I made a mental note to check the pockets before Jason's card went through the laundry.

Jason ushered us out. "Brian, you're to meet up with your class in the multipurpose room. Your field trip will be rescheduled. Maggie, I hear you're going to join the group at Elaine's?"

I nodded and shook hands with Jason.

I walked with Brian as far as the multipurpose room and said goodbye, telling him to call me if he needed anything. Neither of us had been at a school where the principal had died, and I had no idea what the day would hold. I took a deep breath and put my trust in the experience and knowledge of April, the district counselors, and Brian's teachers. I walked across the street and knocked on Elaine's front door.

The meeting at Elaine's began much like the previous one had, with people greeting each other, preparing coffee or tea, and sitting in the same spots in the living room. I sat on the couch, on the end, next to the chair where Tess was already seated. She leaned over and whispered, "I'm so sorry we haven't been able to get together. I've been working my butt off. September is *never* this busy!"

"It's okay," I said. "Maybe we can get together with the dogs this week. Belle needs a good run and I've missed you."

"It sounds like you've had a terrible time of it. Did you really find her?"

I nodded and Tess grabbed my hand and squeezed it. "Stay there. I'll get you coffee and a cookie," she said.

I scanned the room while she waited on me. Everyone had arrived except Dennis DeSoto, who was late again. I frowned, but being late seemed to be in character for Mr. Snooty, who surely believed his time was more important than ours.

Stephen took charge. "Let me tell you what I know about what happened yesterday," he said. "And then we can talk about how we'll proceed." He looked at his watch. "I'd like to get us out of here by ten or ten thirty."

"Before we start, I have a request," I said. "If it's okay with all of you, I'd like to program your numbers into my cell phone and the phones belonging to my boys, David and Brian. For emergencies."

Tess, Elaine, Flora, and Stephen pulled out their phones. After a moment's hesitation, Pauline did too. We spent a few minutes texting each other to exchange numbers—an annoying, goofy, but necessary process.

"Thank you all so much," I said, feeling a catch in my throat. Up until now, I hadn't felt I knew anyone in Orchard View well enough to ask them to be emergency contacts.

"It's important to have an emergency plan," Elaine said. "If only for peace of mind." Everyone else murmured words of agreement, except maybe Pauline.

Stephen took a sip of coffee and looked at notes scribbled on a yellow legal pad.

"Let's start with the basics: Susan Harrier was found dead, alone in her office, at approximately seven thirty last night. Maggie found her. The medical examiner has ruled out natural causes and accidental death and is looking at suicide or homicide."

Elaine gasped. "Homicide? Murder? Here? Are you sure, Stephen? She had a huge number of allergies and asthma, I think. Isn't it more likely to have been an allergic reaction or something like that?"

Stephen rubbed his chin with his hand. "We know Miss Harrier recently filled a prescription for Valium. Based on evidence at the scene, we know she took some of the pills, but not how many. We haven't been able to locate the bottle. Taking all the pills could have resulted in drowsiness or a coma, but likely not death, unless the pills were mixed with alcohol. Asthma could have made the complications worse. The medical examiner will be able to tell us more later in the week."

Elaine leaned forward. "Would it help if I added to the timeline?" Stephen nodded.

"I told the police I saw her drive in at about five o'clock." Elaine said. "I waved to her when I was mowing the lawn out front. She often came in on Sunday evenings so she could start Monday morning ahead of the game. After I finished mowing, edging, and sweeping the sidewalk, the fog was starting to come in and it was darker than usual. The lights in the parking lot across the street came on and I checked my watch. It was close to six thirty, but I don't remember the time exactly." Elaine looked out the window toward the school.

She took another sip of tea and went on with her account. "The lights in the office were flashing on and off, which seemed strange, but not worth checking out. I put away my tools and went inside, but before I could start dinner, I heard a bang or a loud thud. I thought there had been a car accident and went out to see if anyone was hurt. Miss Harrier's car was still where she'd left it, and there were three or four other cars in the parking lot."

Elaine paused, swallowed, and continued, speaking more slowly with a strained and shaky voice. "I saw a man . . . no . . . a person . . . I can't be sure it was a man . . . running from the office down the center corridor of the buildings toward the back of the school. I decided the sound I'd heard must have been that person flinging the door open too hard, or maybe the door got caught by the wind and banged against the wall of the school."

"Do you have any idea how old that person was?" Stephen said. "Could you tell from the way they moved?"

"Younger than I am, that's for sure," Elaine said. "I don't run like that anymore. I waited for a minute to see if Miss Harrier would come out, but she didn't."

Elaine's hands shook as she reached up to smooth the hairs that had escaped her bun. "I should have gone to check on her. If I'd called the ambulance then . . ." She dropped her chin to her chest and a small sob escaped her control.

"You couldn't have known," said Stephen. "Nothing you did or didn't do hurt Miss Harrier."

Elaine lifted her head, straightened her spine, and pushed her hair back. "I went back inside and put some potatoes on to boil, but something just didn't sit right. I called Jason and he said he'd check it out. I was watching out the front window and that's when you pulled up, Maggie."

"Okay, so we've got Elaine seeing and hearing something at about six thirty-five or six forty," Stephen said. "Maggie, can you take us from when you arrived? Do you remember what time that was?"

I looked at my watch as if it would give me the answer. I thought back to late Sunday afternoon—deciding to go to the store, helping the kids with the fire escape, printing out the form. I'd left the house after seven, I thought. I estimated times and moved my finger around the watch face as I ticked off the time required for each task.

"I'm not sure," I said. "After seven, maybe as late as seven thirty?"

Stephen nodded. "That fits with what you told the police last night. I was just checking to see if you'd remembered anything else since you'd had time to reflect. Please go on."

I continued: "The place felt deserted. Spooky. I didn't notice Miss Harrier's car and would have said the parking lot was empty. The lights were on in the main office. I had a form I'd planned to slip under the door, but the door was unlocked, so I added the form to the pile of other papers on the mat. But then I thought I ought to turn off the lights so as not to waste electricity. And then I f-found her."

"What did she look like—" began Pauline.

Stephen cut her off. "The police have asked that Maggie keep that information to herself."

Jason hadn't told me that, but I was grateful to have an excuse to avoid reliving those moments out loud.

"Okay," said Stephen. "That gives us a picture of what happened on Sunday. Now I'd like us to look at what motivations there might have been, either for Miss Harrier to end her own life or for someone else to end it for her."

April sighed. "I know that we're meant to speak well of the dead," she said, pausing to clear her throat and wet her lips. "But above all,

Miss Susan Harrier would demand accuracy. And I don't see how polishing up our feelings into something socially palatable will help us get to the truth of how she died."

April looked at the far wall, avoiding everyone's eyes. She put down her coffee mug and held her hands together, tightly clenched. "The truth is, she was a demanding and frustrating person to work with. I considered killing her myself on numerous occasions. I never would have done it, of course, but when she made me angry I entertained myself by thinking of creative ways to do away with her. She belonged in a military academy, not a middle school."

April's honesty broke the ice and a barely audible sound of muted, embarrassed laughter circled the room.

Elaine chimed in. "I know she could be abrasive. She was dedicated to her career, but she'd never wanted to be a teacher. That was her domineering father's idea. She'd dreamed of being an accountant and had a way of thinking in columns and boxes. She tended to take it personally when something or someone didn't fit in the proper box. But she was also adept at finding funds to maintain services for the kids despite the state budget cuts."

"She did the same thing with the PTA budget," Flora said. "That was Dennis's area, of course, not mine, but he frequently fussed over finding time to meet with Miss Harrier. She requested way more meetings than Dennis felt were necessary and questioned every line item and purchase. She was only trying to help the PTA, but it annoyed Dennis, and he kept reminding her that he was a volunteer, not her employee."

Stephen looked up from his notes. "Does anyone know where Dennis is? He told me he'd be here at nine." We each looked at someone else and shook our heads.

"I didn't see him at school this morning," I said. "He's one of the few people I know, so if he'd been there, I would have noticed."

"I saw him yesterday in the grocery store," Pauline said. "He said he's going into business with his brother Umberto, and it's been taking up a lot of his time. I think it's putting pressure on him too. He looked really washed out and tired, poor man."

Flora looked pale and shivered. I wondered if she had a touch of the flu.

April snorted. Apparently she had little sympathy for Dennis.

Stephen went on. "Maggie and her son Brian had some problems with Miss Harrier at the start of school, and I know that the kids called her Horrible Harrier, but does anyone know of anyone who was obsessively angry with Susan—Susan Harrier?"

Tess frowned. "She hit Mozart with a newspaper one day because he got too close to the office. On a Saturday. I was furious, but I wouldn't have killed her over it."

"Mozart is a decorated veteran," Stephen said, sitting up straight and bristling. "She should have been ashamed of herself."

"Veteran?" Flora said.

"Mozart is one of Stephen's retired Marine dogs," Tess said. "I navigated miles of red tape before I qualified to adopt him."

"Okay, so she rubbed parents, students, and dog people the wrong way," Stephen said. "Anyone else?" The room was quiet with only the sound of cookies crunching. "What about employees? Or members of the community? April, were there odd phone calls or threatening letters? Did you know she was taking tranquilizers? Or why? Or if she had any other health problems?"

April thought for a minute. "Sometimes I think they should put tranquilizers in the water supply around here," she said. "But, no, I didn't know Miss Harrier was taking Valium."

She broke off a small piece of the leg of a gingerbread man and chewed slowly.

"Any other ideas?" said Stephen.

"I could have recommended several soothing herbs and meditation tapes," Flora said. "Valium is truly unnecessary."

Stephen avoided looking at Flora, but glanced at the rest of us in turn. We all shook our heads. Disliking Harrier, or at least being frustrated by her top-down management style, was something everyone seemed to take as a given. Despising her enough to kill her was something else.

I tried to imagine what might have driven her to suicide, but I couldn't think of a thing. I barely knew the woman, yet from what I'd seen, she was self-centered and focused, but not depressed.

"What about the bottle of tranquilizers?" I said. "The one that's still missing? If she'd committed suicide, wouldn't the bottle still be in her office, just sitting there for the police to find? I would think the fact that it's missing would point strongly toward murder."

"Possibly," agreed Stephen. "But suicide is an individualized business." He tapped his ring against his coffee mug. "Let's say Miss

Harrier decided to end her life, but wanted to hide the fact that she'd committed suicide. She could have transferred the pills to another container. Or, the person Elaine saw running from the scene could have taken the bottle for any number of reasons."

"Why?" said Flora. "What would be the advantage of taking the bottle? It was a plain orange plastic pill bottle, I assume?" Flora chewed her lip and pulled at a lock of her hair.

"That's the type of bottle the police are looking for," said Stephen. "As for a motive for taking it? Someone might have wanted to confuse the investigation."

Elaine leaned forward. "Someone who cared about her might have found her body and taken the bottle to protect her from scrutiny and public debate," she said. "They could have thought that taking the bottle would make it look less like a suicide."

"It would be handy to find it in the pocket of the murderer," I said. "After that, they could cut to a commercial, because stuff like that only happens on one of those crime dramas where they wrap everything up before the credits."

I looked at my watch. This process might be important, but it wasn't getting us anywhere. No closer to finding out who killed Harrier, why she might have killed herself, or what else was wrong in Orchard View. I wanted those answers. I wanted to know what had happened to the foundation money and who was willing to put my family at risk to damage my home and the school. I was growing frustrated, but short of jumping up, waving my arms, and shouting "Round up the usual suspects," I didn't know what to do. If I'd known the names of any usual suspects, I might have been tempted. Instead, I took a sip of my coffee, grabbed another cookie, and tried to pay attention.

"What about secrets?" Stephen said. "Could someone have a secret she'd threatened to expose? Could she have had a secret she was desperate to keep hidden?"

Secrets. I leaned forward and looked surreptitiously around the room. Now we might be getting somewhere. Who knew what other secrets were hidden behind the tidy front yards and doors of this town?

"She had access to a lot of confidential information," April said. "She knew who qualified for free lunches and field-trip assistance, whose parents were out of a job, whose supposedly divorced husband was really in prison, which couples were separating or divorcing . . ."

April paused and looked around the room. "Stress is a huge problem for kids and families, and mental-health issues push privacy buttons. We've had kids who were cutting themselves with razor blades, parents who were in rehab programs, kids with eating disorders, and a couple of students who were considering gender-reassignment surgery. Those kinds of things rock families at their foundations. You never know how far a parent will go to protect their child, do you?"

Stephen fiddled with his ring. Flora smoothed her skirt. Elaine shifted in her rocking chair, and April brushed crumbs from her sweater. Pauline Windsor checked her phone. I wondered if we were all thinking about the pressures on our own families.

"What about the vandalism at my house?" I said. "Could that be connected? Jason said it was likely the kid is violent and his behavior is escalating. Could someone that angry be capable of killing a person? Are there children you know of who have those kinds of issues?"

Pauline made a *tsk*ing noise. "Vandalism *again*? We've got a plan to keep an eye on it at school, isn't that enough? You can't really expect us to solve your problem at home too."

As usual, Pauline's words left me speechless. Tess sucked air in through her teeth, but Stephen quieted her with a look.

"That brings up a good point," Stephen said. "Where were the dog walkers who were supposed to be keeping an eye on the school? Pauline, do you have a list of who was scheduled for Sunday?"

Pauline sat up straight, tapped her phone, and scrolled. "We had trouble finding people for Sunday," she said. "Both the Giants and the Forty-niners were playing. It was Big Game weekend for Stanford and UC Berkeley. It was the final day of the Mountain View Art and Wine Festival, and move-in day for new students at a lot of the colleges." Pauline frowned at each of us like a disappointed schoolmarm.

"There were no volunteers last night," she said.

"But Pauline . . ." Elaine began.

Stephen shushed her. "Pauline, let us know if there are any other holes in the schedule, and I'll make sure we've got coverage. In the meantime, now we know there aren't any volunteers who might have been on site and be able to provide information about what they saw Sunday night. That's a big help."

I tuned Stephen out and looked around the room. Pauline knew there had been no volunteers on Sunday. Could she have taken advantage of that information and confronted Miss Harrier when no one could overhear? I knew how volatile Pauline could be over something as simple as a parking spot. Could something else have bothered her enough to drive her to murder? I didn't know.

I really didn't know much about any of these people, and it was making me increasingly frustrated. In Stockton, which was a much larger community, I knew people in a wide variety of fields and it would have been easy for me to tap into expertise and experience that would have allowed me to figure this whole situation out much more easily.

I was aware of Tess's secret alter ego, yet that seemed like an open secret. And Stephen had revealed his past to me, a virtual stranger. But what about the others?

The group broke up soon after that. We'd made no progress, or none that I could see. I looked at my watch. Ten o'clock. I had time to ask a few more questions and get to know these people better.

I moved into the kitchen with Tess and Stephen after saying goodbye to Flora, who had to meet an administrator at her mother's assisted-living facility. Pauline said she wanted to round up more volunteers to patrol the school. Stephen asked her to share the list with the police. April returned to work.

As we'd done after the first meeting, Elaine, Tess, Stephen, and I washed, dried, and put away the dishes.

"You know," said Tess. "I didn't want to mention it while Flora was here, but she has a secret she didn't offer up. Her herbalism business? There's a recurring rumor that says she grows marijuana and isn't particular about who she sells to."

Stephen made a growling noise. "Does she sell to kids?"

"Flora? I don't think so . . . no, she wouldn't do that," Tess said. "Remember, I don't know if the rumor is even true."

"As long as it doesn't involve kids or big business or other drugs, the police aren't that interested," said Stephen. "They have bigger problems to tackle."

Elaine handed Stephen a saucer to dry. "What about April?" she said.

"What about April?" I asked. As far as I was concerned, April could do no wrong. She'd said my son was a good kid.

"She wanted Harrier's job," Elaine said.

"What is her title now?" I asked. "Assistant principal?"

Elaine nodded. "April was the logical choice for principal. She'd been teacher-in-charge and was experienced. When the district offered her the second-banana slot, I told her not to take it. They were taking advantage. She could run a major company single-handedly. But she wouldn't listen. She'd helped interview all the candidates, so she'd met Susan Harrier and had Harrier's number from day one. She wanted to provide a buffer between her and the rest of the school."

Okay, so that made sense. A buffer was exactly the role that April had played to help Brian and me work with Harrier. But financially? And career-wise? If April was qualified to be principal here, she could have found a better-paying job in another district. Was she waiting, hoping Harrier would move on? Had she grown impatient?

These people were friendly and open up to a point, but they all could be hiding something.

I looked at the coffee mug in my hand and wondered how long I'd been drying it. I handed it to Tess to put in the cupboard over the counter.

I picked up another mug from the drying rack. "Stephen," I said, seizing the opportunity to ask a question that had been bugging me for a while. "How come you're always on the spot when things go wrong, day or night? Do you have a police scanner, or do you have an alter ego like Batman or Underdog? How do you have the time for that and your day job?" I looked pointedly at the ring on his left hand. "Does your wife mind your odd hours?"

Elaine stopped washing dishes and stared at me.

Tess turned and looked at him.

Stephen blushed.

My face burned and I stammered, "I'm sorry. I've put my foot in something."

No one said a word, so I stumbled on. "I'm new and I don't know the rules. Do you tell me what I've stepped in or do we move on and pretend I didn't say anything?"

Tess and Elaine looked at Stephen, who shrugged. He took the mug from my hand, finished drying it, and handed it to Tess to put away.

"It's not really a secret," he said. "I'm surprised you don't know. Jason and I were one of the first couples to be married when the Supreme Court made gay marriage legal in California. We've been together many years and I'm proud to be his husband. I think he feels the same way about me."

Yikes. I'd called him my fairy godmother. I held my hands against my face to cool the burn. I wanted to sink into the floor.

Tess snorted. "I can't believe you didn't hear about it, even in Stockton. Jason and Stephen were the poster couple for the news outlets. A front-page picture of them went viral. *Cop marries Marine*, the headline read. The photo showed the two of them looking insanely happy, in love, and drop-dead gorgeous in their dress uniforms."

Elaine patted Stephen's arm. "You're one of the nicest couples I know."

Stephen smiled. "Like I said, it's not a secret. It's just awkward when folks jump to the conclusion that if you're a guy and you're married, your spouse is a woman."

"I try not to jump to conclusions," I said. "Or put people in boxes based on stereotypes. I apologize, Stephen. I like both you and Jason and I hope I haven't offended you. I'm sorry I called you my fairy godmother."

Tess snorted again. "You didn't."

"I did."

"I loved that, Maggie," Stephen said. "And it's not your fault you assumed I was married to a woman. I've done the same thing to guys I don't know. But look, it's like this: You don't walk up to people you barely know and say, 'Hi, I'm Maggie, I'm married to a man.' Right?"

I nodded.

"I don't, either."

"Good point," I said. "Friends?"

"Friends," Stephen said. "Now, do you want to help me set up some wireless cameras and see if we can catch your vandal? If we nab him, we can see if he's connected in any way to Miss Harrier's death."

"Did you get any useful information from this meeting, Stephen?" Elaine said.

Stephen turned to me. I guess he felt the need to explain his role in the investigation.

"My canine partner and I had police training in the Marine Corps, and our first assignment was with a law-enforcement unit. I'm an unpaid police consultant. I know when Jason's called out, of course, and I provide victim support when I can. It's an arrangement that wouldn't work everywhere, but this is a small town and the chief's on board with it. The other detectives call me sometimes too. That's why I gave you the Batman impression, I guess." His blue eyes twinkled. "I need to get a cape."

"I'll make you one, if you want." Elaine slapped Stephen's leg with the end of her dish towel.

"Your teddy bears and quilts are sufficient, Miss Elaine," Stephen said with a slight bow.

Tess explained. "Elaine makes patchwork quilts. Every patrol car has teddy bears and quilts in the back. When kids are in trouble, the officers pass them out and it comforts the kids."

I thought about how soothing a soft kid-sized quilt would be. A comforter, in every sense of the word.

"I know you've got your hands full, Maggie," Elaine said. "But if you're interested in joining our guild or learning to quilt, let me know."

She turned back to Stephen. "So, don't deflect. Do you think you got anything useful out of this meeting?"

"I'm not sure. I'll hand it off to Jason and see what he thinks. Keep an eye on the school for us, will you?"

"As always," Elaine said. "As always."

We said our goodbyes. I cringed when I thought about all the hints I'd seen and heard that pointed to Jason and Stephen's close connection. Hints I hadn't picked up on. Now that I knew, Stephen's professional and emotional ties to the Orchard View Police Department and his commitment to its chief detective made perfect sense.

I walked to the car. I was happy thinking about my growing group of friends and tried not to dwell on the death of Miss Harrier. Unless I could find the pill bottle or wrap up the case in a tidy little bow, there was little I could do for Miss Harrier right now.

Chapter 18

When a job seems infinite, a list can create a number of
finite steps toward progress. Lists aren't for everyone,
but I'd be lost without them.

*From the Notebook of Maggie McDonald
Simplicity Itself Organizing Services*

Monday, September 8, 11:30 a.m.

I was in a good mood, feeling like a combination between Sherlock
Holmes and Lara Croft. I hummed the James Bond theme song as
I drove home.

Stephen and I spent an hour putting up cameras at the front and
back doors of the house. We installed four more to cover the barn.
Stephen suggested I hire an electrician to install spotlights on the barn
and the house to illuminate the yard. I didn't really want our rural
landscape lit up like a parking lot, but I told him I'd think about it.

I had visions of a spruced-up front yard, with driveway lights that
would make it easier to find our address and navigate the path to the
house without tripping. In the back, though, I hoped we could keep it
dark enough to see the Milky Way and teach the boys to identify con-
stellations.

Lights that we could flick on at any sign of trouble wouldn't be
bad, though. Even without vandals and violence and the death of
Javier Hernandez, it was a little spooky not knowing what animals
might be lurking in the yard when I let Belle out at night.

Using computer magic I didn't understand, Stephen showed me
how to access the video feed for the surveillance cameras on my laptop
and my phone. He refused my offer of lunch, but grabbed an apple

from the bowl on the kitchen table and dashed off for an appointment with a veteran interested in working with one of the discharged Marine dogs.

I set to work unpacking more boxes, glancing at the camera feeds every time I passed my computer. I didn't expect the vandal to return in the daytime, but I wanted to get in the habit of checking on things.

An alarm on my phone reminded me it was almost time for school to get out.

David had a trumpet sectional for band after school, so I drove straight to the middle school.

"Mom," Brian said, poking his head in the car window, "can we give Diego DeSoto a ride home? He lives just up the hill from us." I agreed and Brian waved over a young boy, shorter than most of the other seventh-graders, with thick dark hair that hid his eyes.

Diego kept his head down, but muttered "Thanks for the ride" when I invited him to hop in the car.

"Do you want to borrow a phone to text your parents?" I said. "Will they know where you are?" Diego shook his head and looked out the window. I couldn't tell whether he was shy, rude, tired, sick, or depressed. Something wasn't quite right with this kid, but that was the case with most seventh-graders from time to time.

"Mom," Brian said, "we have to call Jason. I thought of something."

"What's that, honey?" I said, barely listening as I navigated the crowd of kids on foot, skateboards, and bicycles, all under the influence of after-school euphoria and hormones. My goal was to exit the parking lot without killing any of them.

"I remembered something that was missing from Harrier's office. Her iPad. Remember how she used to hit and slap it all the time? She was always taking pictures and writing notes. She never went anywhere without it. But it wasn't in her office."

"Maybe the police took it?"

"But what if they didn't? What if it's missing? What if she wrote something in there that the killer didn't want anyone to know? Maybe that's why she's dead. To keep her quiet and destroy the evidence."

We were stopped in a long line at a stoplight, waiting our turn to cross Foothill Expressway. I looked at Brian, sitting on the edge of the backseat, quivering with excitement. Was this some sort of conspiracy theory he and his friends had cooked up at lunchtime to scare themselves silly? Or was his observation the key to breaking the case open?

"Mom, we need to call Jason now. He needs to look for the iPad. That's the key; I know it is. I figured it out during my math class. We had a test and I finished early. I was staring out the window and the teacher was entering grades in her iPad. That's when I remembered. Harrier *always* carried hers with her."

If Brian was right, if Miss Harrier had been murdered and the iPad really was the key, it could be dangerous for him if the killer knew he'd figured it out. Diego knew, obviously, but I wondered if Brian had mentioned it to anyone else. It was definitely time to get the police involved.

"Pick up my phone, Brian. Jason's on speed dial. If you can't reach him, leave a message and call Stephen. And when you're done, make sure their numbers are in your phone. There are a couple more I want you to add later, just in case."

"Is this for real?" Diego said. "You really think this is for real?"

"I'm not sure," I said. "But it's worth checking out."

I looked at Diego in the rearview mirror, and he looked pale, almost gray.

Brian wanted to drive straight to the police station. I wanted to drop off Diego, go home, get Brian a snack, shift the laundry, and let him get started on his homework before it was time to go back and get David. I craved normalcy. I feared growing more deeply enmeshed in what was shaping up to be a murder investigation, but we had an obligation to pass any information we had along to the police. Brian phoned Jason and left a message.

We dropped Diego at the DeSoto house, an overbuilt home with pink walls, a huge courtyard fountain, and a Mediterranean feel. A signpost read *Castillo de las Fuentes*. My Spanish was rusty, but I was pretty sure that meant "Castle of the Fountains," and I wondered where the other fountains were. Most public fountains in California had been turned off during the drought to save water and money. Having a huge fountain like this one running in your front yard seemed to say that the DeSotos felt Orchard View policies about conserving water during the drought did not apply to them.

"Thanks, Mrs. McDonald," Diego said. "See you tomorrow, Brian."

I helped Diego with his backpack. "It's no problem giving you a ride, Diego. Anytime. You know where we live?"

Diego nodded. "It's where my br—" Diego was cut off by Belle's barking. I usually fed her when the boys got home from school, so she wanted to get moving.

"Sorry, Diego, what was that?" I asked.

Diego looked at his feet. "Nothing. Mr. Hernandez let us play there sometimes, is all."

"Well, you'll have to come back," I said. The more I heard about Javier Hernandez, the more I thought I'd missed getting to know a wonderful man. I waited to be sure Diego got in the front door, but I wasn't sure where the front door was. Diego shuffled across the courtyard dragging his heavy backpack and trailed his hand in the fountain as he passed it. No instrument case.

"Did Diego forget his instrument?" I asked Brian. "Should we take him back to get it?"

"His dad thinks music is a waste of time. He won't let Diego join band."

Okay, then. I put another black mark against Mr. Snooty in my mental list of his offenses.

When I turned back to make sure Diego got in safely, he'd disappeared, and I still couldn't figure out where the front door was. The enormous fountain made it hard to see anything beyond it.

I backed out of the DeSotos' driveway and drove to our house. Jason arrived shortly after we did. We went inside and Brian filled Jason in on his suspicions about the iPad and suggested Miss Harrier might have installed an application on it that would allow it to be traced.

Jason confirmed that the crime-scene techs had secured Harrier's phone and computer, but that neither held any documents that helped clear up the mysteries surrounding her death. They hadn't looked for a tablet because they didn't know one was missing. Jason thanked Brian and took his phone out on the porch where we could hear him barking orders to his team to meet him at the school.

"Can I help look for it?" asked Brian.

I started to answer, but Jason walked back in from the porch and beat me to it.

"We'll need to search the entire school, and her home, and go through her car once more," he said. "Don't you have homework?"

"I'll do it before Mom drops me off in the morning. Or I could help you look in Miss Harrier's office then?"

"I'll keep it in mind."

"But . . ."

"For reasons pertaining to bringing charges against someone later, we need to limit the number of people who are involved in the search. If our team finds nothing, we'll see what you can do to help. For now, do your homework."

Brian frowned and rolled his eyes, but turned and ran upstairs.

"Should I be worried for him?" I asked Jason. "What kind of evidence would you expect to find on Miss Harrier's iPad that would be worth dying or killing for?"

Jason rolled his shoulders, then tilted his head from one side to the other, stretching.

"We're the only ones who know that Brian thinks the iPad is a key bit of evidence. If there's a killer out there, he or she might have destroyed it."

Jason brushed his hair away from his face and looked at me, biting his lip and thinking.

"What?" I asked.

"Do you have a minute? There's something else I need to tell you." He gestured toward the living-room sofas. "Can you sit for a minute?"

"What is it?" I asked, sitting on the arm of the couch across from Jason. He stared out the window and looked exhausted. I was reminded of my conversation with Paolo at the gas station, and wondered if getting a word out of Jason this afternoon would prove as difficult.

"Maggie . . ." Jason coughed and started again. "We got the report from the medical examiner on Javier Hernandez's death."

"Right, the guy in the basement," I said.

"It's been ruled a homicide."

My hand flew to my mouth. "Homicide?" I was horrified. A person had been murdered in my home. In an odd way, I felt responsible, as if, because it was my house, I could have somehow prevented it. It was ridiculous, but then, before I moved to Orchard View, I hadn't had much experience with homicide and had no idea what a normal reaction to such dreadful news would be.

Jason nodded. "We're still not sure what happened, or why. But we need you and the boys to be extra careful."

"Are we safe here?" The idea that someone had murdered Javier meant he'd been alive one minute and killed the next. Someone did that to him. Someone who could do the same to the boys or to me, or to one of the animals.

"Is it the same person as the vandal? Could it be the same person who killed Miss Harrier?" I asked.

Jason shook his head. "We just don't know. But we *will* find out. Would you be more comfortable living somewhere else?"

It was my turn to shake my head and I did so with more determination than I felt. "This is our home," I said. "We're staying put."

Jason thought for a moment. "I can step up the patrols, and Stephen and Munchkin will be here for as long as it takes us to find this guy. But be careful."

I walked Jason back to his car.

"You can change your mind any time," he said.

I nodded. Jason climbed into his car and turned the key in the ignition. He rolled down the window. "I'm as excited by the possibility of finding that iPad as Brian is. Please thank him for me. And try not to worry about the crimes. I'm more concerned about the vandal than I am by the murderer. TV is one thing, but in real life, murderers usually don't kill random people."

I shuddered and tried to hide it. Jason either didn't notice or pretended he hadn't.

"Stephen will be by later. We'll have eyes on those monitors all night. And Maggie? No snooping. That's our job."

I thanked Jason, waved to him as he pulled onto Briones Hill, and walked back to the house.

Back in the kitchen, I pulled out a pad of paper. I had time to do a little planning—especially if I picked up a deli meal on the way to or from getting David.

I wrote down everything that I remembered from this morning's meeting, and what we knew about the death of Javier Hernandez and the destructive little lowlife who was targeting our house. I had no idea if the events were connected, but I figured the only way to ensure that we didn't find a connection was to avoid looking for one. I tapped my pen against the pad, leaving tiny dots of ink where there should have been bullet points outlining stirring insights.

Flora was the most recent addition to my circle of friends, so I focused on her first. There was the marijuana angle, but it was a stretch to connect that to Miss Harrier or to the events at our house. Sure, if we'd flung open the doors of the barn on that first day and uncovered a major pot-growing operation, that would help explain why Flora might have wanted Javier out of the way and why she would want to drive us from our home.

And if it had been a major operation that Harrier had somehow uncovered and threatened to expose, and if Flora was in debt to a major drug gang—all that might have given Flora a reason to kill Harrier. But Flora? Part of a major drug ring? A murderer? I couldn't see it. She was an herbal entrepreneur with fairies embroidered on her skirt. I could easily picture her wearing a *Think Global, Buy Local* T-shirt. She'd turned down the big-name coffee at Elaine's. No, if Flora was selling pot, it would be a small, one-woman operation.

What had Flora said at the meeting about her PTA role? Something about not being privy to the treasurer's reports. But that Susan Harrier had wanted to review those reports more often and in more detail than Dennis DeSoto thought was necessary? In Stockton, when I'd had a brief stint as the not-very-organized secretary of the elementary-school PTA, the treasurer's reports were attached to the minutes and filed with them. I had no idea whether all PTAs had similar requirements, but I thought Flora should have access to the treasurer's reports in her role as PTA secretary.

PTA finances would be kept entirely separate from school or district funds and from the foundations that Tess had told me about. So why had Susan Harrier wanted to scour the PTA treasurer's reports? Compared to all the other pools of funds, the PTA budget was small potatoes. Did she suspect Dennis of fiddling with the books? Or did she just have a special project she wanted to suggest the PTA help finance and was hoping to find an untapped budget category? I didn't know, but I thought it was worth finding out more. Someone who might cut a few corners when it came to PTA bookkeeping might not be scrupulously honest in their other dealings, either. And, if Dennis had done something wrong and someone discovered it, they might be blackmailing him into performing other criminal activities. Or it could be that I'd read too much crime fiction.

I wrote *Call Flora* on my pad. I'd call her while I was waiting for

David. If she still didn't have the reports from Dennis, I'd offer to go to his house and pick them up myself. Progress. I had one bullet point. I clicked my pen and made the bullet darker and larger.

I took the pad with me when I drove to the high school so I could take notes as ideas came to me. None did. I phoned Flora, but had to leave a message. When I picked up David, he claimed to be starving and begged me to take him to In-N-Out Burger. Since I'd talked myself out of a slow-cooked meal in favor of a quick stop at the deli, David didn't have to twist my arm very hard.

The line at the drive-through window was enormous, so I parked and walked inside. David stayed in the car to contact a school friend about a homework assignment.

I ordered burgers, including extra for Stephen and for Munchkin. "Maggie?"

I turned and watched Elaine Cumberfield and her cloud of gorgeous white hair approach me. Elaine eats hamburgers? She gave off such an impression of a magical fairy queen that I found myself surprised she ate at all. If she did eat, surely honeysuckle nectar and bee pollen would be her comfort foods.

"I see I'm not the only one on a quest for an easy meal," Elaine said. "There's just too much going on to plan and cook, isn't there?"

I agreed and she went on. "I'm going to grab my burger, plop down in front of the TV, and watch *Castle* reruns. They always wrap up the worst murders in less than an hour. I want some of that in my life, don't you?"

I nodded. *Castle* was a favorite of mine too. "Do you know if they've made any progress on Miss Harrier's murder?"

Elaine shook her head. "What do you think happened, Maggie? As an outsider, you can look at events more objectively than the rest of us."

I laughed. "Jason doesn't feel that way. He's asked me to stay out of the investigation, stop thinking about it, and let the police handle it."

Elaine frowned. "I'm not sure that's the best approach." She looked at my face, which must have showed the skepticism I felt. "Really. I think you could offer a lot. Look at everyone, including me. After all, I probably know the school better than anyone, and my house is in a great position for me to know when I could sneak in undetected."

Elaine placed her order and stood to the side of the front counter, waiting with me. "If we're talking about murder, or even suicide, we're not talking about reasoned behavior, are we? Most rational people will find other solutions to their problems. And we never know what will make an ordinary person snap, do we?"

Elaine was starting to make me nervous. Her comforting cloud of hair was beginning to make her look more like a mad scientist and her voice was growing strident. I'd embraced David's suggestion of an easy meal, thinking it would give me more time to play with my ideas about the cases and discuss some of the possibilities with Stephen. But now, with Elaine exerting pressure to think the worst about the only people I knew in Orchard View, I was increasingly uncomfortable with the idea of digging up motives for murder.

I was relieved when they called my name to pick up my order. I said goodbye to Elaine and tried not to run to the car. David demolished one burger on the way home and another when we sat down to unwrap our dinner.

We ate in the kitchen. Stephen joined us and we had a lively discussion about video games and the one that was everyone's current favorite. I asked the boys to toss their laundry down the chute in the upstairs hall and headed to the basement to start a load of wash. Fall in California, at least until it starts raining, is hot and dusty. With all of us still working on moving chores, and David's long, hot, dusty band practices, I was doing laundry whenever I could squeeze it in.

I'd started upstairs with a basket of clean and folded wash when I heard the sound of breaking glass and a *pop, pop, pop, pop-pop* noise I couldn't identify. It didn't sound good, though. I dashed up the basement steps, skipping several in my hurry to get to the boys.

Chapter 19

If you have an organizational system that works for you,
don't change it.

From the Notebook of Maggie McDonald
Simplicity Itself Organizing Services

Monday, September 8, After dinner

"Brian! David!" Stephen called to the boys from the living room. "Are you okay?"

Both boys answered from their bedrooms upstairs.

"Grab Belle. Move into the hallway." Stephen shouted orders in a voice that left no doubt he was a Marine. It sounded like a good plan to me. "Close the bedroom doors. Sit on the floor in the hall and stay there."

By the time I reached the living room, glass from the front windows littered the window seats and carpet. Stephen crouched next to the front door, gun drawn, peering through the sidelights into the darkness beyond.

I hadn't realized Stephen carried a gun, and I wondered if it was a recent addition to our protection detail. I decided it didn't matter. As creepy as I thought guns were, I was glad Stephen had one. I trusted him. If he thought it was needed, it probably was.

"See anything?" I whispered.

"Nothing. Stay away from the windows. If you want to join the boys, take the back stairs."

I retraced my steps though the kitchen, turning off lights and staying away from the windows. Upstairs, the boys sat in the hallway with Belle, as Stephen had asked, but they sat on the top step of the front stairs, trying to see what was going on outside.

I pulled them both roughly by their shirt collars back to the relative safety of the central hallway. They protested such profound indignity, but I ignored them. Their blue-jeaned–covered bottoms scooted easily on the polished floor.

Pop pop pop-pop pop came the noise from the front yard, followed by crashing and a clunk as something heavy broke through the window above the front stairs. I hoped it hadn't destroyed the wisteria window that had first endeared me to the house, but then I scolded myself for worrying about something replaceable when we were in danger.

"Have either of you called the police?" The boys shook their heads.

I pulled my phone from my pocket and pressed the buttons. Before the line had time to connect, I heard sirens. Stephen or one of the neighbors must have called.

Munchkin barked and we soon heard the voices of officers calling to one another and talking on their squawking radios as they crept through the bushes and patrolled the rest of the property.

After a very long fifteen minutes, Stephen shouted an all-clear.

"Close Belle in your room, David," I said. "Put on your shoes. We'll need everyone to help with the glass."

I crept down the stairs in my sneakers, avoiding as many of the shards as possible. I worried about the cats cutting their feet, but expected that wherever they were, they'd be hiding from the commotion.

I checked in with Stephen to make sure we wouldn't damage any evidence if we began sweeping up the glass. He showed me small rocks that must have been thrown by a slingshot in order to have enough power to break the windows. Small green and white plastic spheres littered the front rooms, creating a tripping hazard that was more dangerous than the broken glass underfoot. Stephen told me the tiny balls were pellets from an airsoft gun, which sounded something like the BB gun one of my brothers had when we were growing up.

Stephen showed me a pale-yellow brick and the note that had been rubber-banded around it: *Go Back To Stockton.*

I was angry. First, I was angry because someone thought they could dictate who was welcome in the neighborhood. Second, that they endangered the stained-glass wisteria window, which had survived, no thanks to them. Third, that the coward wasn't brave enough to show himself. In addition, I thought it was excessive to use three different kinds of weapons—BBs, bricks, *and* slingshots—to attack us.

Of course, my overwhelming fear was for the safety of my family, but that terror was so primal it was beyond words, beyond thoughts. It wasn't so much an emotion as a wash that tinted my entire perception of the world. *This has to stop. And I'm going to have to stop it.*

Paolo Bianchi pulled up to the front of the house with several sheets of plywood strapped to the Subaru's roof rack. He and the rest of the officers covered the broken windows before the boys and I had finished sweeping up the glass. I was sure we hadn't found it all and that we'd each probably have to pick a sliver or two out of our bare feet at some point during the next week. For now, we'd done the best we could.

I put hot water on for tea and invited the officers to debrief in the kitchen. I sent the boys to bed, intending to stay and listen to what Stephen and the police had to say. But I couldn't keep my eyes open. The adrenaline rush had worn off. Despite my anxiety and concern for my family and our home, the stress of it all had simply caught up with me. I was exhausted and for the moment, we were safe. I could get the nitty-gritty details from Stephen tomorrow. The predawn marching-band alarms would be going off way too early and I needed sleep if I was going to have any energy at all tomorrow to get to the bottom of what was going on in Orchard View.

To: Max.McDonald2111@gmail.com

From: SimplicityItselfOrganizing@gmail.com

Hey Hon,

Everything here is much as it has been. We're all healthy and happy. How's our "hospital guy" doing?

Love, Maggie.

To: SimplicityItselfOrganizing@gmail.com

From: Max.McDonald2111@gmail.com

"Much as it has been?" That sounds ominous, considering every-thing that has happened since I left. That, combined with your short email, makes me think things aren't going very well at all. Is everything OK?

Hospital Guy, Veejay, is improving. I may be home within the week. Being so far away is getting old, fast.

Love, Max

Sometime around two o'clock in the morning, both cats had curled under the covers seeking warmth and security.

By morning, I had to dig myself out of the cocoon of blankets the cats and I had created.

The temperature had dropped considerably overnight and there was a hint of the coming winter in the smell and feel of the air. It wouldn't be long before it started raining and we'd need to turn on the heat. I wrote *Get Furnace Checked* on my pad.

I pulled on my uniform for chilly mornings: jeans, T-shirt, hooded fleece, wool socks, and sneakers. I fed the animals and let Belle out the back door after she'd eaten. Stephen, Munchkin, and a patrol officer were conferring near a police car that was parked next to our drive-way near the barn.

I made coffee, heated milk for hot chocolate, and filled our insu-lated travel mugs. I toasted English muffins, spread them with al-mond butter, and added thin slices of apple to change things up a bit. We were getting tired of peanut butter on toast.

I pulled premade lunch bags out of the refrigerator. With a quick glance to make sure Brian and David's backpacks and instruments were waiting by the back door, I called the boys. Belle danced ea-gerly at my heels, but I told her no. I had a number of errands to run, and I didn't want to have to leave her in the car. She slunk to her pouf in the corner of the kitchen, settling in with a heavy sigh—the golden-retriever guilt trip.

I headed to the car to wait for the boys.

My plan was to drop them at their respective schools and then stop at Starbucks to top up my caffeine level and make some phone calls.

School drop-off went without a hitch, and I was quickly on my way. I phoned Tess to see if she wanted to join me for coffee, but my call went to voice mail.

I drove through the parking lot at the local shopping center, watching for cars that might come flying off the expressway and peel into a parking space in front of Starbucks as if there were no one else on the planet. Drivers in Orchard View, I'd learned, are very serious about their coffee.

Once inside the coffee shop, I ordered, grabbed my drink, and found a seat on the outside patio. I rummaged in my backpack for my notepad and my phone. Three sips of my drink and I was ready to dial. Flora first.

"Meadows for Health."

"Flora? It's Maggie McDonald. I met you at Elaine Cumberfield's house."

"Of course. Have you learned anything more about Susan Harrier's death?"

"Not yet. That's why I'm calling. Have you been able to get the treasurer reports from Dennis DeSoto? You'd mentioned at the meeting that he was stalling on those?"

"Not really stalling. He's busy."

I didn't know Flora well enough to know if she earnestly believed that Dennis was busy or whether she was being sarcastic. Either way, I pressed on.

"Would it help if I dropped by his house to pick them up? He lives up the road from me."

"That would be great. You could drop them at school when you get them. I'm sure there's no rush, though. With Miss Harrier gone, I don't know when our next PTA meeting will be."

Flora changed the subject and her voice dropped to a whisper. "I didn't want to say this in front of everyone at Elaine's, but I'm afraid Tess might have had a motive for getting rid of Miss Harrier."

Tess? Tess had said she could have killed the woman. At the time, I'd assumed she was exaggerating for effect, since I'd said much the same thing myself. Could I have been wrong? Could Tess have been serious?

"Miss Harrier found out that Tess and her husband were separated, and that Teddy, their son, was spending a lot of time at his dad's apartment in Mountain View, outside our school district," Flora said.

"Surely that's none of Harrier's business. It's a good thing, isn't it? A boy spending time with his dad?" I was filling space. I hadn't given much thought to Tess's husband or lack thereof, but learning they were separated reminded me how little I knew about anyone. I seemed to be having that thought over and over. I should have it tattooed on my arm: *Things aren't always what they seem and you can't trust anyone.* I shuddered. What a dreadful way to live.

"Maybe," agreed Flora. "But the problem is the school district's residency requirements. Miss Harrier was hoping to cut costs by kicking out any child who didn't live in the district most of the time. She'd talked to Tess about whether Teddy was spending more time with his dad, and whether he should be going to school in Mountain View instead of Orchard View. Tess was furious and defensive, as if Miss Harrier had questioned her fitness as a mother, her supervision of her son, and her choice of career."

"If Harrier was on a campaign to reduce costs, she must have been asking other parents similar questions?"

"Yes, but as far as I know, none of them were as angry as Tess. She has a frightful temper."

I told Flora I would pass the information along to Stephen, but I needed to change the subject. I didn't think Tess was the killer. I was fishing for information, but the problem was I didn't know what I was trying to catch or what to use for bait. I tried a different topic.

"Flora, you know that iPad that Harrier took everywhere with her, slapping it to get people's attention, taking notes, and checking databases?"

"Yes?"

"Do you have any idea where it is?"

"Surely the police have it. Maggie, I'm not Miss Harrier's secretary, I'm the secretary for the PTA and a reluctant one at that. Tess twisted my arm and told me it was my duty to volunteer and I'm regretting saying *yes*. I'm a single mom looking after the health of my family and my business. I don't have time to track things down for you or for the police. I'm sorry Susan Harrier's dead, but I really don't know what that has to do with me. If you're able to get the PTA treasurer reports from Dennis, drop them off in the office with April.

It was lovely meeting you on Monday." Flora's voice grew more shrill and her agitation increased with every sentence she uttered.

I started to ask another question before realizing she'd hung up on me. I shrugged. Flora *was* trying to run a business and could have any one of a number of reasons for hanging up so abruptly.

I hadn't teased much information from her, but I had what I needed most: an excuse to press Dennis for the reports. I wasn't sure why I was focused on them, especially now that the police were on the look-out for the iPad. I just had a nagging feeling, an inkling that there was something hidden in the numbers that would give us a hint about what had happened and why. Flora had said Harrier was pressing Dennis for the reports. If she'd wanted them, and Dennis was withholding them, they must mean something. Besides, I neither liked nor trusted Dennis. Not at all.

Next up, I phoned Adelia to ask about window repairs.

Adelia said she was sure her window guys still had the measurements for the windows they'd previously replaced. They'd bring extra glass and cut the panes for the other windows on-site. She'd let them in and didn't need me to be there.

Walking back to my car, I was surprised to see Flora standing in the doorway of one of the other stores in the rustic strip mail, beckoning me in. I'd completely missed her store when I'd walked past it the first time. A carved wood sign over the door spelled out *Meadows for Health* in gold-embossed letters flanked by beautifully rendered California wildflowers. A similar motif was painted on the store's front window, which was filled with artful but natural arrangements of flowers and plants.

"Come in," said Flora. "Come in, quickly."

Flora was an odd, jittery woman, and apparently prone to mood swings, but her shop was warm, inviting, and very well organized. It smelled fresh and clean, without the overpowering sweetness of a candle or soap store. The shop welcomed visitors to linger, with tea and cookies set out on a low table in the center of a cozy seating area that included a floral-cushioned love seat and two armchairs. Soft flute music mingled with the sounds of rain-forest birds on a hidden sound system.

"Your shop is lovely," I said, scanning the shelves to see if I could spot the medical-marijuana products I'd heard about. I scanned the room, trying to determine at a glance whether there were any profes-

sional services I could offer to help Flora run her business more efficiently. Given the personalized nature of her business, I thought it
would be nice to do away with the grocery store type shelving and install narrow glass shelves that stocked her products one-deep, emphasizing the freshness and uniqueness of each organic product. I
saw gift baskets of bath oils, candles, and wooden massage rollers
that looked like children's toys. Prisms, crystals, and New Age self-
help books. Earrings, yoga mats, and chimes, but none of the smoking paraphernalia I'd expected. And, other than the expensive glass
shelving I could easily imagine, there were no obvious business op-
portunities for Simplicity Itself other than the fact that Flora and I
might have some crossover clientele interested in a variety of self-
help services.

I wasn't sure what a marijuana dispensary looked like nor did I
know for sure whether Flora ran that portion of her business from
here or from home or another location. In short, I didn't really know
much at all. I reminded myself that Flora's pot business, licensed and
legal or otherwise, was an unconfirmed rumor, not a fact.

"I'm sorry I hung up on you earlier," said Flora, whispering.
"Elisabeth DeSoto came in for a massage, and I didn't feel comfortable talking about Dennis and the treasurer's reports while she was
here. I can't afford to insult *any* of my customers."

"But I just spoke with you a few minutes ago," I said, thinking
that was the world's fastest massage.

"She's in the back with Jenelle, my massage therapist. You
should come in for a session. It would take care of that stress you're
building up in your shoulders and neck. The first one is half price. I
have Jenelle's cards here somewhere."

Flora stepped behind the counter and rummaged in a box next to
the cash register.

"I know a great product for keeping track of loose business cards,"
I said. "Did I tell you that I'll be launching my own business in the next
few months? It's Simplicity Itself and my goal is to find ways for all
my clients to operate their homes and businesses more efficiently.
Please let me know if there's anything you'd like my help with. I have
my own card right here."

I'd stuffed a few of my cards into my bag last night on a whim,
since business cards seemed to be part of even the most informal
meetings in Orchard View.

Flora apparently hadn't heard me because she ignored my out-stretched hand.

"Aha," she said. "Here you go. Jenelle keeps her own schedule, so you can call her directly."

I took the card and added it to the stack I'd collected and secured it with a rubber band.

"Flora, was there a reason you pulled me in here?" I said, once again offering her my card.

"Oh, right," she said, patting the pockets on her work apron and pulling out a fist-sized set of keys. Flora selected a key from the ring, one with a green plastic bumper around the head of the key.

"Come through to the back," she said. "I wanted to give you the PTA binders so that you'll know which of the treasury reports I'm missing. When you get them from Dennis, you can pop the new ones in and give the whole thing to April."

"Can't I just give the reports to April?"

"You could, I guess, but it seems better to keep the whole binder together," Flora said, bustling through a curtained doorway to the back of the store. I followed behind her like a baby duck following its mother. We passed a restroom and two doors marked *Whisper, Please. Therapy in Session.* A utilitarian stockroom and office fol-lowed, with a short row of purse-sized lockers secured with combi-nation locks. Next to the lockers was a towel rack around which an additional collection of locks was fastened.

Flora saw me looking at them. "That's Jennifer's project," she said. "My daughter. She's a huge fan of *Elementary*, and wants to be able to pick a lock faster than Joan Watson."

The hallway ended in a door that opened onto a delivery alley with spots for owners to park behind their shops.

I wasn't going to argue with Flora. I was the newcomer. She was the old hand. I knew enough about PTA politics to avoid rocking the boat. If she wanted me to put the reports in the binder before I gave them to April, that's what I'd do. It wasn't a battle worth fighting. And Flora seemed emotionally brittle, somehow. I wasn't sure why, but I felt she needed protecting, like a baby bird.

She unlocked the passenger door of a vintage, hunter-green VW bug in mint condition, with blue, purple, and rainbow-colored bumper stickers saying *Co-exist*; *Tolerance*; *Respect*; and *Namaste*. The little car was adorable—a throwback that spoke of frugality and painstaking maintenance.

Flipping the seat forward, Flora rummaged among school sweatshirts and dance clothes in the backseat, searching, I guessed, for the binder.

I peered over her shoulder to see if I could help. "If you can't find it, Flora, it's not a problem," I said.

"It was here this morning," Flora said. "It must be here now."

She pushed past me, muttering a quick "Excuse me," and attacked the clutter in the backseat from the driver's-side door. I was reminded again of a fluttering baby bird and moved to help her look.

The clutter was girl clutter, with lots of purple and pink: a pair of tap shoes, a teddy bear wearing a pink tutu, and some sparkly hair ties. At the bottom of the pile, something black and clunky fell from the seat to the floor.

I reached down, wrapped my hand around the handle, then pulled it up and stared.

"You have a gun?" I said.

Chapter 20

Gossip often reveals more about the gossiper than the gossipee. Organizing professionals can use that knowledge to their advantage in getting to know their clients.

From the Notebook of Maggie McDonald
Simplicity Itself Organizing Services

Tuesday, September 9, Late morning

I stared at the gun, which became weightier as I held it.

"Is that safe, just sitting out here like this?" I didn't know anything about guns, but I was sure there were laws that said you couldn't carry one around in the backseat of your car.

"That's Jennifer's," said Flora.

"Jennifer's? Your eighth-grade daughter?"

I turned the gun over. It was definitely a pistol—heavy and black. But someone had drawn polka dots on the side with fuchsia nail polish.

"Jennifer's?"

"Got it!" said Flora, grabbing a massive black binder and standing. She banged her head on the roof of the VW.

Breathing hard, she hefted the book out of the car, lifted it up and let it drop on the roof. She pushed the binder across the roof to me, but I was still holding the polka-dotted gun.

"Oh, just shove that back under the sweatshirts," said Flora.

"Seriously?" I couldn't for the life of me reconcile the fact that the woman I'd pegged as a liberal earth mother tolerated handgun ownership among children.

"Oh, for Goddess sake," she said. "Hand it over."

I did, happy to be rid of it.

"See this?" she said, sticking her index finger into the barrel like a cartoon character about to get her arm blown off. "This orange tip means it's an airsoft gun. A toy. I'm not a big fan of toy guns, but Jennifer bought it herself with money she earned doing chores for the other shop owners after school. The hobby shop next to her dance studio has a target range. She practices there sometimes while she waits for her dad or me to give her a ride home."

"May I see?" I said, changing my mind about handling the gun. Flora handed it over. I'd never seen an airsoft gun before. Most of what I heard wasn't good. Besides the fact that Stephen had said one was used in the shoot-out at our house last night, news reports in Stockton about airsoft guns usually focused on the fact that they looked just like real guns. Tragedy ensued when police mistook airsoft guns for real guns or vice versa.

The orange end was pretty small, and I approved of Jennifer's efforts to differentiate the pistol from a real handgun by painting it with fuchsia dots. Maybe she should have gone a step further and painted the whole thing purple.

I didn't like it. I knelt and wrapped the handgun in a purple sweatshirt with *Namaste* printed across the front in pink glitter. I stuffed the bundle as far as I could under the front seat and packed frilly dance clothes around it.

I sucked in my cheeks, not wanting to lecture Flora on the danger of handguns, real or pseudo-real. Orchard View wasn't as close to California's growing gang problems as we'd been in Stockton. Children here didn't wake up to the sound of gunshots and wonder whether one of their classmates would be missing from school on Monday because their uncle, older brother, or neighbor had been killed.

In the northern part of Stockton where we'd lived, we'd been insulated from that trouble for the most part, although Brian's first-grade teacher had lost her brother in a drive-by shooting.

Here in Orchard View, maybe kids only associated guns with target-shooting or video games, and a handgun could be separated from tragedy, fear, danger, and death if it sported a fluorescent orange tip on the barrel. It was a question for another day.

All I knew for now was that Flora seemed like a good soul and an unlikely killer. She worked the long hours required of a single mom and small-business owner who volunteered in the local school. Neither Flora nor her daughter had likely spent yesterday night at our house shooting out our windows with a purple polka-dotted handgun.

I took the black binder from Flora and promised her I'd be back to visit the shop. It seemed like a great place to pick up birthday presents for my nieces, and a massage was definitely going to be part of my future as soon as I could squeeze in the time.

We were walking back to the shop when Flora froze. I turned toward her. Her face was pale, her eyes were wide, and her teeth were clenched. She made a short hissing noise and fisted her hands. I was about to ask if she was in pain and needed help, when I realized she was staring down the alley. I turned to see what she was looking at. A black SUV with darkly tinted windows drove toward us. Flora put out her arm and pushed me back toward her store like a mother trying to keep her child from hitting the dashboard. I stepped back and watched the scene unfold. Flora was clearly upset, to the point of barely being able to breathe or talk. The black SUV kept coming, but slowly. It didn't seem like a threat to me.

As the SUV drew abreast of us, the rear window rolled down, and a man with a round face and cheery smile leaned out.

"Morning, Flora!" he said. "How's the family?"

Flora still looked sick, but she answered, "Doing fine, Umberto. It's good to see you."

"Do you have that order ready for me yet?"

"On Thursday, Umberto, just as we discussed."

"Great! I'll see you then."

Flora and I stood in the shadow of the building and watched the SUV until it reached the end of the alley and turned onto the main road. I wondered if this Umberto could possibly be Dennis DeSoto's brother, the one who ran their family foundation. I discarded the thought. There was little to no resemblance between rail-thin Dennis and the more rotund Umberto.

Flora let out a deep breath and walked back into her shop. She sank down onto the sofa in the front window, poured a glass of iced tea, and drank most of it before looking up. Beads of sweat dotted her forehead.

"I'm sorry, Maggie. Would you like a glass?"

I shook my head. "Is there anything I can do for you, Flora? That man upset you. Do you want me to call someone? Are you safe here?"

"He's just a client," Flora said, finishing the rest of her tea. "Please sit down, Maggie. There's something I need to tell you."

I sat, thinking that she was going to tell me who Umberto was and why he scared her. I was wrong.

"At the meeting the other day we were talking about who had secrets, and who had a motive for murder," Flora said. "Do you remember?"

"Of course I remember. What about it?"

"Pauline Windsor is telling people that *you* had the best motive for murder, and that *you* were furious with Miss Harrier for changing Brian's schedule. She says that Orchard View was a quiet town with zero murders on the books until you moved in and 'found' a dead body in your basement. She's suggesting you brought the body with you, that you killed Harrier, and that you're faking the vandalism at your house to deflect attention."

Flora looked horrified, but I laughed, assuming she was kidding. "Seriously? She doesn't even know me."

"It's awkward telling you about it. Maybe I shouldn't have? I thought you'd want to know. Stephen said we needed to share everything and look at the big picture if we were going to learn anything."

Flora sounded hurt. I thanked her and assured her she'd done the right thing. I glanced at my watch.

"Are you sure you're okay?" I asked. "I need to get home, but I could call someone for you."

Flora convinced me she was fine, so I returned to my car and reviewed the odd behavior of the only people I knew in town. First, there was Elaine pushing me to investigate.

Second, there was Flora, who accused Tess and Dennis, but was driving around with an airsoft gun in the car—an airsoft gun like those that had done so much damage at our house. And who was Umberto, who was chauffeured in a black SUV like a movie mobster and terrified Flora, but seemed nice enough to me?

And what was with Pauline, who'd been accusing me of all sorts of nefarious activities starting with parking-spot stealing?

And where was Tess? Why hadn't she returned my call?

Flora had said there was friction between Tess and Miss Harrier over Teddy's eligibility for school. Tess, like most mothers, was ferocious in support of her son. How far would she go to secure the best education possible for Teddy?

The text alert on my phone went off as I reached the car. Juggling my backpack and my keys, I pulled out my phone. I'd assumed it was Tess, but the alert said it was the middle school.

Assuming the news was bad, I unlocked the phone and read the text. It was from April.

Brian's fine. No rush, but please call me when you get a chance.

I had to admire an administrator who led with *Your child is fine.* What parent didn't panic at a message from school during school hours?

I texted back:

On my way.

I pulled into the school parking lot, which seemed empty now that the emergency vehicles had left. The crowd of concerned parents had dispersed and the students were safely ensconced in their class-rooms.

April, in her canary-yellow garb, stood behind the front counter sorting papers.

"Oh, hi Maggie," she said. "Thanks for coming. I didn't mean to alarm you. We could probably have covered this over the phone or after school."

"I was in the neighborhood."

April looked around. "Hmm. We can't meet in Miss Harrier's of-fice. Let's go to the table in the break room. This will only take a minute."

I followed April out the back door of the office and across the open-air corridor to a teachers' break room. Counters filled with copiers, laminating equipment, and stencil machines lined the room, which held the smell of stale coffee and microwaved popcorn.

April pulled out a chair and asked me to sit in the chair opposite.

"What's up? You said Brian was fine."

"He is . . ."

"But?"

"I don't know if this is anything to worry about, but I know your family has been under a lot of stress, so I thought I'd mention it."

"You're scaring me."

"Brian's eyes were super-red this morning and he fell asleep in math and music. I know those are his favorite classes."

"I hope he's not coming down with something. Although things have been so crazy at our house, he may not be sleeping well. And then there's our move, I guess, though I've kind of lost sight of how that might be affecting the kids, what with everything else going on."

April raised her eyebrows as if she were asking whether I'd finished what I had to say.

"Sorry," I said. "Tell me more about your concerns."

"Falling asleep in class could mean a number of things, including that he's a normal middle-school boy who is growing fast and needs more sleep than he's getting," April said. "It's one of the signs we watch for. I don't think it's anything serious in Brian's case, but it can mean that things are rocky at home, that a child is experimenting with drugs, that they're depressed, studying too much, texting too late, or reading to the end of a great book."

"But . . ."

"I asked Brian to come see me at lunchtime and asked him how things were going. I offered him a soda—which the kids know is pure contraband around here—and asked him why he was so tired."

"And . . ." I was desperate to hear her answer, but worried too.

"He told me that you and Stephen set up spy cameras to watch for the crooks who've been trashing your house."

"That's right."

"Could Stephen have said he wanted eyes on the cameras all night? Could Brian have overheard that?"

I thought for a moment and nodded. "Not Stephen, I don't think. But Jason." Of course Brian could have heard him. Kids hear everything. Jason, Stephen, and I hadn't tried to keep anything from either Brian or David about efforts to catch the local miscreants in the act.

"Apparently he stayed up all night watching the feed on his computer."

"That's just like Brian—taking on more than he can handle, trying to single-handedly manage chaos. I'll talk to him, April. Thanks."

"No problem, Maggie. It's what I'm here for. You seem tired yourself." April leaned forward and whispered, "You wanna soda?"

I laughed and said I was fine, but I was glad to know where I could score a cola if I needed one.

I drove home and pulled into our driveway, cringing as the car lurched from pothole to pothole. I'd have to move resurfacing the driveway higher up on my list of necessary renovations.

I sat on the back porch to eat my lunch and keep an eye on Belle—and so she could keep an eye on me. I texted Tess. My previous messages had been purely social. Now, I was growing desperate to talk to someone about how crazy things were getting. I was worried about the murderer and the vandals who threatened the security of my home and my family. I was concerned that the police were making no progress in the investigation into any of the crimes. And I worried about the toll that sleepless nights and the chaos were taking on all of us, particularly Brian.

And I still had the nagging feeling that I was missing something—something important.

Chapter 21

One of my guilty pleasures is watching *Game of Thrones* with Max. I love that the Stark family motto is based on being ever vigilant, organized, and prepared for what's ahead.

From the Notebook of Maggie McDonald
Simplicity Itself Organizing Services

Tuesday, September 9, Afternoon

After lunch, I phoned a heating and air-conditioning technician Tess had recommended. As soon as I mentioned Tess's name, he said he'd drop what he was doing and come out. In some of the first good news we'd had in a long time, he gave our system a clean bill of health. He cleaned the filters, tested the main unit, examined the ducts, and said it was all ready to turn on as soon as the weather grew cold enough. Usually, that was sometime around Halloween, but the weather could turn nippy before then.

Of course, having a working furnace probably assured us of the warmest fall on record. But it was nice to know *something* in the house—and in my life—was working as expected.

I checked my phone. Still no answering text from Tess. I needed to ask about Pauline and Dennis. At minimum, they were odd birds. But were they dangerous? I needed to talk to someone who knew them. I wanted to bounce some ideas off Tess and hoped that I could convince her to call another meeting to help us shine some light into the darkest corners of Orchard View. Those corners almost certainly hid one or more people who might be murderers—or at least be thriving on spreading the kind of fear that tears communities apart and keeps young boys and their mom awake at night.

My phone rang. I glanced at the screen. Tess.

"Tess, I've been trying to get hold of you all day. How are you?"

"Sorry, Maggie. I had a client meeting, followed by a meeting with Teddy's dad, trying to figure out how to fit in all the after-school activities he wants to try, and still have time for each of us to see our kid."

"Teddy's dad?"

"My husband, Patrick. He's a love."

"I didn't know you were married."

I did, of course, Flora had told me. But Tess didn't know that, and I didn't want her to know I'd been talking about her behind her back.

"Oh, we don't live together. He lives in Mountain View, in an apartment with a building concierge to look after him."

I wasn't quite sure what to say to that. While California was full of people living alternative lifestyles, the vast majority of couples I knew were pretty darn ordinary. A married couple living apart was new to me.

"We love each other and we love Teddy. We just can't stand living together. I'm a complete slob at home, but want my clothes picture perfect when I go out. He's the exact opposite. To tell you the truth, I'm not sure I understand our relationship, but it works for us."

I heard slurping, as if Tess was sucking down a smoothie. As an organizer, my job is often about developing systems to help households of diverse personalities and cleanliness standards get along. But now did not seem the time to mention that to Tess.

"So, spill. What's so important that you sent me three texts?" she said.

"Do you have time to meet me before school gets out?" I asked. "David's got band, but I've got about forty-five minutes before I need to pick up Brian."

"Not really. That client meeting? It's for a firm bringing in a bunch of engineers from Texas. They're flying them in tomorrow and I have no idea what to show them. I've got tons of research to do."

"Rats. I've talked to a bunch of people lately, many of them strange, and I wanted to get your take on them, since you've known them longer.

I was also hoping you could call another meeting for me. They'll show up for you."

"Maggie, I'd love to help, but I don't have time this week. Can we meet on Monday for coffee after the kids are in school?"

I didn't want to wait that long. For all I knew, the vandals might have destroyed our house by then and more people could be dead. But that wasn't Tess's fault. She had a business to run with meetings that couldn't be rescheduled or postponed. I was disappointed, but I understood.

"Okay, Tess," I said. "I'll let you get back to it. See you Monday?"

"Monday," said Tess. "With the dogs."

I hung up the phone and spent a good three minutes feeling sorry for myself and hunting for cookies in the cupboards.

I couldn't find any cookies, didn't really need any, and it was almost time to pick up Brian. If I couldn't have Tess as a sidekick, I'd need to tackle the problem myself. I'd talk to the people I knew. If that didn't work, I'd try to find some other leads.

It wasn't until after both kids were home, finishing their homework after dinner, that I had time to talk to Stephen over tea in the kitchen.

I filled him in on what April had told me about Brian and asked Stephen to talk to him and assure him that several officers were keeping on eye on the camera feeds. I'd tell Brian the same thing, but I thought it might mean more coming from Stephen. I hoped we'd both be able to reassure him enough so that he could get a good night's sleep.

"Is Jason making any progress?" I asked.

Stephen grabbed one of the chocolate-chip cookies he'd brought over—leftovers from a meeting at the VA hospital. He looked thoughtful or as if he was going to try to dodge the question. I wasn't sure which.

He surprised me. "Some new evidence has come to light," he said, smoothing out the corner of a place mat and aligning it with the edge of the table. "Fingerprints."

"Whose fingerprints?"

Stephen cleared his throat. "Here's the thing," he said. "Jason's team collected fingerprints from your basement when he investigated Javier Hernandez's death. They did the same in Harrier's office."

"And?"

"Fingerprints belonging to Tess Olmos and her son Teddy were found at both locations."

"Tess?"

"And her son, Teddy."

"That's ridiculous. It can't be them."

"I agree. But let's look at it as if we didn't know them. Teddy's parents are separated. They both want the best for their son. Like a lot of Silicon Valley parents, the message is that they expect their kid to do well—really well. Some kids crack under that kind of loving pressure. There are kids all over town who are cutting or self-medicating. Teddy could be one of them."

"But we don't think he is, right?" I said. I hadn't met Teddy yet, but the quirky lifestyle of his parents seemed to be a model for being the person you wanted to be and finding ways to make it work. But what did I know? Tess and Patrick's parenting methods could have backfired and Teddy might be letting off steam by blowing up porta-potties. And if I really stretched, I could concoct a scenario in which a group of kids convinced themselves it would be funny to get their principal unknowingly drunk. Liquor, combined with tranquilizers they didn't know Harrier was taking, could have resulted in an unintended consequence, a deadly consequence.

But it didn't fit. Not with the Tess I thought I knew.

"No, I don't think Teddy is guilty," Stephen said. "But sometimes, trying to stretch your brain to make sense of evidence is a good exercise. Sometimes, it brings other possibilities to light."

Stephen stood and started pacing. Munchkin lifted his head, wagged his tail, and went back to sleep with a sigh. "For example, maybe Teddy didn't do it but some other child did. If that's the case, how did soda cans and water bottles with Tess and Teddy's fingerprints make their way to the office and your basement?"

"Tess volunteers in the office . . ." I said. "But she seemed mesmerized when I showed her around the house. If she'd been here before, I don't think it was recently. It's a good question to ask."

"Don't get that glint in your eye," Stephen said as I picked up a pen to make a note on my legal pad. "And don't make a note to ask Tess or Teddy. Jason told you to stay out of it."

"Surely there are kids in town living under more pressure, in much worse circumstances than Teddy?"

Stephen thought for a moment. "Well . . ." he began. "No, never mind. Forget I said anything. Leave it to Jason."

To: Max.McDonald2111@gmail.com

From: SimplicityItselfOrganizing@gmail.com

I've attached the schedule for David's performances. Can you make any of them? It would mean a lot to him.

I got the furnace checked out and it's perfect. Not so the roof, according to the building inspector. I've attached his report too.

I'll ask my friend Tess for a roofer recommendation—all the people she's referred so far have been wonderful. We'll need to get it attended to before it starts raining. It won't be a fun project like the floors were, where we could see a massive improvement immediately, but we'll be glad we took care of it. And, once we do, we won't have to worry about it for years.

I'm hoping I can convince some of these people to work with me and Simplicity Itself. Getting my go-to people lined up will be a big step toward opening up my shop here in Orchard View.

Love, Maggie

To: SimplicityItselfOrganizing@gmail.com

From: Max.McDonald2111@gmail.com

Are you OK? Your writing sounds tired . . . or at least less perky than usual. Please don't try to do too much. And don't get discouraged. I'll be home soon and I'm sure it won't take long for the Orchard View police to nab the guys causing all the trouble.

Veejay is up and around and improving quickly—but still on too many painkillers to run the office.

Please let me know if there's anything I can do to help from here.

And don't be too frustrated by the delays in getting Simplicity up and running. I can help with that when I get home. I owe you. I know that my trip here has put a huge strain on you and the boys—but despite that you've made enormous progress on the house.

Love you!

Max

Chapter 22

If you're investing in home furnishings, from major appliances to window coverings, paying for installation can save time, energy, and headaches. Installers will have the appropriate tools and experience to complete the job in less time than it might take you to read the instructions and gather your tools.

From the Notebook of Maggie McDonald
Simplicity Itself Organizing Services

Wednesday, September 10, Morning

My phone rang the following day just after I'd finished dropping off Brian. I was on my way to a decorator fabric store Adelia had recommended. I glanced at the screen: Tess. I pulled the car to the side of the road and answered the phone.

"Maggie, I'm so sorry about yesterday. I didn't want to put you off. I've carved out some time this morning and wondered if you'd like to walk the dogs."

"I'm doing some errands. If I don't get them done, I'll be holding up Adelia's schedule. Would you be willing to meet later this morning? Maybe ten thirty at Starbucks?"

"Great! See you then."

Tess must still be rushed. By the time I said goodbye, she'd disconnected. It was one of the fastest conversations she and I had ever had. But it made sense—we were getting together shortly. Anything we had to talk about could wait.

The fabric store I visited was a treat for the eyes and fertilizer for ideas I didn't have time to put into action. Steeling myself against distractions, I found likely samples for curtains and cushions. I plunked down a deposit for three sample books and made an appointment to have a sales rep measure for curtains and suggest hardware options.

I finished more quickly than I expected, so I drove straight to Starbucks and found a table in the shade. I ordered a medium latte, a spinach-cheese croissant, and a giant cup of water for Belle. Belle slurped. I sipped and pulled out my yellow pad to examine my lists while I waited for Tess.

I needed to ask her about Pauline and Dennis. Were they benign oddballs or as volatile as they seemed? And how did Tess and Teddy's fingerprints get on the soda cans at school and in my basement? Had they been in our house? Did they know Javier? If so, why hadn't Tess told me?

If Tess had known Javier Hernandez and neglected to tell me, what else might she be hiding? What else might she know? And who else might have known him and also neglected to tell me? I needed to start finding out more about him. I shivered and savored the comforting warmth of my coffee cup. I hated the idea that someone might have murdered an elderly man and gotten away with it.

"Maggie!" Tess called from the doorway of Starbucks, waving and making hand motions that seemed to indicate she'd get her coffee and then join me.

"No Mozart today?" I asked as Tess plopped purse, coffee cup, and keys on the table and dropped into the chair opposite me.

"Nope. Not in the BMW and not with clients. I think Belle's been wearing him out. He's at home, asleep with his head under the couch looking like he's nursing a hangover."

Belle's tail thumped at the sound of her name.

"I'm sorry about yesterday," Tess said. "You sounded like you needed to talk. What's up?"

"I feel like I need an anthropologist to decrypt the local culture," I said, shaking my head. "I just don't get some of these people."

"Ahh. Which people?"

"Pauline Windsor and Dennis DeSoto, for starters."

Tess laughed. "Pauline is harmless. She has no filter on her mouth, a bit of an entitlement complex, and can be self-centered. Err, not self-centered exactly . . ."

Tess took a sip of her coffee and I told her about how Pauline berated me on the first day of school and said I'd stolen her parking space.

"What an introduction to Orchard View," she said, shaking her head. "Like I said, she's not self-centered exactly—she's always drumming up money for various charities and she'll take on projects that everyone else has refused. It's more like once she's involved in a project it becomes the most important thing in the world, and she's astonished that other people might have other things to do."

"And the parking space?"

"She bought the right to park there in a silent-auction fund-raiser when her oldest child was at the middle school. It was meant to be a six-month permit, but she's staked a permanent claim."

"Can she do that?"

"No, but we let her because she takes on the really nasty volunteer projects and raises a ton of money."

"Okay, I get it. Don't park there unless you want to take over Pauline's volunteer responsibilities."

"Exactly."

"And Dennis?"

"Oh boy," said Tess. She leaned back in her chair, took a sip of her coffee, and looked around to see whether anyone was in earshot. There was no one near us, but she leaned forward, lowered her voice, and whispered.

"That whole DeSoto family is a piece of work," she said. "I'd tread carefully."

"Why?"

"The DeSoto family is the closest thing Orchard View has to an aristocracy. Their family goes back to the days of the Spanish dons and land grants from the king. They used to own all of the land on the west side of Interstate 280 between Stanford and Cupertino. Even now, the DeSoto family members are the biggest landowners in Orchard View. They're generous to the community, though. Dennis's brother Umberto runs that foundation I told you about. His sister is on the board at the children's hospital. Colleges and universities all over California have DeSoto buildings." Tess stared into the distance. "There's something, though . . ."

"What kind of something?"

"In the last six months or so, Dennis has changed. Normally, he's a big presence at school and town-council meetings. It's like he gets a kick out of thinking that you can't plan a project or run a meeting without him." She paused for a moment, leaning back in her chair. "You know how every high school has a kid who tries to be in every yearbook picture? That's Dennis. He's always got his picture in the local paper: breaking ground, cutting a ribbon, presenting a check, shaking hands with a dignitary. Dennis is the king of the grip-and-grin photograph."

"But you said something changed?"

Tess nodded. "Last spring, he was late to a bunch of meetings. This fall, he's missed meetings completely. I heard that his oldest son was in trouble and maybe ran away from home, but it was hushed up. It was one of those rumors that comes and goes too quickly for most people to notice. I'd forgotten about it until now."

"I remember that when we met at Elaine's, Dennis kind of blew in and then blew right back out again."

"Exactly. That never would have happened a year ago. He would have come in and taken charge of the meeting."

"What do you think changed?" I asked.

"I'm not sure. It could be almost anything. It's a big family—very proud and very secretive. Someone could be sick. Someone's business could be in trouble. It's impossible to say. They stick together, the DeSotos. Dennis was a year ahead of me in school, and one of his sisters was two years behind me, so I didn't know them very well. But Umberto was in my husband Patrick's class. Patrick always uses Umberto as an example when he's talking to Teddy about how to shut down bullying."

"Does this Umberto have a driver and ride around in a big SUV?" I asked. "I saw someone like that outside Flora's shop. She called him Umberto."

"One and the same. He was arrested for driving under the influence a few years ago, but I think he likes the look of being important enough to have a driver. He still likes to throw his weight around."

Belle scrambled to her feet as if she'd just realized we were entertaining. She pushed her nose into Tess's lap. Tess laughed and rubbed Belle behind the ears.

"Once a bully, always a bully?" I asked. "Do you think Umberto could still be terrorizing people?" I thought of how afraid of him Flora had been when he drove down the alley in his intimidating car.

She hadn't wanted to talk about it, but she'd been terrified to the point of shaking. He'd seemed like an okay guy to me, but at the time I didn't know he had connections to anything else.

"Maybe," said Tess. "Like I said, tread carefully. If he *is* still a bully, he might be dangerous. If what Patrick says is true, he had a mean streak that went beyond pranks and harassment."

Tess took another sip of her coffee and shifted the subject away from Umberto. "You said you'd talked to a bunch of people. Who else is on your list to psychoanalyze?"

I started to protest, saying I was just trying to get a sense of who was who, but then I recognized Tess's teasing for what it was.

"I talked to Elaine, and she suggested that I consider everyone a suspect, even her. But I can't imagine Elaine killing someone. Or nailing a squirrel to the wall."

Tess shuddered. "That whole squirrel thing creeped me out even more than the possible murder. It makes me sound callous, but think about it. At least on TV, when there's a death, there's a motive. Something happens that leads a damaged person to believe that the only option open to them is arranging someone's death. But killing a squirrel? What did a squirrel ever do? And you've got to stalk one in order to kill it. You could hardly claim a squirrel killing was a crime of passion or revenge."

I laughed although Tess was right. It wasn't funny. It was disturbing.

"What about Stephen?"

"*Stephen?*"

"Well, Elaine said to look at everyone."

"Okay, she's right." Tess continued stroking Belle's ears, and Belle was nearly groaning with pleasure, her eyes half closed. "Stephen . . ."

"Would he kill to protect Jason?"

"Maybe, if Jason's life was at stake. But honor is a pretty big deal to him. I think if he'd killed someone he would admit it and take the consequences."

"What else might make him angry?"

"Anyone who didn't respect the contribution those military dogs have made," she said. "He works so hard with them."

She tapped the side of her coffee cup with her index finger. "Probably the angriest I've seen him was when he was working with me and Mozart before I adopted him. Stephen wanted to make sure that Mozart and I were a good match and that I took my responsibilities seriously. We were talking and Mozart was sniffing at some bushes. Miss Harrier came out of nowhere, hit Mozart over the head with a newspaper, and told Stephen to keep his scruffy dogs and their stinking poop off of school grounds. Stephen turned, I dunno, purple? And then went pale. He called Mozart to heel, took on that extreme military honor-guard posture, and in a very low, very quiet voice he told Miss Harrier that Mozart was a decorated war hero and deserved her utmost respect."

"Oh, God. What happened then?"

"He said he hoped he would never hear her disrespect a veteran again. He clipped Mozart to the leash and the two of them marched off with military precision. And Miss Harrier was speechless. Literally. She walked back to her office without saying a word. She treated Stephen very carefully after that."

"So you don't think she'd do anything else to make him angry enough to kill?"

"Not knowingly," Tess said. "But . . . no, I don't see it. Stephen has said he saw too much warrantless killing in Afghanistan. This is a hard thing to say, but I honestly believe he'd kill himself before he'd kill someone else."

"Which brings up the suggestion of suicide in Miss Harrier's case. Was she the same way?"

Tess ran her hand through her hair. "I don't know. Miss Harrier was an extremely difficult person and difficult to get to know. She was prickly. You didn't want to get too close."

None of my questions had uncovered anything to move the investigation forward. Should I mention the fingerprints to Tess? Jason and Stephen hadn't told me to keep the information from her, but on TV, the detectives always held something back from the suspects, and letting that information out damaged their ability to make an arrest.

I picked at the lid of my coffee cup. I was being ridiculous. Tess could not be involved in any murder.

"Tess," I began. "I talked to Stephen. He says they've identified fingerprints that showed up at both my house and in Miss Harrier's office. They may prove a link between the two crime scenes, but they don't make a lot of sense . . ."

I felt awkward, as if I were accusing Tess of not one crime, but two. And not only Tess. Teddy's fingerprints were in all the same places Tess's were. I tried to think how to continue without damaging our friendship.

I needn't have worried. Tess got a text message on her phone, glanced at it, drained her coffee cup, gathered up her purse and keys, and smoothed her skirt. As usual, her business came before mysteries, murder, and gossip.

"I'm sure they'll figure it out," Tess said. "Orchard View PD is small, but the best. Sorry, Maggie. Got to go. Are we still on for Monday with the dogs?"

I nodded, uncertain whether to feel happy that her departure had saved me from continuing a difficult line of questioning, or frustrated because Tess had dodged questions to which I still needed answers.

Chapter 23

Make sure you manage your time for the world you live
in. On a perfect day it might take fifteen minutes to drive
to work. But that doesn't mean you've got a fifteen-
minute commute. In the real world, your commute is
more realistically twenty to thirty minutes.

Allow for a thirty-minute commute and relish the rare
day when the universe turns the lights green and gives
you the gift of an extra fifteen minutes.

From the Notebook of Maggie McDonald
Simplicity Itself Organizing Services

Wednesday, September 10, Lunchtime

Belle and I walked to the car. I hoped to catch Adelia at the house
and talk to her about getting quotes from a landscape architect
and a roofer.

I was unlocking the car when I heard my name.

"Yoo-hoo! Maggie!"

Yoo-hoo? Who says "yoo-hoo"?

Flora waved from the front of her shop where she was watering
flowers in the containers that flanked the doorway. She turned off the
water and started toward me, then stopped, looking back at the door.

I guessed she was there alone and didn't want to leave her business unattended.

Belle looked at me and whined. I felt the same way. I wanted to
get home. But Flora beckoned again.

"We'll just be a minute, Belle, I promise," I said.

I walked back toward the buildings and approached her store.

"I baked some cookies last night," Flora said. "I wanted to give some to you and the boys. Come inside."

I held up Belle's leash. "I'll stay out here. I don't like to tie her unless I have to."

I sat outside in front of the display window on a green bench painted with wild flowers. Flora disappeared into the shop and brought out a cellophane bag of chocolate cookies tied with a crisp blue ribbon. I wondered if they might be "special" cookies made by adding weed, but I didn't want to ask.

"No special ingredients," Flora said.

"I didn't—" I began.

"You did," Flora said. "I know that rumors abound about my business, but honestly, I don't approve of kids using weed." She pointed to the cookies. "The only drugs in those are fair-trade chocolate, organic butter, and sugar."

"My drugs of choice." I eased a cookie from the crackling cellophane bag, took a bite, and smiled from my ears to my toenails.

Flora beamed, but shifted her focus away from her cookies. "Any news from Stephen or Jason about their investigations?" she asked. "Everyone who's come into the store has been talking about it, but no one seems to know anything."

I shook my head and discreetly put the half-eaten cookie back in the package. It was delicious and would taste better with cold milk, later. "'Fraid not," I said. "At least not that I've heard. Do you have any ideas? Anything come to mind since the last meeting?"

Flora looked thoughtful, checked the parking lot to make sure we were out of anyone's earshot, lowered her voice, and whispered, "I've had some thoughts about April."

"April?"

"She's wanted to be principal for years," Flora said. "She's followed a systematic campaign to make it happen, including taking time off to take some classes she needed. At least, that's what she said. But I heard that she may have been in rehab when she was supposedly in school."

"That can't be right." In my mind, April could do no wrong. She'd helped Brian, and that was good enough for me. But it couldn't hurt to listen, so I nodded.

Flora shrugged. "It's what I heard. She apparently had quite a problem with prescription drugs. Hard to break a habit like that. Really hard."

"Hmm," I said, not wanting to add anything that might seem disloyal to April. There was something distinctly ironic about Flora, the suspected pot distributor, pointing fingers at others for using drugs.

Flora continued. "So, think about it. What if she relapsed, needed to finance her habit, and turned to selling as well as using? And what if Harrier found out and threatened to tell? Killing Harrier would solve both problems for April. The principal's job would be posted and she could reapply. No one would know about her drug problem. On the other hand, if she *didn't* stop Harrier, she'd almost certainly have lost any chance of the principal's job, here or anywhere else. And she'd have risked arrest and prison time."

Flora made a good case, but her evidence was flimsy.

"But your scenario only works *if* she had a drug problem, *if* she relapsed, and *if* Harrier found out. That's an awful lot of *ifs*, Flora. Who is your source? And how reliable is the information?"

Flora shrugged in a gesture that was becoming annoying. If she cared so little, why was she telling me about it?

"I'm just repeating what I heard, is all. You asked if I had any theories. Stephen asked us to pass along anything we heard, no matter how off the wall it sounded. Will you pass the information along to Stephen, at least?"

I agreed, but I doubted that Stephen would give the information more than a passing thought. There wasn't any substance behind it. I stood up and disentangled Belle's leash from the legs of the bench. Picking up the bag of cookies and starting to say goodbye, I thought of one last question.

"Flora, did you ever meet a man named Javier Hernandez?"

"Of course," she said. "He was the custodian at the middle school most of the time that Elaine Cumberfield was principal there. Such a nice man. The kids loved him and he always seemed to have a kitten in his workroom. Even after he retired, we'd hire him to help out at after school and evening events. He was supersmart. His daughters went to Caltech. I think one is doing cancer research."

"Wow. Thanks, Flora. And thanks for the cookies."

She waved and disappeared into her shop.

I wasn't sure why I'd thought to ask the question about Javier, nor why I hadn't asked about him earlier. I needed to ask Jason how the police investigation into his murder was progressing. I couldn't shake the feeling that his death was linked to the other problems—embezzlement, property damage, and Miss Harrier's death.

Even if it wasn't connected, I needed to learn more about the man who had cared for our house. He'd called the police when the windows were broken and when someone tried to start a fire on the second floor. He'd performed the ongoing maintenance that made us all refer to the house as perfect when we'd seen it back in February. Someone had deliberately ended his life on our basement floor and left his body there for us to find. I owed it to him, and to my family, to honor his work and his memory by uncovering more about who Javier Hernandez had been when he was alive, and who might have wanted to kill him and Miss Harrier.

Chapter 24

Many people have the sense that professional organizers
are miracle workers. They believe that if they hire one of
us, or if they own enough books about reducing clutter,
or if they own enough plastic storage bins, they'll finally
be in control of their lives. The truth is that much of our
lives are out of our control. Organization can help you
pick up the pieces and roll with the punches, but it can't
help you control the uncontrollable.

From the Notebook of Maggie McDonald
Simplicity Itself Organizing Services

Thursday, September 11, Morning

I was starting to feel as if I had a manageable routine: Drop off
David. Drop off Brian. Run errands and learn more about Orchard
View secrets. Become more confused.

Thursday morning after I'd dropped off Brian, I saw April helping two students put up the flag in front of the school. September 11.
I wondered if the flag would be set at half-mast in remembrance of
those who'd died in 2001 or in remembrance of Miss Harrier.

I watched as April and the students pulled the rope to bring the
flag to the top of the pole. I thought that was best. Most of us didn't
need any help remembering.

The students joined other groups of kids, and I caught up to April
before she returned to her office.

"How's it going?" I asked.

April smiled. "Okay, I guess. We're finding our way. Miss Harrier was very organized, so the logistics are easy. The hard part is the number of times a day that I think of something I want to double-check with her, and find myself halfway to her office before I remember she's dead."

"You miss her."

"More than you can imagine. I don't think most people had any sense of how much she did around here. She never gave herself credit, and the rest of us didn't, either. We tended to focus on her more abrasive attributes." April pinched her lips together and shrugged.

"Do you have any idea who might have done it?" I asked.

April shook her head. "Have they definitely decided she was murdered? I thought they were considering the possibility that she'd accidentally overdosed or killed herself. Is there new evidence?"

Interesting. April was one of the few people I'd spoken to recently who was still talking about the possibility of suicide. Did she know something the rest of us didn't? Or had the rest of us watched too many television mysteries and used our dislike of Miss Harrier to jump to the wrong conclusion?

"You're right," I said. "I don't think they have decided. Next time I see Jason, I'll ask."

"He's stopping in at lunchtime in uniform. He thought it might help the kids feel more secure and give them an opportunity to talk to him about her death."

I bit my lip. I wanted to ask April whether the reports of her drug addiction were true. I hesitated, because I didn't want to sound like a tattletale or a gossip.

April looked at me and laughed. "I've interrogated enough middle-school kids to know when someone is holding back. You've got something to ask me or tell me that's making you feel awkward. What's bothering you?"

I let out a breath I hadn't known I was holding in. "It *is* awkward. Here's the thing: I've heard that when you said you were on a leave of absence studying, you were *actually* in rehab battling drug addiction. That rumor has led to speculation that you relapsed and Miss Harrier found out and—"

April sat on a bench in front of the school, shaking her head. She held up one hand to shield her eyes from the sun. The other hand patted the bench beside her.

I sat and she looked me directly in the eye. "Do you want the truth or do you want to spread the story?"

"The truth. I don't believe the story."

"But you don't know me well enough to be confident enough to deny the story."

"Umm . . ."

"Never mind. That's admirable, I guess. The truth is, I wasn't in rehab, but I *was* hiding something about that leave. I should know by now that it's impossible to keep any secrets from middle-school kids."

"You don't have to tell me, April. You deserve your privacy."

"No, it's better if the truth is out there. I had surgery, chemo, and radiation treatment for a very aggressive form of breast cancer. When I came back, I was still very tired, which is why I took the assistant-principal job. I'm hoping to move into a full-time principal's position if the cancer stays away. Filling in for Miss Harrier is a temporary gig, but it's already wearing me out."

"I'm so sorry . . ."

April put her hand on mine. "Don't be. They caught it early, the district took good care of me, and I had the best treatment possible. Miss Harrier covered for me if I needed to rest. My chances are good. Besides, I think the odds are better for beating cancer than they are for conquering a drug habit."

I smiled, enjoying April's wry sense of irony and humor. "Is it okay if I spread the word? Or would you rather let the drug rumors die out on their own?"

"Spread the word, please. I only kept it a secret because middle-school kids get so squirmy around words like *breast*. I didn't want them staring at my chest all the time, wondering when I was going to kick the bucket. But I don't want them thinking I'm the poster child for functioning well under the influence, either. Can you imagine the sneering they'd do on Just Say No day? No, better they know I had my boobs removed."

"Will do. With pleasure. I love shutting down rumors. Do you need any help picking up the slack until they find a replacement for Miss Harrier?"

April shook her head. "There's a retired administrator who will come on at the end of the month to fill in. I can manage until then, but thanks."

I stood and squeezed her shoulder. "Let me know if you change your mind about help. Brian and I owe you."

April stood and walked to the office doorway. She opened the door and turned back toward me, still holding the door.

"Thanks," she said. "But you owe me nothing. I was doing my job."

Chapter 25

When you're researching a new product, decorating a
room, or learning a new skill, take notes. Keep product
flyers, measurements, and fabric samples. Carry them
with you until the project's finished. You never know
when you'll stumble upon something that might pull the
project together if you can be sure it will fit.

From the Notebook of Maggie McDonald
Simplicity Itself Organizing Services

Thursday, September 11, Midmorning

I was running out of suspects. Everyone's story seemed to hold together and explain why they couldn't have killed Miss Harrier.

And each person, except for April, had pointed me toward someone else. Were they giving me legitimate leads or were they feeding
me red herrings, hoping I'd become distracted and stop weighing
their own motives and opportunity?

In the past, I'd prided myself on my ability to read people, to figure out what they *meant* rather than what they *said*. I'd used that skill
in my work, getting to know my clients and figuring out what organizational strategies would work best for them. But many of my
clients were people I knew. If I didn't know them, they were people
who worked in or around the university, and I understood their jobs.

Here in Orchard View, I knew only a handful of people.

When a job seemed too daunting, my strategy was to break it
down into manageable chunks. I needed to find a way to do that with
all the mysteries that were plaguing us. If we had any hope of leading
the life we intended to lead when we moved to Orchard View, we

couldn't continue to be afraid of vandals and murderers. I had to look at the problems in a whole new way.

Walking back to the car, I heard my name called. Across the street, Elaine Cumberfield waved from atop a ladder where she appeared to be cleaning her gutters in an outfit that included a purple floppy hat with electric-blue flowers. A lime-green T-shirt and purple overalls completed her ensemble.

I waved back, then looked at my watch. I'd done enough snooping for today, and I was ready to get back to work on the house, but Elaine was right here. And Flora had told me Javier worked at the school at the same time Elaine did. Elaine might even have hired him. She might know more about him than anyone else in Orchard View.

I opened the car door, attached Belle's leash, and we crossed the street together.

Elaine climbed down the ladder and brushed the hair off her face with a gloved hand.

"Ah, Maggie. How are you? It's warming up quickly this morning."

"Morning, Elaine. Your garden is beautiful."

"Gardening is my version of step aerobics, but I'm ready for a break. Do you and Belle have time for lemonade? Would Belle like to play with Mackie for a bit?"

Belle did a small hop, step, bounce toward Elaine at the sound of her name, and we laughed. "I think that's a yes," I said.

Belle and I followed Elaine through the house to the kitchen. I let Belle and Mackie out into the fenced backyard, where Belle's first stop was to get a loud, slurping drink from a charming fountain/birdbath/sculpture of a heron.

The beauty and delicacy of the heron, caught in the act of spearing a fish, was lost on Belle. Finished with her drink, she barked and bowed to Mackie with her front legs splayed out and her rear and tail in the air: a clear invitation to play. And they were off, chasing each other around the garden, where Mackie had made a clear running path.

Elaine put two glasses on a tray, along with a small pitcher of pink lemonade and a plate of her gingerbread men.

"Let's take this outside," she said. "It's warming up in the sun, but I think it will still be pleasant on the back patio in the shade."

Elaine invited me to sit on one of three folding camp chairs surrounding a rustic pine table. The setting was much less elaborate than Tess's red-and-black deck, but equally soothing.

She poured two glasses and passed me one, along with the plate of cookies.

The formalities observed, we leaned back and sipped, watching the dogs.

"How are you and the boys settling in, Maggie?" Elaine asked. "Are the boys happy in school?"

"They seem to be adjusting quickly," I said. "We're doing well, except for the murders and vandalism, of course."

"What a terrible introduction to our village you've had."

It was the first time I'd heard anyone refer to Orchard View as a village, but the term fit. It was a close-knit town with essential shops and businesses, but no big box stores or industry.

"In a sense, though, it's been nice," I said. Elaine's cheerful outlook on life was contagious. "We've been thrust into the thick of things. We know the police and emergency personnel, and I've made friends with the important people." I lifted my glass to her, honoring her role as one of the most influential people I'd met so far.

"Thank you, my dear. Now, is there anything I can help you with? Understanding the school system? Finding a dentist? Locating a store? Or can you find all that on your smart phone these days?"

I laughed. "I'd trust your opinion over the saccharine voice on my phone. But there is something I wanted to ask you about. . . ."

"Yes?"

"Did you know Javier Hernandez? Flora told me he used to work at the school."

"You missed meeting a wonderful man, Maggie. Javier was one of my favorite people. A true scholar. He and his wife and I used to have lunch together every Sunday and talk about books we were reading or problems at the school. He was great with the kids, and a better listener than some of the trained counselors the school district employs. He was especially good with troubled kids."

Elaine paused and sipped her lemonade. "I'll miss him terribly. We all will. But how distressing it must be to have all this happen just as you're moving in. What a dreadful way to spend your first day in a new town."

"I'm sorry for his family and his friends. He sounds like a saint. In trying to come to grips with his death, I'm trying to learn more about him." I shook my head and wiped tears from my eyes, a little surprised at how emotional I'd become.

"We were upset, naturally, but I'm afraid I thought more about the problems created by the situation than about the man he'd been. Max knew him as a child, of course. They renewed their friendship while we were planning our move. But I hardly knew him, aside from talking a few times on the phone. I'm trying to fix that now, even if in a very small way." I was also desperate to identify the murderer and protect my family, but I didn't say that out loud. I wasn't sure why, other than that both Elaine and her backyard exuded peace and kindness. That atmosphere encouraged me to keep murder out of the conversation as much as possible. I also thought Elaine might be more forthcoming if I encouraged her to reminisce about Mr. Hernandez without feeling it was part of an investigation.

Belle bounded up and nudged my hand with her nose, planting her head in my lap. Elaine refilled my glass and handed me a clean, pressed handkerchief to dry my tears. The delicate white cloth of the hanky smelled of lavender and looked like it had sprung, fully formed, from the depths of a Victorian novel. Not for the first time, I had the impression that Elaine was a time traveler who might be more at home in a different century.

"I think I have pictures of him working at school and with his family at Christmas parties here at the house. Would you like me to see if I can dig them out?"

I nodded and sniffed.

"He was my ally in those years I was teaching and being principal," she said. "Even after he retired, he would serve as a chaperone at dances, or stop by on Sundays for a chat and fix things the current custodian hadn't had time to tackle. The kids created this alter ego for him, claiming he had superpowers. He could smell pot a mile away and always knew who was experimenting with drugs. He'd tilt his head, look them in the eye, and they'd confess immediately. I think the story they told was that he used to be a Colombian drug lord and if you lied to him . . . there would be retribution and it would be bad." Elaine laughed. "I think I half-believed the story myself. But it's odd; I don't think the kids ever specified what might happen if you lied to him. Just something so bad that . . . they couldn't imagine it." She used her index finger to swirl the condensation on the outside of the glass. "Middle-school kids are funny old things. Betwixt and between. Some days they're small children and the next day young adults. They ride a roller coaster of hormones and emotions that are mostly out of their control."

"Do you think one of the students could have hurt Miss Harrier?" I asked. I stumbled over the words, swallowed wrong, and coughed. I couldn't bring myself to use *students* and *murder* in the same sentence.

Elaine put down her glass. "Is it murder now?"

"I don't know," I admitted. I suddenly felt I was in middle school again, being interrogated by the principal. "But if it's suicide, we already know who did it."

"Well, to answer your question, absolutely not. I'm not saying none of those kids have problems, including tendencies toward violence. But Susan—Miss Harrier—was an astute judge of character and very good at identifying and helping the troubled kids. She wasn't universally liked, I'll give you that, but among the troubled kids and their parents, she was idolized."

"A side of her most of the community never saw."

"That's right." Elaine wiped up crumbs and put the plate, pitcher, and glasses back on the tray. It was time for me to leave.

I stood.

"I'm sorry to shoo you out, Maggie, but I want to finish cleaning the gutters."

"No problem. This was a wonderful visit and break. Thank you." I held up the crumpled handkerchief. "I'll get this back to you shortly."

"Toss it on the tray. I'm doing wash later, anyway."

"Are you sure?"

"About something like a handkerchief? Absolutely. About what's going on in Orchard View that's resulting in murder, fraud, and vandalism? Not so much."

I laughed, called to Belle, and attached her leash. We followed Elaine into the house and she walked us to the front door while Mackie whined and nipped at Belle's feet. Asking her to stay, I guessed. But both Elaine and I had things to do. Another doggy visit would have to wait.

I was outside the door and halfway down the walk when Elaine called to me. She closed the door behind her and scurried down the walk. "Javier Hernandez was one of those people who used to be called 'salt of the earth.' He truly believed that money was at the root of evil—at least around here. It really bothered him when the parents of kids in trouble would drive their expensive cars to school-counseling sessions about their troubled kids and say, 'We have to work,' as if that were an excuse for ignoring their kids."

Elaine shook her head. "It made him sad and he made an effort to be around for those kids as much as possible. I'm glad you're trying to get to know him, even now."

"Thanks, Elaine," I said. "Are there any other historical tidbits you've got that might help? Maybe not about Javier, but someone else?"

Elaine thought for a moment, surprising me. Up until now, she'd seemed reluctant to pass along anything she'd learned in her role as principal. She bit her lip and nodded quickly, as if she'd made an important decision. She looked up at me, shading her eyes from the sun.

"There's been something odd going on with Dennis DeSoto over the past few months, and I haven't trusted his brother Umberto since he was a seventh-grader. He stole a master key, opened the girls' gym lockers, moved their street clothes to the shower block, and turned on the water. They had to go to class in their PE uniforms—mortifying. It took Javier to get Umberto to confess. I don't know if that means anything. I haven't seen Umberto in years. But he runs the foundation whose funds have been frozen. I wonder if everything dreadful that's been happening boils down to a problem with money."

"Do you think Umberto could have embezzled funds from his own family's foundation? That would be pretty risky for him, wouldn't it? From everything I've heard about him, power and prestige are everything. Would he take a chance on tarnishing his family's reputation?"

"Everyone has their price," Elaine said, shrugging.

"But what motive would he have for damaging our house or the school? The incidents have gone beyond juvenile pranks, but they don't seem the work of a mature adult, either. Why on earth would Umberto, the big and powerful, bother himself with something so small-time? And if he's embezzling, why involve his brother Dennis?"

Apparently, Elaine had said all she had to say on the subject, at least for this afternoon. She turned and walked back to her front door, opened it, waved, and then closed it firmly.

I shook my head. I was uncovering more questions than answers and it was time to go home. But I continued to muse over the hints

Elaine had dropped. Could everything that was going wrong in Orchard View come down to something as simple as following the money?

Elaine had encouraged me to take a look at the person I'd suspected from the start, Dennis—Mr. Snooty, who I'd seen examining our mailbox minutes before it exploded. Could the solution be that simple? Could the most obvious person really be the culprit? Not on TV. And not in a book. But maybe in real life?

Chapter 26

Moving is a process that isn't completed until long after
the moving van delivers your furniture. You need to
arrange furniture, put things away, and develop the
patterns you'll use in your new life. Where's the gas
station? The grocery store? Who is your doctor? Who
are your friends? Allow the process the time and
energy it deserves.

From the Notebook of Maggie McDonald
Simplicity Itself Organizing Services

Friday, September 12, Evening

By Friday afternoon, the boys and I were exhausted. Even without
the turmoil caused by the vandalism, deaths, and Jason's investigations, we'd have been tired.

The boys were still getting to know their school campuses, remembering names, and making friends. David faced a steep learning curve and long hours in marching band. Brian was still, I suspected, waking up to check the security cameras in the middle of the night.

David had texted me to ask if he could stay at school for a trumpet-section meeting. I agreed.

I picked up Brian and we stopped at the hardware store for more lightbulbs, a special cloth that I knew would make it easy to wipe up tiny slivers of glass, and other odds and ends. I stopped at Starbucks for a small latte while Brian walked around the corner for frozen yogurt. Fortified, we drove to In-N-Out Burger and ordered.

We were eating too much fast food and I vowed we'd get back to our normal, healthy diet soon. Tess had promised to take me to the

Mountain View farmers market and show me which vendors she preferred.

Tonight, though, we needed fast fuel and an early night. If Purina had made something called "Tired Family Chow," I would have served that with a little ketchup and everyone would have been happy. Failing that, it was yet another order of In-N-Out Burger for us.

By the time Brian and I picked up David, the wind had come up, the fog had rolled in, and the warm day was cooling off fast. We showered, threw on sweatpants and T-shirts, and watched our old standby favorite, *The Princess Bride.*

Stephen arrived at eight o'clock and found us all nearly asleep on the sofas. I pointed him toward the burgers. The boys and I stumbled up the stairs to bed.

After a few hours of blissful sleep, I awoke to the all-too-familiar sound of breaking glass, Belle's barking, and a houseful of smoke. *Not again!*

I grabbed Holmes, who'd snuggled under the covers next to me. Shoving my feet into my sneakers, I called to the boys.

I found them both in the hallway rubbing sleep from their eyes. I made a snap decision.

"Remember the rope ladder in the attic? Time to use it," I said. "Get out. Go straight to the car and meet me there."

"What about you?" Brian asked, eyes wide.

I lifted Holmes. "I'm grabbing the cats. We'll meet you at the car."

"Come on, squirt." David grabbed Brian's hand and pulled him up the attic stairs. "It'll be fun. Just like we practiced."

Holmes squirmed, and I braced myself for cat scratches, but he was only burying his head in my armpit, apparently trying to pretend he was back under the covers.

"Stephen?" I called, breathing in smoke and coughing as I dashed down the front stairs. The treads were covered with glass shards. I avoided looking at the wisteria window. If it had broken, I didn't want to know.

"Here, Maggie," Stephen called to me from the front door, coughing and wiping his streaming eyes with a handkerchief. "Where are the boys?"

"Fire escape. Where's Watson? Belle?" I looked at Stephen's side, where I was used to seeing Munchkin, with his head nearly glued to Stephen's thigh.

"Belle, Watson, and Munchkin are in my car. Fire department is on the way. They've called out mutual aid countywide. The whole hillside could go."

I grabbed my backpack from the hall table and wasted no time getting out. My chest felt tight, but I couldn't tell if it was because of the smoke or because I was terrified.

I pushed the *unlock* button on my key fob over and over as I ran to the car. I was relieved to see the boys were in the car with their seat belts on, waiting. I opened the passenger door and handed Holmes to David.

"Stephen's got Belle and Watson," I said.

My phone rang as I jumped in the driver's side and fastened my seat belt. I tossed my backpack to Brian.

"Find the phone and answer it, please." I put the key in the ignition, started the car, and put it in *drive*, planning to move us all back into the barn. I cursed the inept electrician who must have goofed up the wiring, neglecting to resolve the problem that had made our fuse box so dangerous back when we'd moved in.

As I pressed the accelerator and looked up to see where I was going, I slammed on the brakes, pressing hard enough and fast enough to engage the automatic braking system. The pedal throbbed and the car came to a skidding halt.

Flames shot from the roof of the barn. The field and hillside were dotted with small fires started by sparks.

My heart sank and my lower lip trembled. I cleared my throat and fought back tears, trying to avoid upsetting the boys any more than they already were. What I'd thought had been a fire restricted to the house was now an imminent disaster. Everything we'd fought for was at risk: our home, the barn, the view, and Max's dreams of taking the boys backpacking from our back porch to the coast through oak chaparral and redwood forests. We'd all worked so hard to move, to settle in, and to make the house a home. I now had to face the very real possibility that it was all going to go up in smoke.

But first, I had to get the boys to safety. My hands shook as I shifted the car into reverse.

"Stephen says to follow him," Brian said. Anything else he might have added was lost in a fit of coughing. We'd all inhaled too much smoke. I had to get us out of here.

Chapter 27

Emergency plans need to include strategies for
protecting people and grabbing shoes, keys, animals,
and critical medications. Organization is essential and
can save lives.

From the Notebook of Maggie McDonald
Simplicity Itself Organizing Services

Friday, September 12, Near midnight

I followed the taillights of Stephen's car, trying not to panic. Sweat
coated my face as a result of fear, or heat, or both.

Fire trucks screamed past on the other side of the road: red from
Mountain View and white from Orchard View and Santa Clara County.

"David, call Stephen and ask if he's alerted the Open Space District. The barn was sparking and starting fires on the hillside."

David dialed, relayed the message, and listened.

"Okay . . . good . . . okay . . ." he said to the phone and hung up as
I was about to ask him to put it on speaker.

"We're headed to his house off Grant Road," David said. "Paramedics will meet us there to check for smoke inhalation and lacerations from the glass. He says the county takes charge of wildfires in
the Open Space District and they've alerted other local departments
to stand by in case they need help."

At Jason and Stephen's house, David and I were examined and
quickly released from the paramedics' care. Brian's coughing had
improved, but they hooked him up to an oxygen sensor, listened to
his lungs, and kept an eye on him for a little longer.

After an hour they released Brian too, with instructions to head straight to the emergency room if he grew worse. Stephen grabbed blankets and pillows and I tucked the boys in on the sofas in Jason and Stephen's front room. David fell asleep immediately. Brian stayed awake a little longer. Belle curled up on the floor next to Brian's couch. His arm dangled over the side, patting Belle's head in a gesture that appeared to be soothing them both.

Stephen had hospitality down to a science, even at two o'clock in the morning. While I settled the boys in, Stephen had transferred the cats from our cars to a cozy den at the back of the house. Clearly, this was where the couple spent most of their time. Rust-colored recliners were positioned in front of a wide-screened television set. A complex sound system and speakers filled shelves behind the chairs.

Stephen had filled a mixing bowl with water and found a plastic dishpan that would do as an emergency litter box for the cats. He ripped up newspaper in place of kitty litter.

"Is this okay?" he asked. "We're not well fixed for a feline bathroom."

I nodded. "They'll have to make do like the rest of us."

I plopped down on the end of a pullout sofa bed Stephen had made up for me. I sniffed at my sweatshirt and wrinkled my nose at the smoky smell.

"I'm sorry," I said. "Everything in your house will smell like a campfire."

"Forget it. I'm glad we're all safe. Do you want tea? Jason will be calling with a report soon."

I shook my head. I'd resigned myself to losing everything. I didn't need to wait to hear Jason confirm it. Lists of to-do items ran through my head: call Max, contact insurance . . . it was too much.

"At this point, I just want sleep," I said. I was tempted to climb into the bed, throw the sheets over my head, and hide from the world for a week. A part of me managed to hope this was a horrible dream from which I'd awake, wondering why I was at Stephen's house.

"Of course. Sure you don't want water?"

I shook my head and Stephen nodded, leaving the room and closing the door behind him.

He reopened the door and stuck his head in. "Wake me if you need anything."

I nodded, he closed the door, and I slipped between the sheets. I wiped tears from my cheeks and wished Max were here, but I was awake only long enough to feel Holmes burrow under the covers while Watson curled up behind my knees.

Chapter 28

Organization does not prevent disasters, but it can help
you bounce back from a crisis more quickly.

From the Notebook of Maggie McDonald
Simplicity Itself Organizing Services

Saturday, September 13, Nine o'clock

The next morning I awoke to a knock on the door.
"Nine o'clock, Maggie," Stephen said. "The boys are up and
breakfast is ready."

I ran my fingers though my smoky hair and hawked up ugly gray
mucous. *Gross!*

I followed the sound of laughter broken up by coughing. In the
kitchen, Stephen flipped pancakes while Jason sliced strawberries.
Brian sipped a cup of tea and David was juicing oranges using a me-
chanical device with a whirring motor that drowned out any attempt
at a conversation.

Jason handed me a cup of steaming coffee.

"Let me give you the highlights before you bombard me with
questions," he said. "The fire department's primary job was to keep
the fire from spreading. They plowed firebreaks on the hill and ex-
tinguished grass fires before they could spread. Any damage to the
hillside will repair itself quickly after the next rain."

"The barn?"

"Unsalvageable," Jason said. "Insurance should cover a rebuild,
though current environmental regulations may require you to relo-
cate it."

I took a deep swallow of coffee to fortify myself and asked, "The house?"

Jason leaned back in his chair and smiled. "Nearly one hundred percent undamaged," he said. "Smoke bombs. You've got another broken window. There may be a residual smoke smell, but nothing that opened windows can't handle. Your house is fine."

I sighed heavily, unaware until then that I'd been holding my breath. I bit my lip and fought back tears. It seemed like tempting fate to ask about the wisteria window, but I sat up straight, squared my shoulders, and asked.

"Wisteria window?" Jason said.

"That stained-glass window in the stairway. Mom loves it," David said.

Jason shook his head and my heart sank. If only I'd taken a picture of it; we could have found an artist to re-create it.

He must have read my expression. "Maggie, I'm not saying it's destroyed. I don't know. Chances are your stained glass is fine. It survived the last attack, didn't it?"

I nodded and wiped tears from my eyes. I felt ridiculous crying over an endangered window. My kids were safe. The animals were fine. No one was hurt. Our house was mostly undamaged and definitely livable. The barn was something we could rebuild.

"What about the cameras?" I asked. "Did the security cameras show who did this?"

Jason frowned. "We took a quick look at the footage. We could see a hooded figure dressed in black who faced away from the camera. The techs are taking a closer look, but for now we can't see enough to identify anyone."

Stephen refilled my coffee mug and flipped three pancakes from the pan to my plate.

"I'm sorry, Maggie," he said. "I'm not doing a very good job of protecting your family."

"That's ridiculous, Stephen, of course you are," said Jason at the same time I said, "I shudder to think where we'd all be without your help, Stephen." I glanced at my two boys and tears filled my eyes. I didn't want to say any more in front of them. I didn't want them to know how worried I was, nor how close a call it had been. I wanted Stephen to know, however, that I owed him everything.

He must have gotten the message, because he put his hand over his heart and bent his head in a combination of a nod, a bow, and a benediction.

David looked at the clock. He lurched from the table, nearly up-ending a pitcher of orange juice. "I'm late for band practice. We've got to go *now*. I need my trumpet and water bottle and sunscreen and I need to change. I'll boil in sweats—it's like a million degrees on that fake grass on the field. I need to call my section leader and explain why I'm late."

I offered David my phone, but he didn't know the older boy's number by heart. He'd programmed it into his phone, which he'd left at home.

I took two bites of my pancakes, thanked Stephen, and confirmed with Jason that we could get back into the house. The boys and I hit the bathroom. Stephen offered to keep the cats until I could bring their carriers down. Within seconds we were headed back home.

"No exploring when we get to the house. No sightseeing. Brian, you're staying in the car. David, you're getting your band stuff, changing, and coming right out. I'll grab the cat carriers. Pretend it's a timed race-car pit stop. Go."

We were in and out in record time. David plugged his phone into the car charger and checked in with his section leader. Brian and I dropped him off and were back home in time to meet Jason and the fire department's investigative team.

The wind blew steadily from north to south, carrying any lingering barn smoke across the creek toward the hills. I opened the downstairs windows while Brian tackled the ones upstairs. I climbed the front staircase, pausing on the landing to check the wisteria window. Small chips and cracks were visible in the vines, but the majority of the window remained intact. I took a picture of it with my phone, guarding against another attack. For now, though, I took comfort from its beauty, and from its strength in withstanding assaults that had twice destroyed the window beneath it. I made a note to find an expert to repair the damage.

I knelt to brush my fingers across soot stains left on the stairs from the smoke bomb. From what I could tell at a quick glance, the bomb hadn't damaged the stairs or the finish. The walls and ceiling, however, were marked with stains that smeared under my fingers.

We could try washing them down with trisodium phosphate like we had the mailbox, but I suspected that might only be a prelude to painting. I sighed.

I was tempted to sit on the stairs and wallow in my misery, but we had work to do. I turned on the attic fan. From the small window overlooking the backyard, I could see Brian talking to the firefighters and poking at the edges of the burned beams with a stick.

Walking down the hill to the barn, I got the full impact of the devastation from the fire. Black splotches marred the hillside where sparks had tried to start a wildfire. Firefighters had done an amazing job of limiting the damage to the barn, protecting our house and the Open Space District. Autumn in California was fire season. Hillsides and wooded areas were tinder-dry and would stay that way until the winter rains dampened them sometime near Halloween.

"Morning, ma'am," said one of the firefighters, turning a soot-stained face toward me. "Are you the homeowner?"

I nodded. "Maggie McDonald. Is it still burning?"

He periodically sprayed the wreckage.

"I'm Jackson. Those hay bales are still smoking. We're using water and a wetting agent to make sure they're out. There are hot spots that need cooling before our chief can clear the site." He nodded to an older, heavier man talking to Jason and taking photos on the other side of the wreckage. "He'll want to ask you some questions."

The chief looked up, waved, and he and Jason walked toward me. Jason introduced us.

"I've got a few questions for you, when you're ready," the chief said.

"And I've got questions for you too. I'm sure you're thirsty. Would you like lunch?"

"I wouldn't say no to iced tea if you've got it, but no lunch. And if we could sit on your steps there, I could keep an eye on the fire."

I nodded. I was happy to turn my back to the devastation. Last night, I'd mourned the loss of everything—the house, the barn, the soothing view, and the plans Max and I had made. Today, I was angry. And I was determined to do something about it.

To: SimplicityItselfOrganizing@gmail.com

From: Max.McDonald@gmail.com

Hey Babe,

Jason sent me a note about the barn. I'm so sorry. He also told me that none of you were hurt, thank God!

Oh, Mags, I can't shake the feeling that if we'd stayed in Stockton, none of this would have happened.

Please be careful. We can talk about moving back. The good news is that I will definitely be home within the week. Details to follow!

To: Max.McDonald@gmail.com

From: SimplicityItselfOrganizing@gmail.com

What a mess! I've got tons to do, so I'll keep this short.

I'm thrilled you're coming home and so are the boys. We're managing fine without you here, but I know we'll all feel more secure once we're all together under one roof. It's been one thing after another around here and we're all exhausted.

I've thought a lot about moving back, but I've decided I don't want to. This house is amazing, the boys love their schools, and we're all making friends.

The barn is a disaster, but maybe that's a good thing. I know you talked about providing housing for a Stanford student the same way Aunt Kay used to do. Maybe we can rebuild the barn with that project in mind. Or an office, or even a business office, studio, and showroom for Simplicity Itself. Don't worry, I'm not galloping ahead with plans. I'm just looking for an upside among all the soot and ashes.

See you soon!

Love,

Maggie

Chapter 29

When you consult a professional, be honest with them
and with yourself. It does no good to have a doctor
prescribe treatment you refuse to follow. The same goes
for a professional organizer. If I suggest a plan that my
client doesn't embrace, I hope he will let me know so I
can make adjustments. If he doesn't, he's wasted his
money and my time.

From the Notebook of Maggie McDonald
Simplicity Itself Organizing

Saturday, September 13, Midday

The fire chief confirmed that the fire was arson. Someone did not
want us in Orchard View. That much was certain. Maybe someone
was threatened by my meager investigations into Javier Hernandez's
death, Miss Harrier's death, the vandalism, and the embezzlement. But
scare tactics and a campaign to oust us from our home made it clear
they didn't know me very well. I was more determined than ever
not to give in. Maybe I didn't know the town, or the people, or what
they were hiding. But my ignorance was not going to make me
give up.

What did Max's Aunt Kay say? "Play to your strengths."

I was best at bringing order from chaos. I'd done it for friends,
strangers, hoarders, and hopelessly disorganized professors. I could do
it with what I'd learned during my investigation. And if I couldn't, following familiar procedures would soothe me. While Adelia's team
wiped down and repainted the staircase, Brian played video games and
I ran our smoky-smelling clothing and bedding through the wash; I

pulled out my colored index cards, my colored markers and high-lighters, and got to work.

I made cards for the key players, along with wild cards for persons unknown. Flora, April, Pauline, Dennis, Tess, Elaine, Stephen, and Jason each had a card. I didn't want to think that anyone I knew could be hiding the kind of anger and desperation that would lead them to arson or murder, but I made cards for everyone and hoped I'd soon be able to rule them out.

I wrote the locations on cards too—the school buildings, our house, the barn, and the foundation that had taken a hit in the embezzlement scheme. I didn't have any details on the fraud and I wasn't even sure that any of these things were connected, but I wrote them down anyway. Elaine had suggested I follow the money. I added cards for the other sources of school funding: PTA, the DeSoto Foundation, the Orchard View Foundation, and regular state funding. If one pocket of school funding had proved lucrative for a crook, I wanted to try to make sure they weren't all vulnerable. I knew that school districts near New York and Chicago had been the victims of comprehensive frauds that took advantage of lax accounting and auditing practices. I didn't know enough about the Orchard View school-district administration to rule that out, here.

My organizing process required taking a good, hard look at everything my client was dealing with, so that we could make realistic improvements and changes, creating a system the client could maintain. I was literally putting my cards on the table, or in this case, laying them out in a riot of color on my living-room floor.

I made cards for the times when we thought each crime had occurred. That was the hardest part. Everything that had happened since we'd arrived seemed to have run together into one major nightmare. Separating them made me face each event individually, including those that might or might not be accidents.

As I'd hoped, when I reduced each horrifying episode to a few words that fit on a cheerful pink 3-by-5 card, they seemed much more manageable.

I moved the cards around based on who could have been in each location at the time the crimes had occurred. I made duplicate cards for the key players, making each one a different color: red for the Tess cards, green for Flora, blue for Dennis, etc.

If I was positive that someone had access to a crime scene and had no alibi, I put their card below the crime-scene card. If their presence was possible, I put their name above the scene.

I still didn't know much about the events of the past two weeks or the secrets that people were hiding. But patterns were emerging. Both Tess and Dennis had easy access to all the crime scenes. I clung to the concept of Tess's innocence, so I focused on Dennis.

Dennis had proximity to our house. Of all the suspects, he lived closest. He'd offered to sell our house, which seemed to indicate he'd be happy to see us go. His brother ran the DeSoto Family Foundation, and Dennis was the PTA treasurer. He'd told me himself that he was an active volunteer in a wide variety of school organizations. His son, Diego, had seemed uncomfortable when we gave him a lift home. Unlike the others, Dennis offered no help with our brainstorming sessions after the vandalism at the school and Miss Harrier's death. Miss Harrier had been asking for his PTA treasurer reports and Flora said he'd seemed reluctant to provide them.

I'd told Flora days ago that I'd pick up the reports from Dennis. Making good on my promise would be the perfect excuse to visit him and ask him a few more questions.

If two weeks in Orchard View had taught me one thing, though, it was that baked goods were currency. If you were saying thank you, asking for help, apologizing, or saying hello, unwritten Orchard View rules dictated that cookies be provided. My cupboards were nearly bare, but I still had the cookies Flora had given me earlier in the week. I'd frozen them when I'd been under the temporary delusion that we had more than enough cookies to last us into next spring.

I pulled them from the freezer and arranged them on a plate. While they thawed, I picked up the piles of index cards, set them aside, and went to tell Brian I was going to the DeSotos'.

But when I checked on Brian, I found him sprawled on his bed, fast asleep, with Belle curled up next to him. His breathing was still raspy, but it was more relaxed and even than it had been. I left a note for him on the bathroom mirror and left Belle to keep him company.

I walked down the driveway and checked the mailbox. I still wasn't sure when our mail was delivered. Like the vandal, the mail carrier came and went without me seeing him. The box was empty.

Overhanging live oak branches shaded Briones Hill Road and made the walk toward Dennis's house cool. I drew my sweatshirt around me and felt alone.

My calves burned from the steep climb by the time I reached the ostentatious lampposts that marked the end of the DeSotos' driveway. Dennis had made it clear that he thought of our house as a dump, so I felt free to entertain snarky comments about *his* house, as long as I kept them to myself. The drive itself was paved with sand-colored stones that probably had a special name, but I didn't know what it was.

I tried not to let the house intimidate me, but it wasn't easy. When I walked past the fountain, I wondered how I'd missed seeing the front door when we'd dropped off Diego. A two-story entryway with double doors and the largest brass doorknobs I'd ever seen dominated the courtyard. Through clear sidelights and windows above the door, I could see a staircase that curved upwards, encircling a giant chandelier. I wondered who dusted it.

I felt very small, as if I should be selling Girl Scout cookies. I reminded myself I was more than forty years old and a mother of two. I stood as tall as I could in my jeans and sneakers and rang the bell, which was so large I had to hit it with the heel of my hand instead of my finger.

Chapter 30

Magazines work hard to sell the idea that women need to develop a personal style for their hair and clothing. The same principle works for organization. What works for one person might be ridiculously onerous for the next.

From the Notebook of Maggie McDonald
Simplicity Itself Organizing Services

Saturday, September 13, Afternoon

Elisabeth/Demi answered the door. I introduced myself and stepped into the marble-tiled front hall, asking if Dennis was available. Elisabeth called up the stairs to him and we chatted in the circular room, which was notably barren of skates, balls, rackets, shoes, books, backpacks, and any other evidence that five children lived in the house. I assumed that there was another dumping ground for kid paraphernalia at the back of the home, probably closer to the kitchen.

"Of course, you're the new neighbor," Elisabeth gushed. "For a second there I was sure that Laura Linney, the actress, was standing on my doorstep. Has anyone told you that you look just like her?"

I rubbed my hands over my face, unsure how to reply. I assumed Elisabeth was being sarcastic and trying to tell me I still had smears of soot on my face.

Elisabeth wore full makeup and was carefully coiffed, wearing a tailored butter-yellow shift and matching heels. She asked about the fire and expressed relief when I told her no one had been hurt. We waited for Dennis . . . and waited for Dennis . . . and waited some more for Dennis.

"I'm not sure where he is," she said. "Come through to the kitchen and I'll give you coffee while we wait. He may be on the phone. I'll text him."

Text him? In his own home? Elisabeth led me down a narrow hallway filled with school pictures, framed awards, and bookcases filled with sports trophies. I relaxed a little, more comfortable here than I'd been in the cold and showy front hall.

Elisabeth invited me to sit at a large square table in the corner. A right-angled cushioned banquette provided seating on two sides of the table. Diego sat at one end, supporting his head with his left hand and slurping Cheerios from the spoon in his right.

"Hi, Diego," I said. "No soccer today?"

Diego looked up through his thick bangs and I gasped.

"Oh, honey," I said. "I'm so sorry. What happened to your eye?" A dark purple bruise covered the left side of his face, and his eye was swollen closed.

I put down the plate of cookies I'd made up from the batch that Flora had given us, and hoped they'd had time to thaw.

"Have a cookie," I said, looking up at Elisabeth to confirm that it was okay to offer her son a treat. She nodded, staring at her phone. She was waiting, I assumed, for an answering text from Dennis.

"Tried to catch a soccer ball with his face," Dennis said from the hall. He came in to the kitchen holding a sparkly purple leash in his left hand.

Attached to the leash was Belle, looking embarrassed by the blingy leash.

In his right hand, Dennis held a gun pointed at Belle's head.

"Belle!"

Belle pulled toward me. Tugging back on the leash, Dennis slipped on the slickly waxed floor, waving the gun as he lost his balance.

I grabbed for Belle, trying to get her away from his gun. I fought to grasp her collar. In doing so, I banged my head hard on the metal edge of the kitchen table and hissed in pain.

Belle snarled and growled at Dennis. It was unusual behavior for Belle, but I was terrified of the gun and injured. Belle may have picked up on my fear. She was in a strange house, with strange people, and she was protective. Especially when she thought someone might be threatening me.

"What is going on here?" Dennis said. "Has the whole world gone nuts?"

"Honey, the gun," Elisabeth said.

Dennis looked at the floor and knelt to pick up the gun.

"Diego, take this gun outside with the rest."

Before Diego could take the gun from his dad, Dennis changed his mind. "Never mind. I'm keeping it until we can repaint the tip orange. It's not safe to have a toy that looks this real. Go on upstairs and get ready for the doctor." Dennis turned, still holding the gun, and looked at me.

Diego grabbed a handful of cookies as he left the kitchen.

"Demi's taking him in to make sure there's no serious damage to his eye."

He looked at the gun in his hand and at me.

"Oh, hell, Maggie. Did you think this was real?" Dennis sank onto the cushioned bench. Elisabeth handed me an ice pack wrapped in a kitchen towel.

"You ought to have that wound looked at," she said. "You could use a few stitches."

I reached up to feel the cut above my eyebrow. The skin was thin there over the bone and I'd hit the table hard. It was a classic injury I'd seen in both my boys. I could feel the swelling now and the pain, along with blood that left my fingers dripping and red.

"Head wounds always bleed a lot," I said. "I'll slap some Steri-Strips on it when I get home." I started to move toward the door, wishing I'd never decided to visit the DeSotos.

Elisabeth pushed me gently back onto the banquette. She placed a glass of ice water in front of me.

"Drink that, first," she said. "And let me check you for a concussion before you go."

"Demi was a nurse before I married her," Dennis said. "I'd listen to her if I were you."

"What was Belle doing with you, Dennis?" I asked, still shaky from the image of him holding the gun to Belle's head. I hadn't known it was a toy. Like Belle, I'd been quite sure he'd been threatening both of us.

"She was running on the road," Dennis said. "It's rural here, but you really can't let her out without a leash."

"But how did she get out?" I said. "I locked up before I left."

"Might want to get those locks checked."

"Thanks. I'll do that." I had no intention of discussing our ongoing security problems with Dennis, who, if my index cards were right, might be the main cause of our problems.

Elisabeth checked me for a concussion. She said I was fine, but recommended I consult the doctor and get stitches. She offered to drop me off at home while she took Diego to the doctor, or to take me to the doctor so I could get stitches at urgent care.

I refused both offers, but asked if I could hang onto the ice pack.

"Keep the towel too," she said.

"If you're insisting on walking home, sit a few more minutes and finish your water," Dennis said. "And tell me why you're here. Elisabeth said you wanted to see me."

Belle sighed and laid her head on my foot, her eyebrows raised as if to say, "What on earth are we doing here and why aren't we going home?"

"Are you ready to sell that white elephant house of yours?" he said. "Silicon Valley can be a bit much for some folks. I'd be happy to take it off your hands for you."

I shook my head. "I'm here on an errand for Flora Meadow," I said. "She asked me to pick up the PTA treasurer's reports."

"Treasurer's reports?"

"Flora said Miss Harrier had been asking for them. She wanted to include them in the PTA binder. The audit is coming up soon, and Flora's afraid that if she doesn't provide a complete binder . . ." I was embellishing and had run out of inspiration. Luckily, Dennis didn't seem to notice.

"But Harrier's dead and the audit isn't for ages. Flora must be confused."

"Flora wants to get everything in order for the next principal. She said Miss Harrier had been asking for them for months, but that you kept forgetting to give them to her because you're so busy. I thought I'd help by picking them up."

"Oh, that's not necessary. I'll have Elisabeth drop them off at the school."

"I'm afraid Flora insisted," I said. Flora hadn't, of course, but the more Dennis sidestepped this simple request, the more I was certain the answer to everything lay in something as simple as a monthly PTA report. Hadn't Elaine suggested I follow the money? Had she known there was something to find?

I looked around the kitchen. Every appliance was fancier than any I'd seen outside of a showroom or a magazine, but the overall effect was cold and sterile—literally sterile—more like a laboratory than a family kitchen. French doors led to a slate terrace. It looked like most of the family's real living was done out there. Built-in benches formed a low wall, separating the patio from a lush lawn. The benches were covered with piles of hockey sticks, stray socks, baseball gloves, shin guards, small orange cones, tennis rackets, swim bags, and soccer cleats. All the detritus that said *kids live here*, and that I'd missed seeing in the front hall.

In the middle was a rifle with the telltale orange tip. Next to it was a slingshot. *An airsoft rifle and a slingshot.* I remembered the brick that went though the staircase window and realized how close a match it was to the sand-colored stones that paved the DeSotos' driveway. *Uh-oh.*

Could the DeSoto kids be our vandals? Or Dennis himself? Could he have murdered Javier Hernandez? Or Miss Harrier? I shuddered and felt sweat drip down my sides. The police had moved away from thinking of the vandals as exuberant kids. We'd started thinking of them as unpredictable and dangerous criminals.

If the vandals did turn out to be Dennis or his offspring, I'd made a big mistake coming here. Whoever had been damaging our property wasn't concerned about who he or she injured and probably wouldn't stop at hurting one of us, if they had also been responsible for Mr. Hernandez's murder. My gut was telling me I didn't belong here. Belle woofed softly in agreement, as though she could read my mind.

I looked from Elisabeth and Dennis to the various exits—out the patio door and over a wrought-iron fence with a gate that was probably locked or back through the hallway and fumbling with the giant doorknob. I sighed. There was no easy escape, not if I wanted to take Belle with me. I was already here. I might as well ask my questions. I had lost patience with subtlety and decided to be as direct as possible.

"Airsoft guns?" I said. "And yellow pavers in the front drive? Have you been targeting us? Was the vandalism at our house your idea? What about the school? Was that to deflect attention from what you'd done at our house?"

Dennis sighed and took a sip of water. "I've been meaning to talk to you about the damage to your house."

I could hear the clock ticking on the wall, Belle's heavy breathing, and my heart thumping. I pushed my back hard into the cushions of the banquette, eager to put as much room as possible between Dennis and me.

Elisabeth shifted her weight from one foot to the other and checked her watch. "I need to leave to make Diego's appointment. If you're sure you don't want a ride . . . ?"

I shook my head and she left.

"It's my oldest son . . ." Dennis began.

Chapter 31

Sometimes, life gets in the way, and there are other
things far more important to attend to than being
organized.

From the Notebook of Maggie McDonald
Simplicity Itself Organizing Services

Saturday, September 13, Afternoon

I spent an uncomfortable half hour with Dennis as he explained that
his oldest son had complicated mental-health issues and that they'd
enrolled him in a boarding school for troubled teens earlier in the
week.

"He'll be under the supervision of doctors and counselors," Dennis said. "He's very angry with us right now, but Demi and I are hoping that it will eventually turn out to have been the right thing to do."

"His name is Dante," Dennis added. "He's sixteen."

Dennis looked up at me, then quickly away. He rubbed at an invisible smudge on the table.

"Maggie, I'm so very sorry for all the trouble he's caused you.
H-he wanted me to tell you that he never would have done anything
to seriously threaten you and your family."

I wondered about that statement, considering the seriousness of the
attacks on our home. Maybe Dante was trying to deny everything he
could. Maybe he had been forced to admit to vandalizing our house,
but was still trying to dodge accusations of endangering our lives?

I made sympathetic sounds, trying to think about how hard it
must be to come to grips with the idea that your child needs more

help than you can possibly give them. But my empathy didn't miti-
gate the relentless harassment and damage Dante had inflicted on our
house and the school.

"He wanted to make sure everyone knew that the squirrels were
dead when he found them on the road," Dennis said, rubbing his eyebrow and swallowing hard. "He didn't t-torture them."

I shuddered at the idea of a teen coolly planning far enough in ad-
vance to collect dead animals from the roadway to use later, but I
was relieved he hadn't tortured the creatures.

"When did he leave, Dennis?"

"Wednesday."

"But . . . the fire . . ." I shook my head. Dennis had implicated his
oldest son in the vandalism. But if Dante had left town on Wednesday, that meant he couldn't have torched our barn, thrown the smoke
bombs, or broken our windows. I needed to look for another suspect.
Maybe more than one. I needed to tell Jason and the fire investigator.

I stood and Dennis did too. "If you can wait a minute," he said,
"I'll get you those reports you wanted. And I'll wash that plate for
you." He pointed to the cookies on the table.

"No rush on the plate," I said. Dennis left the room to get the
binders, and I picked up a cookie and nibbled it. What would make a
kid angry enough to inflict the kind of damage Dante had? And why
did he direct his anger at my family? As far as I knew, we'd never
met.

Dennis came back with two giant binders. He handed them to me.

"Thanks, Dennis," I said. My lip twitched as I tried to wrap my
arms around them and I recognized the irony in suddenly feeling
overburdened by the information I'd been trying so hard to get hold
of. "I think."

"You're welcome. With so much going on around here, I've
gotten a little behind. Dante ran away about a month ago. We were
terrified. Demi and I and all the kids have been stressed-out by the
tension in the house. I rushed through the accounting and could easily have missed something. It's probably a good idea to have Flora
look the accounts over. She's done bookkeeping for her own business and is great at catching unintended discrepancies."

I smiled, nodded, and left with Belle, promising Dennis that I'd
have the cut on my forehead attended to and would check on our

locks to discover how Belle had escaped. How *had* she escaped? We were airing out the house with the windows open. Could she have broken through a screen? Or were the new door locks not working?

"Maggie, wait," Dennis called after me when I was halfway down the driveway. He ran to catch up with me and handed me the purple rhinestone-studded leash. He shrugged. "I know it's not her style, but it will keep her safe until you get home. Drop it in the mailbox when you get a chance. We have more. My daughter likes to buy them—the more sparkles, the better."

I took the leash, clipped it to Belle's collar, and thanked him. I sensed he had something more to say, but he seemed hesitant to speak. Dealing with Dante's crisis had shaken Dennis's confidence.

"What is it, Dennis?" The cut on my forehead was throbbing and I wanted to be home. I also didn't want Brian to wake up, find me gone, and worry.

"It's about the damages. This is awkward . . . but I-I want you to know that we'll see you're reimbursed, that Dante puts things right. We don't need to involve the police . . ."

"Thank you, Dennis, but would you mind if we talked about this another time? I need to get home."

"I-I also need to apologize for how rude I was when we first met. When Dante ran away, he broke into your vacant house and hid there for days. I blamed everything on that house and, by extension, you and your family. It wasn't fair."

I touched Dennis's arm, but could think of no appropriate response.

He nodded. We'd said all we could think of to say. I nodded back and walked briskly down the hill. I appreciated his apologies and promises that Dante would take responsibility for his actions, but I had no intention of hiding anything from the police. Jason needed the information about what Dante did or didn't do if he was going to figure out who'd burned down our barn.

Belle and I stayed on the shady side of the street. She sniffed bushes and threatened to take chase when a hare bounded out of a thicket and disappeared up the hillside. I was glad Dennis had loaned me the leash.

My encounter with him had run contrary to my expectations in so many ways. After an initial reluctance, he'd handed over the PTA reports eagerly. I no longer suspected he was hiding unusual account-ing practices.

Flora and Elaine had both suggested Dennis might be the culprit, but he had easily explained the anomalies in his behavior that had worried them. Dennis had been preoccupied by Dante's issues and fell behind on his responsibilities. His son was responsible for at least some of the vandalism.

I remembered how uncomfortable Diego had been when we'd given him a ride home and we'd talked about the vandalism and Miss Harrier's death. Was he stressed-out by the tension at home? Did he think Dante was behind Miss Harrier's death or had killed Mr. Her-nandez? What a horrible burden for a kid that would be. It was al-most too painful for me to contemplate a boy Brian's age thinking his brother might be a murderer. The most Dennis was responsible for was delaying getting help for Dante and putting a stop to his es-calating vandalism. But being a slow-to-act parent wasn't a crime.

I wondered what had caused Dante to turn to destroying property. I'd heard that kids sometimes became destructive when they were acting out frustration caused by abuse or other problems at home. Dennis was not my favorite person, but was he abusive? I didn't think so.

My "investigation" was getting nowhere. I'd have to go back to my index cards and see what else and who else they suggested.

I checked the mailbox before I walked up the driveway, but no letters, bills, packages, or junk mail had been delivered. No bombs either, thank goodness. I checked my watch. Three o'clock. Almost time to pick up David. I hoped Brian was awake. Maybe the boys and I could go out to dinner.

As I drew close to the house, I could see Flora's VW parked next to my van. Perfect timing! I couldn't wait to give her the heavy binders and tell her what I'd learned from Dennis. I expected Flora to climb out of the car and meet me, but she didn't. Could Brian have let her into the house? In theory, he wasn't supposed to let people in the house when Max and I weren't home. In practice, however, that rule had always applied to other kids, and Brian might have thought an adult was an exception to the rule. Was Flora down at the barn ex-amining the fire damage?

I heard dishes clattering in the kitchen as I climbed the back steps.

"Hey, Flora," I said as I walked into the kitchen. "What on earth are you doing in my house?" I wrinkled up my forehead and dropped the binders on the table.

Flora was disarmingly matter-of-fact and hummed as she bustled about.

"I'm making coffee," she said. "And more cookies."

What the hell? Orchard View really was another planet if people like Flora took for granted that they could pop in unannounced and take over another person's kitchen as if they owned the place. I was going to have to make it clear to everyone that while I was all for neighborliness and casual, friendly behavior, I would draw the line at intrusions like this.

"How did you get in, Flora?" I asked. "I'm sure I locked the door." I put down the binders and unclipped the hideous purple leash. Belle sniffed at Flora and went straight to her water bowl, lapping up as much as she splashed on the floor. I walked back to the door to examine the lock and the strike plate, neither of which showed signs of damage from being wrenched open by an intruder.

"The first batch is almost finished," Flora said. "Doesn't the house smell wonderful with the cookies and the coffee?"

"How'd you get in?"

"Sit down, Maggie, sit down." She put a place mat on the table and set it with a napkin, spoon, plate, and a steaming mug of coffee.

"You look exhausted. Coffee and a cookie will perk you right up, I'm sure."

I *was* exhausted. And while I was still determined to get to the bottom of Flora's strange behavior, I figured I could just as easily do it while drinking her coffee. Or was it *my* coffee? I sat down and took a deep sip. Coffee, like most things, tasted better when someone else made it for you.

Flora slowed her bustling and humming long enough to get her first good look at my face. Her hands flew to her own forehead and she gasped.

"What *happened* to you?" She ran to the sink, grabbed a clean washcloth, wet it, wrung it out, and handed it to me in what seemed like a single motion.

I took the washcloth from her and held it to my head as the timer on the oven went off. I took another sip of coffee. Flora pulled one tray of cookies from the oven and put another tray in.

Maybe my head wound was worse than I'd thought. I had a growing sense that nothing was as it should be. I wanted to make sure that Brian was okay, but something prevented me from mentioning him until I figured out what Flora was doing here. She seemed more at home and in control of her surroundings in my kitchen than she'd been in her own shop. Yet I was sure I'd locked the door, and we'd just changed the locks, so there was no way Flora could have a key. Even with Belle home, I wouldn't have left the door unlocked with Brian asleep upstairs.

"Wasn't the door locked when you arrived, Flora?"

Flora moved cookies from the hot baking sheet onto a plate and set it in front of me. She poured herself a mug of coffee, then opened the refrigerator door, took out a carton of cream, and poured a hefty dollop into her mug.

She sat at the table next to me, sitting a little closer than I'd expected her to. I scooted my chair away, and she scooted hers closer. All sorts of alarms were going off in my head. I didn't have the foggiest idea what was going on, but I had a growing certainty that something was wrong. I felt more uncomfortable now, in my own home, than I'd felt at Dennis's. I scooted my chair away and made a move to stand, patting the pockets of my jeans to find my phone.

Brian was upstairs. I thought back, trying to remember whether I'd told Flora he was home. I didn't think so. I hoped he was still asleep and would not walk into the middle of whatever was happening here. Even if he did come down to investigate, I knew that there was no way I would let Flora bother, worry, or hurt Brian. My kids had been through enough.

Flora put her hand on my arm. "Don't bother yourself, Maggie," she said. "Take a break. Drink your coffee. Have a cookie. That's why I'm here. To give you a rest. You've been working too hard, getting settled in your house, seeing bad guys where there aren't any, chasing down clues. It's too much." She nudged the plate of cookies toward me. When I didn't move to take one, she put two on my plate.

Belle came to the table and thrust her snout between us, jostling Flora's arm.

The forceful intrusion of Belle's big, insistent, golden-retriever head must have knocked Flora a bit off balance, because she gasped and grasped the edge of the table. When she opened her hand, dozens of white, five-sided pills spilled on the floor and across the table. The last time I'd seen similar pills was when I'd found Miss Harrier dead in her office.

I picked up my cup and looked into it, then stared at Flora.

"Flora, did you drug my coffee? Susan Harrier's coffee?" I formed the words and heard myself say them, but I couldn't quite wrap my head around the concept that Flora the earth mother, the PTA treasurer, the herbalist who only drank fair-trade organic coffee, could also be a murderer.

"Did you kill Miss Harrier?" I asked. "Tell me you didn't."

Flora shook her head, scrambling to pick up the pills and shove them into the pockets of her shapeless sweater.

"I didn't kill her. It was an accident. I didn't mean for her to die." Flora buried her head in her hands and sobbed. "She accused me of selling marijuana to the middle-school kids. She was going to tell the police. I could have gone to jail, Maggie. I don't have money for lawyers. Who would take care of Jennifer and my mom if I landed in jail? What could I do, Maggie?"

"What happened? Were you selling drugs at the school?"

"Not at school. Not to kids," Flora explained. "Oh, God. I can't believe this happened. My mom has Alzheimer's. After my divorce, she took care of Jennifer during the day and later after school, so I could start my business. She moved in with us so we could save on expenses. I bought the house. But then Mom had trouble looking after Jennifer. For awhile, they looked after each other, but Jennifer was getting more involved in after-school activities and evening dance classes. Mom was on her own more and things fell apart."

I pulled a stack of napkins from the holder on the table and handed them to her. She dabbed at her eyes and blew her nose. I felt dizzy and confused, but I wasn't sure whether it was because of the drugs Flora had put in my coffee, or because I couldn't wrap my head around the situation. Flora as a murderer? Flora was the last person I would have suspected.

"It wasn't safe for Mom to be alone during the day when I was working. Jennifer was in school during the day and in dance classes at night. We moved Mom to assisted living and, for a while, everything was fine. Money was tight, but my business was doing well."

"And then?" I prompted.

"I'm not sure how it started. I grew cannabis for Mom when she was undergoing chemotherapy for breast cancer ten years ago. It helped her so much that she told friends in her support group about it and they came to me too. I wanted to help them feel better so they'd stick with their treatment regimens. So many people give up because they can't stand the side effects."

Flora stopped, took a big gulp of coffee, and coughed. "I didn't want this, Maggie. I only wanted to help people."

I heard a *thump* from upstairs. Brian must be up. I prayed he wouldn't come down. If Flora had murdered Miss Harrier to stop her from telling the police about the drug sales, what would she do to me and to Brian to stop us from telling the police she'd confessed to murder?

I patted Flora's hand. "But something changed?"

She sniffed and nodded. "More people found out that I was growing it and wanted me to bend the rules for them. I was growing more, but we had plenty of room in the basement of our old house. I used the same setup that I'd once used to grow flower seedlings to plant in the spring."

Flora rested her elbow on the table and leaned her head against her palm. "These folks are desperate, Maggie. It's horrible what chemo does to them. And some people around here have a lot of money. One man offered to pay me two thousand dollars a week if I could supply his wife with enough pot to help her eat without vomiting."

She balled a napkin up in her hand. "At first, I limited my sales to those with medical-marijuana cards. I didn't have a license to sell, but it was so much easier for them to buy from me than to drive to one of the dispensaries in the city. Even if the cards looked bogus, I figured I could say I'd been fooled into thinking they were real, and that I was in the process of applying for a permit. But then Jennifer announced she wanted to go to college, to a conservatory back east, to study classical dance. And the home Mom is in said she'd have to move to a memory-care unit with skilled nursing. In the space of a week, my budget went from manageable to completely out of reach."

Flora looked up, wringing the napkin with her hands. "What could I do, Maggie? I had to take care of Jennifer and Mom. I had to.

I was keeping the store open as many hours as I could. We'd pinched every penny and economized in every way possible. All three of us had been doing that for years. I mentioned my troubles to Dennis after a PTA meeting, and he suggested I talk to Umberto about a short-term loan."

"Did Umberto help you?" I asked. "I'd heard he was all business."

Flora sneered. "You could say that. He was nice and comforting and wrote me a check as soon as I asked, but a week later, he made it clear that there were strings attached." Tears welled up in her eyes and spilled down her cheeks. "He threatened Jennifer and my mom. Nothing overt, but he made it clear that Jennifer or Mom might have a serious accident if I didn't do as he asked. He wanted me to double my production and do more direct sales."

Flora shuddered. "He had this way of talking as if he were referring to massage oils, lavender, and herbal tea, but we both knew exactly what he meant."

"So you branched out?"

"Yes. I sold to kids from the high schools and at Stanford. Word got around. I could spot them easily—people who came into the shop looking over their shoulders and spent way too long looking at products I knew they couldn't use. My underground business doubled in less than two months, and I started saving for Jennifer's college and paying my mom's bills. Overnight, my money problems disappeared."

"But Umberto kept pressing?" I guessed.

Flora was watching me closely, so I was afraid to reach for my phone to call 9-1-1. I considered running for the door, but was afraid that would create a disruption that would bring Brian downstairs. And the last thing I wanted was to have Brian anywhere near a desperate woman who had killed at least one person. I didn't want her to think about the risks she was taking confessing to me. I had to keep her talking.

"Go on," I said.

"He wanted a little more each week. That's what he was asking about when we saw him in the alley. It was always a stretch to make up his order. But he made it clear there'd be consequences if I didn't."

Flora's eyes roamed the room like those of a trapped and frightened animal.

"I never sold to the middle-school kids," Flora said. "*Never.* He wanted me to, but I didn't."

"But what happened with Miss Harrier?"

"She overheard kids saying they knew where they could get some weed and they mentioned my name. She confronted me and said she was going to call the police. I knew all hell would break loose with Umberto if she did that. I wanted to talk to her, Maggie. To convince her to give me another chance. To make her understand that I'd never sold to the younger kids and never would. I had no idea she was taking tranquilizers. Or that she had asthma. She was such a private person."

Flora gazed at me with a look that I interpreted as a plea for me to believe her story and to understand that her actions were unavoidable.

I nodded in what I hoped was an encouraging and supportive way.

"The doctor at the care home had prescribed benzodiazepine for Mom. Her memory loss terrified her and was making her frantic. I thought the pills would make Miss Harrier less worried about the pot too. So I ground up the pills in coffee I'd spiked with coffee liqueur and sugar. She liked really sweet coffee, did you know that?"

I shook my head. "You didn't worry that there could be complications? You're an herbalist. Aren't you trained to look for interactions between medications like pharmacists are?"

It was the wrong thing to say. Flora scowled. Her skin, her expression, and her entire demeanor took a dark turn.

"One of the joys of herbal medicine is that treatments don't have the side effects and complications that Western medicines do," she said.

I doubted the truth of her statement. Even water can kill someone if they ingest too much. But I apologized quickly, hoping she'd calm down. I couldn't follow her logic, though. Even if herbal medicine *didn't* have side effects, Flora had given Miss Harrier benzodiazepine, which no one would consider a natural product.

"Of course you're right, Flora. I'm sorry. Please go on."

"I took her cookies that I'd doctored too."

Flora was now shredding the napkins instead of balling them up in her hands. "I looked benzodiazepine up on the Internet after Harrier was found dead—after I learned she had asthma. Overdosing is really rare, and I was sure that someone had snuck in afterward and killed her. I truly hadn't meant to kill her, just change her mind. But between the medication she was taking, her asthma, the alcohol, and the pills in the coffee and cookies—I gave her way too much. She got really dizzy and nauseated, and stood up, saying she needed the restroom. She started to fall, and I tried to grab her, but the desk was in the way. Her head hit the corner of the filing cabinet with the most horrible sound."

Flora pointed to the side of her own head. "You know how head wounds are, Maggie. They bleed like crazy. There was blood everywhere. I panicked and ran. What if I'd been arrested? What would happen to Jennifer and my mom? They need me, Maggie. I can't go to jail."

"But what if you'd called an ambulance right away?" I asked the question as gently as I could. "Miss Harrier might still be alive."

I heard sirens in the distance and hoped they were headed straight to my house. Maybe Brian had overheard part of the conversation and called the police.

"And the fire?" I said, thinking that arson went way beyond the vandalism Dante had confessed to. I didn't want to believe Flora would do that, but I had to know. "Did you break our windows and burn our barn?"

Flora hung her head. "I hoped you would think it was too dangerous to stay here or continue investigating. I didn't want to hurt anyone. The insurance company will replace your barn."

"But that smoke bomb did a number on Brian's lungs, Flora. You endangered my son. You terrified all of us." I was angry now. Angry at the way that Flora had tried to manipulate every situation to suit her family and herself, without considering the impact on anyone else. Her problems had overwhelmed her, but I was sure there was help out there for people like Flora, if only she'd asked. She was wallowing in self-pity and blaming others, but the truth was, she could have turned the situation around at a number of key junctures if only she'd trusted someone other than Umberto with her story.

"Did you kill Mr. Hernandez too? What did *he* have to do with all of this?"

Flora pulled a floppy, quilted handbag from the floor and rummaged in its daffodil-printed depths. I pushed my chair back when she pulled out a gun and laid it on the table between us. It was a real gun. No orange tip. No purple-glitter polka dots.

The sirens grew louder.

Flora shook her head. "I can't let them in here, Maggie. I can't let them arrest me."

I put my hand over Flora's. "It's going to be okay, Flora. They'll understand. Tell them what you've told me."

It was an odd thing to say, I thought, as I listened to the words fall from my mouth as if they were coming from the mind of someone else. But I meant every word. Amid my anger and my terror for myself and my kids, I understood Flora's desperation. I didn't understand the solution she'd come to and didn't approve of her decision, but I understood the stress she'd been under, trying to care for her family alone when she'd previously been able to rely on her mother for help. I understood the knife-edge she'd balanced her life upon, and how any change could have made her feel trapped in an unmanageable situation.

I pushed the gun out of Flora's reach and took both her hands in mine. She held on as one might hold the railing on a storm-tossed ship, and I grasped hers almost as tightly. I wasn't sure what might happen if either one of us let go. And, while I was somewhat sympathetic, I was also practical. This woman's emotions were all over the place. She'd proved she was desperate and making terrible decisions. I had no idea what she was capable of or what she'd do next. I needed to keep her calm and holding onto her hands to prevent her from doing any more damage couldn't hurt.

"It's too late, Maggie," Flora said. "I've poisoned us both."

My mouth went dry and my chest tightened. "Poison?"

Flora nodded. "No pain. We'll just drift off to sleep and be done."

Oh, God. What would happen to Brian and David? And Max. I would never see him again. Never have a chance to watch the boys graduate and pursue their dreams. I listened as the sirens grew louder and then cut off as the emergency vehicles turned into the driveway and pulled to a stop at the side of the house in what must have looked like a reenactment of the activities on the day we'd moved in. I heard boots clomping up the back-porch steps and Jason pushed the door open slightly. I nodded to him and he lifted his eyebrows in an unspoken question. I nodded again, and he came into the room with his pistol drawn.

I shifted my gaze to the gun on the table. Jason holstered his weapon, shoved the plate of cookies aside, and picked up Flora's gun using one of the napkins she'd left unshredded.

The cookies. Flora said she'd ground pills into the cookies she'd made for Miss Harrier. Could she have done the same to this new batch? Or the batch she'd given me earlier? The ones I'd taken to the DeSotos' house and Diego had eaten?

"Jason," I said, with my mouth feeling as though I'd been shot full of numbing solution at the dentist. "The cookies. Diego. Poison. Call Lizbef."

Chapter 32

Even professional organizers have days when they can't organize their own thoughts, let alone anything else.

From the Notebook of Maggie McDonald
Simplicity Itself Organizing Services

Saturday, September 13, Late evening

Several hours later, after the paramedics and a stellar emergency-room team had stitched up my head and put me through an unpleasant series of treatments to clear the tranquilizers from my system, Jason drove me home and filled me in on what I'd missed.

"Brian called in the cavalry," he said. "He heard Flora's car and looked out the window, expecting to see you. When you didn't answer and he heard her fiddling with the door and talking to herself, he suspected something was wrong."

"Is Brian okay? What about Diego? He ate Flora's cookies."

"Brian's fine. Diego was on the way to the doctor to get his eye looked at when he began vomiting in the car. You told us about the drugged cookies before you passed out—or gave us enough clues, anyway. The police phoned both Elisabeth and Dennis, and Diego was treated immediately. He'll be fine."

"And David? He got home okay?"

"Stephen phoned Tess. She picked David up from band practice. Her son Teddy and your two boys are at your house wearing out the buttons on your video-game controllers."

"What will happen to Flora and her family? She was so worried about her daughter and her mom."

"Her daughter is with Flora's ex-husband. He's determined to work things out for Jennifer, Flora's mom, and Flora, for that matter." Jason tapped the steering wheel with his fingers. "We're going to do everything we can, under the circumstances. Her mother's doctor has been watching her condition carefully and thinks she may have been given medicines to make her more confused than her condition warranted. We're working to prove that Umberto had a hand in that, and was coercing Flora into some of the actions she took. Flora's helping us with the case against Umberto."

I fell silent, unable to voice any of my other questions and worries. What Flora had done was unconscionable, but I could sympathize with her struggles.

"Do you have enough to arrest Umberto?" I asked.

Jason frowned and accelerated. "I think so, to arrest him, anyway. After that it's in the hands of the district attorney." He shook his head. "Umberto's a slippery bastard."

I thought that *bastard* was too mild a term for a man like Umberto.

Chapter 33

When bringing contributions to a potluck, label
your serving dishes so you can be sure to get them
back, and so your host will know who to ask for your
wonderful recipe.

From the Notebook of Maggie McDonald
Simplicity Itself Organizing Services

Sunday, September 14, Morning

By Sunday morning, dozens of neighbors had dropped off casseroles, expressing their sympathy for our destroyed barn and wanting to hear the story of Flora's arrest. By noon, our refrigerator was full, the countertops were crammed with covered dishes, and I'd met nearly everyone who lived in the neighborhood.

The boys and I texted, emailed, or phoned dinner invitations to everyone who'd left their contact information with their casserole. The plan was to hold a potluck–open house on Sunday evening from five to seven o'clock, tell our story a few times, and encourage our guests to take their dishes home. We invited Adelia and her team, Stephen and Jason, Tess and Teddy, Elaine, April, and the boys' new friends.

I was about to make a list of beverages, chips, and other items we might need, when Stephen called. He offered to stop by the big-box liquor store and pick up everything. I readily accepted.

Before the party had officially started, our backyard was crowded with adolescents eyeing the remains of the barn and listening to Brian and David's story of their daring escape down the rope ladder.

I overheard kids exchanging plans for rebuilding the barn as a water park, a safari experience, a skateboard park, a clubhouse for young teens, or a horse-boarding facility. I decided I wouldn't be missed and returned to the house.

Stephen had opened bottles of wine and put cans of soda and bottles of water on ice.

He looked up as I let the screen door bang shut. "There are a few more six-packs," he said. "Want to take care of them?"

I bent to pick up a twelve-pack of cans from the floor and my stitches throbbed. I'd ended up with six stitches above my eyebrow, along with a lingering headache and a garish purple bruise.

"How 'bout I do the chips instead?" I grabbed a few bowls and a pair of scissors. "When did chip bags become impossible to open without scissors?"

I looked up at Stephen. "Can you answer a few questions before everyone else gets here?"

"Fire away, but I don't believe you have only *a few* questions."

I smiled. "How did Flora get into my house? I'm sure I locked the door."

"Lock picks. Her daughter is a big fan of *Elementary*, the Sherlock Holmes show. Holmes has a wall of locks he uses to test his lock-picking skills and Jennifer wanted a similar setup. She left the pick set her dad bought her at Flora's store, and Flora taught herself during lulls between customers."

I'd seen the locks at the store, and Flora and I had even talked about them, but I'd never incorporated the glaring clue into my index-card analysis. I slapped my forehead with the flat of my hand, and winced. "So, Flora filled the dishwasher with laundry soap."

Stephen nodded. "She told Jason she'd wanted to keep you busy and away from the investigation from the beginning. She hoped anything she did would be blamed on the vandal and you'd decide to give up your detective work or leave Orchard View."

"I nearly did." I nibbled absentmindedly at a chip, realized what I was doing, and pushed the bowl away.

"So, more questions . . . did Jason ever figure out how Tess's and Teddy's fingerprints ended up on the cans and bottles in my basement and Miss Harrier's office?"

Stephen laughed. "That one confused us, but it shouldn't have. Javier Hernandez helped out at school functions. If an event generated too much recycling for the bins at school, he'd bring bottles and cans back here and put them out on garbage day. We figure a few cans from a school event escaped the recycling bins and they happened to be ones with Tess's and Teddy's fingerprints."

"And Harrier's office?"

"Flora raided Tess's recycling bin on a Sunday evening and planted the cans to confuse Jason."

"And Miss Harrier's iPad? Did Jason find it?"

Stephen nodded. "Thanks to Brian. When your heat came on, the vent in his room rattled and he dug out a screwdriver to fix it. The whole process reminded him of the rattling vent in Miss Harrier's office. He figured it made perfect sense that it would be rattling if Flora had decided to hide the iPad in the ventilation shaft and was screwing the cover back on when she was interrupted by a visitor. He called Jason to tell him to look there.

"Jason located the tablet pushed way in the back of the air-conditioning duct in Miss Harrier's office. He found it just before he got the second call from Brian to come up here to rescue you from Flora."

"I did *not* need rescuing," I said, but I smiled. Brian had been determined to find the iPad. Jason had put him off, but in the end, Brian had been instrumental in finding it and in getting the police to the house to arrest Flora. I was proud of him, but I knew that, more importantly, he was proud of himself.

"Did the iPad help at all?"

"It was a gold mine. Harrier had uncovered Umberto's fraud scheme and documented everything on the iPad," Stephen said. "Finding her notes was a major break. Umberto was running scams full-time, from pushing Flora into illegal pot sales to absconding with funds from his own foundation, and to fraudulent contracts with the Orchard View school district. He created maintenance companies under false names. Those companies would bid low on district contracts and then perform shoddy work. His pest-control company sprayed water instead of pesticides. The water created mold problems, so another of his companies performed mold abatement. Where contracts required three coats of paint, his company would apply one. If a job called for ten nails, his guys would use eight. I'm guessing the Internal Revenue Service, the Federal Bureau of Investigation, Cal-OSHA, and the state Department of Education will be crawling over the investigation before the week is out. Umberto and some of the other DeSoto siblings had a widespread scheme to bilk the city and the state out of thousands—possibly millions—of dollars of school funding."

"So when Brian and other kids complained Miss Harrier spied on them at lunchtime . . ." I began.

". . . Harrier was taking pictures of peeling shingles and other evidence. It was all on the iPad," Stephen finished.

"Why put the iPad in the vent?"

"We don't know. Her iPad calendar showed she'd had a meeting with Umberto and folks from the school district to coordinate the schedule for renovating the playing fields."

Stephen stopped speaking for a moment while he crushed empty soda cartons and put them in the recycling bin. "She could have been hiding the iPad from Umberto."

"That's the best you've got? Wouldn't a desk drawer or her briefcase have taken care of that? What does Jason say?"

"Honestly? He has no idea. He's just glad to have found her notes."

Grabbing another bowl and some pretzels, Stephen opened the bag without using scissors and without damaging any pretzels.

I thought for a moment. I was still angry about all the trouble Dante had caused. We'd fallen into the habit of referring to him as the lowlife brat. But he was only a few years older than David and had grown up on our street. His parents were my neighbors.

"What about Dante?" I said. "Does Jason have any idea why he was so angry? Why he decided to terrorize us?"

Stephen shook his head. "It's an incredibly tragic story. Dante and his brothers spent a great deal of time with their uncle, Umberto, who pressured them into running errands for him that ranged from unethical to illegal. Dante sold drugs to middle-school kids and vandalized stores in a protection scheme."

I was shocked but thought about Flora's fear of Umberto and Diego's discomfort in talking about the events at the middle school. I wondered whether his black eye had truly been the result of a soccer accident or if Umberto had something to do with it. I gritted my teeth. I'd change a lot of things in the world if I ran the place, but bringing trouble to those who hurt children was at the top of my list.

Stephen continued. "When Dante balked, Umberto threatened him *and* his little brothers."

"Go on," I said.

"Jason thinks that Umberto found out that the boys were hanging out here with Mr. Hernandez and grew concerned that the caretaker's positive influence on the boys might undermine his own power over them. Dante told Jason that it was Umberto who forced him to start breaking the windows and inflicting other damage so it would look as though Mr. Hernandez wasn't doing his job. With Javier gone, Umberto figured he could use your house to store some of his illegal commodities. He told Dante to step up the damage or he'd hurt Elisabeth and make sure Mr. Hernandez was arrested for child abuse. Umberto told Dante and Diego that they'd go to jail too."

It sounded to me like the scenario Umberto had painted for the kids was a complete falsification, and that any case against Javier Hernandez would have fallen apart when exposed to the light. I frowned and shook my head.

"Poor Dante," I said. "If he'd confided in any adult other than Umberto, he probably would have gotten the help he needed to turn the situation around." I swallowed hard and asked the question that was the most difficult for me. "Did Umberto kill Javier Hernandez?"

"We think so," Stephen said. "Dante told Jason that Javier was going to drive Diego and Dante to the police station to talk to someone about what was going on. Umberto arrived at the house just as they were leaving. Dante thought quickly and told Umberto they were off to get ice cream, but Umberto told the boys to wait in the truck while he had a few words with Javier. They went into the house and after a few minutes, Umberto returned and told the boys that Mr. Hernandez had changed his mind about going for ice cream. Umberto kept Dante and Diego away from the house after that, and they never saw Javier Hernandez again."

I laid both my palms on the table, trying to steady myself. I was shaken by Dante's story and by the horror of Umberto DeSoto. Stephen massaged Munchkin's ears and was otherwise still. I heard kids shouting and laughing in the backyard, while adults gathered in the front room and on the front porch. I needed at least a moment to regroup.

Like most situations, the truth behind the vandalism at our house was more complicated than I'd imagined. I'd thought of Dante as a lowlife brat instead of as a young man caught in a dreadful situation. Javier Hernandez befriended Dante and helped him look for a way out of his mess. He'd served as Dante's lifeline and Umberto had killed him. Dante had a right to be angry.

I wasn't ready to feel warm and fuzzy toward Dante, although I understood what had happened. I hoped he would get the help he desperately needed.

Stephen put his hand on my shoulder. "Jason suspects Dante will eventually confirm that Umberto has been systematically abusing the boys for years."

I felt sick. "Not sexually?"

Stephen shook his head. "Probably not. Jason says Umberto has been a bully since grade school. He thinks intimidation was Umberto's game. Despicable, but not sexual."

"Did the police ever find Javier's wallet and car? Did they figure out why he had no identification?"

"Jason's not sure," Stephen said. "He thinks Umberto hid the car and the wallet to complicate the investigation. He's hoping Dante will help us find them."

"And what about Javier?" I asked. "Why didn't anyone report him missing?"

Stephen rubbed the top of his head with his hand. "He told his wife he was going to stop by here to fix the windows and porch, and then he was headed off on a three-day fishing trip, alone. His wife only began to worry when he didn't come home on time."

I pulled my hair back from my face and my head drooped. What a horrible, tragic mess.

"Will they be able to convict Umberto on any of this?"

"Jason's investigation has uncovered a ton of solid evidence. With help from Flora and Dante, and the information on Miss Harrier's iPad, he thinks the chances are good. That's the district attorney's job, though."

Stephen picked up the tub of soft drinks and ice. "Jason asked me to pass along his thanks to you and Brian. You should take that as a great compliment, especially since he's been forced to admit that your snooping around was really helpful to the investigation."

I snorted. "What on earth is he talking about? Flora nearly killed me and it was the police who filled in all the blanks. I didn't do anything."

"Not so. Flora wasn't a part of the investigation until after Jason picked her up here in your kitchen. He'd given up on locating the iPad but Brian made sure he kept pursuing it. Without Brian he wouldn't have found it. And without the information that you provided from your conversations with Flora and Dennis, Jason wouldn't have had enough evidence for a warrant to arrest Umberto and search his home, businesses, and computers. You broke this case wide open and the police know it. Jason's not happy that it put you in danger, but even he has to admit that you provided a whole new line of inquiry."

I started to respond, but Stephen cut me short. "But don't expect to get more than the thanks he's already given you. He told me to thank you and then to kill you. He's that angry."

He put the tub of drinks on the counter and offered me his hand to help me from the chair. "That's enough of crime and mayhem. I'm starving, and I'll bet those kids outside are hungrier still. Grab those chip bowls and take them out. I need to check on the grill."

I nudged the back door open with my foot and pushed the screen door open with my back. I turned and my jaw dropped.

On the back porch, right where I'd imagined them on our first day at the house, were two classic porch rockers with blue cushions, comfy-looking throw blankets, a small side table, and a giant sign reading *Welcome to Orchard View*.

Elaine took an unflattering picture of me with my mouth hanging open, followed by others of me hugging Stephen, Jason, Tess, April, and the boys.

"You're one of us now, Maggie," Elaine said. "We're giving you the welcome you deserve. We're not letting you go back to Stockton, even if you want to."

Chapter 34

When you own your own business, especially if you
work from home, the first thing you need to learn is how
to turn work off and relax. Family time is family time.

From the Notebook of Maggie McDonald
Simplicity Itself Organizing Services

Monday, September 15, Before dawn

On Monday morning, a text from Max woke me before dawn. It
was worth it. He'd be home Wednesday.

Excited, I got up, fed the animals, and brewed a pot of coffee. I
took a mug out on the porch and curled up on one of the rockers.
Belle's tail swayed above the tall grass as she hunted good doggy
smells. I needed to get the field mowed, but I didn't make a note of it.
There would be time for that later.

For now, I shifted my rocker so the burned-out barn was out of
my field of view. I watched shadows lift from the hills as the sun rose
and tinted the clouds the colors of rainbow sherbet.

I'd grown to love the house and Orchard View, despite our troubles. Dreadful things had happened, but we'd made friends who'd
pulled together to help us out. Orchard View had its villains, but it
also had some generous souls: April, Stephen, Elaine, and Tess tops
among them. I sipped my coffee and tore the corner off a slice of ba-
nana bread left over from the party the night before.

That's the kind of community we'd found in Orchard View. It
wasn't perfect. Neither was the house. I was sure David was right
when he'd bet that the house had bats. But once Max was home and
I had a little more time, I planned to talk to Tess about whether she'd

recommend me to her clients when I reopened my Simplicity Itself Organizing Services in Orchard View.

As a newcomer to town, I hadn't had the background on my neighbors that would have helped me solve the crimes more quickly. But it turned out that I had a good nose for clues that were out of place. Brian did too. And my clue-organizing strategy had led me to question Dennis and the answers I'd gleaned from him had given the police what they needed to carry the investigation to a satisfying conclusion.

My skills had helped us make our way through the morass of evil that Umberto had created and I hoped we'd seen the last of him. While it was satisfying to learn that my problem-solving skills transferred easily to murder investigations, I was hoping never, *ever* to stumble over another dead body.

Don't miss the next book in the Maggie McDonald Mystery series,

Scheduled to Death

Available in January 2017 from Lyrical Underground!

Chapter 1

We don't use the word *hoarder* in my business. It holds
negative connotations, few of which are true of the
chronically disorganized.

From the Notebook of Maggie McDonald
Simplicity Itself Organizing Services

Monday, November 3, Nine o'clock

I couldn't be sure where the line was between a mansion and a
really big house, but I knew that I was straddling it, standing on
the front porch of the gracious Victorian home of Stanford professor
Lincoln Sinclair. The future of my career here in Orchard View
straddled a similar line—the one between success and failure.

I rang the doorbell a second time and glanced at my best friend,
Tess Olmos. She was dressed in what I called her dominatrix outfit—
red-and-black designer business clothes and expensive black stilettos
with red soles. I wore jeans, sneakers, and a long-sleeved white T-shirt
over which I wore a canvas fisherman's vest filled with the tools of my
trade. I'm a certified professional organizer and my job today was to
finish helping the professor sort through three generations of furniture and a lifetime's collection of "stuff" he was emotionally attached to.

The professor was a brilliant man on the short list for the Nobel
Prize in a field I didn't understand, but his brain wasn't programmed
for organization and never would be.

And that's where I came in. Organization is my superpower.

I looked at my watch. It was 9:10 a.m. We had arrived promptly
for our appointment at nine. Tess had arranged to use the house for

her annual holiday showcase to thank her clients and promote her business, but she wanted to double-check our progress on clearing things out before she scheduled her team of vendors. All but one of the rooms was empty, but Tess had a sharp eye and might well spot something I'd missed. If she had questions about anything Linc and I had done, I wanted to be on hand to answer them immediately.

Participating in Tess's holiday event would give my fledgling business a huge boost. Endorsements from Tess Olmos and Linc Sinclair were likely to bring me as much business as I could handle.

"We did say nine o'clock, didn't we?" I asked Tess. "I wonder if he overslept after that storm last night?" A rare electrical storm had coursed across the San Francisco Bay Area the previous evening, bringing buckets of much-needed rain. With it came winds that downed trees and power lines. Thunder shook my house to its foundation.

"What did the weather folks predict? 'Isolated storm cells with a chance of lightning.' The morning news was showing footage of funnel clouds in Palo Alto. My dog whined all night." Tess bent to peek through one of the front windows. "Wow, you've really made a lot of progress in there," she said. "I can see clear through to the dining room."

I smiled as I stepped off the porch and onto the fieldstone path running across the grass and past the chrysanthemums and snapdragons that edged the front garden.

"Linc's been working hard," I said. "All that's left, beyond a few boxes, is his upstairs workroom with all that electronic equipment and research papers. I'm hoping to organize most of that today and take it to his freshly cleaned and cataloged storage unit. If it goes well, we'll tackle his office at Stanford too."

I looked up and down the street. No professor.

"Where is he?" asked Tess, echoing the question I'd already asked myself.

"I'll take a look 'round back," I said. "He may be working in the garden or kitchen with his headphones on and can't hear the bell."

I followed the flagstone walk around to the side of the house and let out a yelp. My hand flew to my throat and my heart rate soared.

"Oh my, sorry. I'm so sorry," I said to the woman blocking my way. I fought to regain my balance after my abrupt stop. "You startled me. Can I help you?"

"Humph!" said the woman, straightening as if to maximize her height. "I could ask you the same question. Does Professor Sinclair know you're here? He appreciates neither visitors nor interruptions." Her face was overshadowed by a gardening hat the size of a small umbrella. Green rubber boots with white polka dots swallowed her feet and lower legs, which vanished beneath a voluminous fuchsia skirt splattered with potting soil. A purple flannel shirt completed her outfit.

Tess's stilettos clicked on the path behind me. With one hand on my shoulder, she reached in front of me, holding out her hand to greet the woman.

"Tess Olmos," she said. "I'm Linc's Realtor and this is Maggie McDonald, his professional organizer. We're here for an appointment."

I scrambled in my cargo vest for a business card as the woman picked up the business end of a coiled garden hose. I had the distinct impression she was waiting for an excuse to turn the nozzle on us. I found a card, plucked it from my pocket, and handed it to her.

"I was checking the professor's house for damage after that storm last night," the woman said as she took my card and put it in her pocket without looking at it. "My nana would have called it a *gully-womper*. Nice to meet you ladies, but I need to get to work. For twenty years, the Sinclairs have allowed me to use their water in my community garden plot." She waved her arm toward an overgrown hedge at the back of the half-acre property. "In exchange, I provide them with fresh vegetables."

"Of course," Tess said as if she knew all about the arrangement. "And you are?"

"Oh, sorry." The woman wiped her grubby hands on her pink skirt before shaking Tess's outstretched hand. "I'm Claire Domingo, but I go by Boots. I'm the president of the Orchard View Potters Garden Club. We run the community garden in back of the house."

Before any of us could say anything more, I heard the screeching of bicycle brakes. Linc careened around the corner with his legs outstretched and his jacket flapping behind him. His Irish wolfhound, Newton, loped beside him and made the turn easily.

Out of breath, Linc jumped from the bike and let it fall to the ground beside him as if he were an eight-year-old who was late for lunch.

"Sorry, sorry, sorry," he said, scurrying toward us. "I had an idea for a new project in the middle of the night and I rode over to the university. Time got away from me. Sorry to keep you waiting."

Newton barked in greeting and lunged toward me.

Linc unhooked the dog from the bicycle leash he'd invented ten years earlier, but had never sought a patent for. Once he'd created it and proved it worked, he'd lost interest.

Newton barreled in my direction. I stepped back and knelt to give him more room to slow down before he plowed into me. Linc had trained him well, but his exuberance sometimes got the better of him. I scratched him behind the ears in a proper doggy greeting before turning my attention to Linc, who picked up the bicycle and leaned it against the fence.

"No problem, Linc," I said. "You're here now. Shall we get started?"

Linc patted the pockets of his jacket, his jeans, and his sweatshirt and looked up, chagrined. "I'm afraid I've forgotten my key again."

Tess, Boots, and I each reached into our own pockets and plucked out keys labeled with varying shades of fluorescent tags. I laughed awkwardly and headed toward the back porch, knowing that the lock on the kitchen door was less fussy than some of the other old locks on the house.

"Let's add installing new locks to the list of jobs," I told Tess.

Boots followed us. We stepped carefully around some of the boxes of donations that awaited pickup by a local charity resale shop. I unlocked the door and we trooped in.

Linc shifted from one foot to another, took off his glasses, and cleaned them with his shirttail. He looked around the room, blinking as if surprised to find he was no longer in his Stanford University lab. I flicked the light switch, but the room remained dim. Last week I'd brought over a supply of bulbs to replace several that I'd found burned out. I must have missed this one.

"Did you lose power in the storm?" I asked.

He answered with a shrug. "I'm not sure; maybe. I was at my lab working on my project."

Boots pulled open the refrigerator door and plucked a bag of lettuce from the darkness within. It had turned soggy in the bag.

"I'll take this for compost and bring you back some fresh spinach this afternoon," she said. "The kale's coming along nicely too."

"Can I get you all a cup of tea?" Linc asked. It was a delaying tactic I recognized from experience. Sorting and organizing was nearly painful for this man, who was said to have several ideas that could reverse the effects of global warming.

"Let's get started upstairs," I said. "I want to show Tess how much progress you've made."

Boots rummaged in the refrigerator. "I'll see what else needs to be tossed, Linc. Go on. I'll let myself out."

"I can't withstand pressure from all three of you." Linc shrugged and turned toward the staircase that divided the kitchen and living room. I started up the steps behind him, then stopped and called over my shoulder. "Tess, I'm going to show you Linc's workroom first. He's been working in there while I've been tackling the other rooms." I mouthed the words *praise him* to her. Linc hadn't actually made all that much progress, but he *had* agreed on broad-based guidelines for culling the equipment and organizing some of his papers.

Newton nudged past us to lead the way up the stairs. When I reached the hall landing, it was dark. *Right,* I thought. *The storm. No electricity.*

Newton growled, low in his throat, then whimpered. Linc moved down the hall toward his office and workroom. In the doorway, he gasped and froze. His mouth dropped open. His eyes grew wide. He stepped back, but leaned forward with his arm outstretched.

"Whatever it is, we can fix it," I said, rushing toward him, terrified I'd tossed out something of great value. "Everything we moved out of here is still in the garage."

Peering over Linc's shaking shoulders, I bit my lip, swallowed hard, and grasped his arm as he tried to move forward into the room. We couldn't fix it. Not this.

"No, don't," I said, pulling him back. "Tess, get the police. An ambulance."

Tess moved forward in the narrow hall, apparently trying to get a look at whatever had shocked Linc and me. I shook my head and whispered, "It's Sarah. Just dial. Quickly."

I hoped my voice would carry to the kitchen. "Boots, do you know where there's a fuse box or electrical panel? Can you make *triple sure* the power is out all through the house?"

"What's going on?" shouted Boots.

I couldn't think of an appropriate answer, but I gave it a shot.

"We've got a problem up here, Boots. Can you make sure the power is off, *now*? Please? Right now?"

" 'Kay," said Boots, though I could hear her grumbling that she wasn't our servant to command. Her voice was followed by the creak of old door hinges and the sound of her rubber boots galumphing down the basement stairs.

I forced myself to look at Linc's workroom again. Nothing had changed. Sarah Palmer, Linc's fiancée, lay sprawled on the floor in a puddle of water. Sarah Palmer, one of my dearest friends, whose caramel-colored skin normally shone with warmth and health, lay face down with her hand outstretched and clutching a frayed electrical cord.

Worst of all, the body that had once been Sarah's looked very, very dead.

Photo Credit: Dylan Studios

Mary Feliz has lived in five states and two countries, but calls Silicon Valley home. Traveling to other areas of the United States, she's frequently reminded that what seems normal in the high-tech heartland can seem decidedly odd to the rest of the country. A big fan of irony, serendipity, diversity, and quirky intelligence tempered with gentle humor, Mary strives to bring these elements into her writing, although her characters tend to take these elements to a whole new level. She's a member of Sisters in Crime, Mystery Writers of America, and National Association of Professional Organizers. Mary is a Smith College graduate with a degree in sociology. She lives in Northern California with her husband, near the homes of their two adult offspring. Visit Mary online at MaryFeliz.com, or follow her on Twitter @MaryFelizAuthor.

Made in the USA
San Bernardino, CA
25 August 2016